The Deal Maker

OTHER BOOKS BY LOUISE BAY

New to Louise Bay? Start with Mr. Mayfair

or The Boss + The Maid = Chemistry

Colorado Club Billionaires

Love Fast

Love Deep

Love Hard

New York City Billionaires

The Boss + The Maid = Chemistry

The Player + The Pact = I Do

The Hero + Vegas = No Regrets

The Doctors Series

Dr. Off Limits

Dr. Perfect

Dr. CEO

Dr. Fake Fiancé

Dr. Single Dad

The Mister Series

Mr. Mayfair

Mr. Knightsbridge

Mr. Smithfield

Mr. Park Lane

Mr. Bloomsbury

Mr. Notting Hill

The Royals Series

The Earl of London

The British Knight

Duke of Manhattan

Park Avenue Prince

King of Wall Street

The Players Series

International Player

Private Player

Gentleman Series

The Wrong Gentleman

The Ruthless Gentleman

The Nights Series

Indigo Nights

Promised Nights

Parisian Nights

Stand-Alones

An American in London

The 14 Days of Christmas

Hollywood Scandal

Love Unexpected

Hopeful

The Empire State Series

For more, visit www.louisebay.com.

The Deal Maker

LOUISE BAY

This is a work of fiction. Names, characters, organizations, places, events, and incidents are either products of the author's imagination or are used fictitiously. Otherwise, any resemblance to actual persons, living or dead, is purely coincidental.

Text copyright © 2026 by Louise Bay
All rights reserved.

No part of this book may be reproduced, or stored in a retrieval system, or transmitted in any form or by any means, electronic, mechanical, photocopying, recording, or otherwise, without express written permission of the publisher.

Published by Montlake, Seattle

www.apub.com

Amazon, the Amazon logo, and Montlake are trademarks of Amazon.com, Inc., or its affiliates.

EU product safety contact:
Amazon Media EU S. à r.l.
38, avenue John F. Kennedy, L-1855 Luxembourg
amazonpublishing-gpsr@amazon.com

ISBN-13: 9781662532122 (paperback)
ISBN-13: 9781662532115 (digital)

Cover design by Logan Matthews
Cover image: © Michelle Lancaster PTY LTD; © zxvisual / Shutterstock

Printed in the United States of America

The Deal Maker

CHAPTER ONE

Lucy

My sister, Katherine, looks exactly how a fiancée should look. Deliriously happy, hopelessly in love, and perfect in all other ways. Perfection is nothing new for Katherine, but now she's engaged—to the perfect man, obviously.

"I can't believe you haven't met Ed's best man until now," Katherine says, pushing her mascara wand back into the tube. "You're going to love Hunter."

No doubt Hunter will be perfect. Just like Ed, my soon-to-be brother-in-law. Ed is from a good Boston family that can be traced back at least fifteen generations. He's "in finance"—whatever that means—just like his father. He and Katherine enjoy wearing coordinating Ralph Lauren, and of course, they never argue. Their future will be full of perfect children who make perfect grades, and they're all going to live the perfect lives my mother foresaw when Katherine was born. According to Mom, Katherine's first word was "please." She never complains, gets angry or irritated. The story goes that Katherine came out of the womb serene and peaceful, like she already possessed enough wisdom to know crying wouldn't get her anywhere with our mother.

In contrast, my mother likes to tell people I could be heard crying in her womb before I was extracted via C-section—far from a perfect start. I've always been the Pig-Pen to Katherine's Snoopy. The Beast to Katherine's Beauty. The Elizabeth Bennet to Katherine's Jane Bennet.

"Lucy," Mom calls from the bottom of the stairs. "It's time you two came down. I don't want you making your sister late."

"Mrs. Jones!" my father bellows. "Where's my tie?"

My mother insists on being called Mrs. Jones by anyone she hasn't known a couple of decades, and Dad likes to tease her about it. At least, I think he's teasing. Obsessed with Jane Austen, Mom thinks she's living in a Regency drama. I wouldn't be surprised if she and Dad have a few costumes hidden at the back of the closet that they sport in private when Katherine and I aren't around. Pass the mind bleach. Our mother watched the adaptation of *Pride and Prejudice*—the one starring Colin Firth—on a loop while pregnant with Katherine. According to my father, that's when the obsession with Jane Austen in general, and *Pride and Prejudice* in particular, really took hold. At least we weren't named Lizzy and Jane. Katherine is far too beautiful to be named Jane.

I scoop up her hand from where she's fussing with the perfect bow in her hair, and we head downstairs. "You look beautiful." She's wearing a sugar-pink grosgrain dress with matching Ferragamo pumps. She looks like a doll.

"You too." Katherine grins, squeezing my hand. "I don't know if he's here yet, but I told Ed to make sure you're introduced to Hunter right away. After all, you have to get to know each other to organize the joint bachelor/bachelorette party."

I hide my sinking dread behind a polite smile. As maid of honor, I'm in charge of all the arrangements. The problem is, I want the party—or more accurately, the weekend-long prewedding event—to be as perfect as Katherine herself. I'm not sure that can happen with me in charge. I'm concerned I'll forget something fundamental, like restaurant reservations or a bride-to-be sash, or cause some kind of chaos. That's what everyone will expect me to do. I have to remind myself I'm no longer the rumpled little kid stumbling after my lithe, elegant sister in the school corridors anymore. I grew up. I moved to New York and upgraded my wardrobe, along with my organizational skills. It's just that whenever I go back to Massachusetts to visit my family, I seem to regress. I become the girl I used to be rather than the woman I am.

As we get to the bottom of the stairs, Ed appears with a guy I don't recognize. Ed's eyes sparkle as his gaze fixes on my beautiful sister.

"Katherine, you look gorgeous," he says.

"Absolutely stunning," the stranger says.

"You too, Lucy," Ed says, and I smile at his forced compliment.

I glance at the stranger, expecting to field another canned compliment, but he's looking over his shoulder at what's happening in the garden rather than back at me. Oh well, at least he's not faking it.

"This is Hunter," Katherine says.

He's slightly taller than Ed and has inky-black hair, which is swept back like he's just pushed his fingers through it. Despite his very broad shoulders, his blue suit fits him like a glove, and the white shirt makes his face look like he's just flown in from a two-week vacation in Aruba. He's handsome—there's no doubt about that—but I'm determined to put his looks to the very back of my brain. I just need his help and cooperation for this party. So long as I get that, I don't care what he looks like.

"We were just talking about how you and Lucy are going to be arranging our bachelor/bachelorette party." Katherine greets Ed at the bottom of the stairs with a kiss on the cheek, and Hunter gives Katherine a reserved hug. "Maybe the two of you can get together after the party or even back in the city. Hunter lives in New York, just like you, Lucy."

I narrow my eyes, suddenly suspicious. Why is Katherine so invested in getting the two of us to meet up? Doesn't she trust me to put together a great bachelorette party? Katherine has always been the one in my corner, sticking up for me. Telling Mom not to be so hard on me, telling me I'm just as pretty as she is. But maybe she never really believed it. Maybe she thinks I'm not capable of doing this for her.

Well, she'll find out soon enough that she's mistaken. Just like everyone else who ever knew me growing up and still doubts me to this day. I'm going to prove everyone wrong.

Katherine and Ed head into the garden, leaving Hunter and me alone. I stick out my hand to shake his. "I'm Katherine's sister, Lucy." I give him my best Massachusetts grin. It's full of clapboard houses, ocean breezes, and a sprinkling of Kennedy confidence.

But my smile isn't returned. Hunter's mother clearly wasn't an Austen fanatic when she was pregnant. She probably saw the glint in her son's eyes when he was born and decided on his name. He's looking at me like he wants to kill me.

"Lucy," he says, scowling and shaking my hand.

"Have you got any ideas about the joint party?" I ask as we follow Katherine and Ed out into the garden. The light is dazzling, and I pull my sunglasses from my pocket. "We have to make it absolutely incredible. They're such a great couple, aren't they?"

"What?" Hunter snaps. His tone sends a jolt of shame through me. Did I say something wrong?

"The party," I say, a little more tentatively. "I wondered if you had any ideas. I think Katherine and Ed want it to be in Massachusetts, on the beach, but other than that, we have free rein."

He groans in response but doesn't say anything else.

I turn to see if he's heard me, but it's like I'm not even there. Like I'm invisible.

He clearly has no interest in listening to me or organizing the party.

Asshole.

Well, he's not going to destroy my opportunity to publicly reinvent myself. Everyone's going to see that I'm Katherine Jones's perfect sister, and Hunter over here isn't going to sully my brand-new reputation.

"Lucy!" my mother calls from across the lawn. I ditch Hunter and head over to where she's looking fraught. "Lucy! Where is that girl?"

"Right here, Mom. You look lovely." She's wearing a powder-blue pantsuit.

She turns and takes in my outfit. "Oh, you went for the lemon in the end."

I fan out my skirt with my thumb and fingers, waiting for a compliment that never arrives. "It's pretty, right?"

She sighs. "It's fine. I want you to move this stack of trays over to the table with the champagne on it."

I glance down. "But I might get a stain on my dress." Mom and Dad were desperate to host the engagement party in their very pretty garden. Ed and Katherine have had to wait five months since they got engaged for this official celebration, thanks to the weather, but at least Mom's happy. It also means the wedding is only two months away. Massachusetts and I are going to get reacquainted. Despite being relatively close, I don't get back much. Katherine often comes down to New York with Ed when he has business in the city, so I get to see her without coming back home. My school friends and I aren't really in touch. There's nothing much to pull me back.

"Wear an apron. Come on. Guests are going to be arriving any minute."

Maybe I should go and change quickly into something more suitable for lugging around catering equipment. All Katherine's friends from school will be here soon, along with Mom and Dad's friends, who have known me since I was born. I don't want to greet them looking like a disheveled mess. It's exactly the opposite impression I'm trying to portray. I'm not the kid sister who used to go everywhere on a skateboard, wearing bashed-up sneakers and an oversize Nirvana tee. I'm a serious, sophisticated New Yorker. Okay, I'm not a banker. But I'm a paralegal. That's a serious job.

"Lucy!" my mother scolds. "Come on. Get those trays moved."

My shoulders drop as I realize I don't have time to change.

Just as I'm about to pick up the huge stack of silver trays, Ed interrupts. "We'll do that," he says.

I turn and come face-to-face with Hunter. He still looks murderous and he doesn't say anything, but at least he takes the stack of trays and ferries it over to the other side of the garden.

I turn and find my mother rolling her eyes at me. "I told you to be quick," she says. "Now poor Ed has to do the donkey work."

"Rather than me, the actual donkey, right?" I don't wait for Mom's response, which is sure to be an eye roll anyway. I've had enough. I need a couple of minutes to regroup before the guests arrive. I head to the bathroom and try to find my Massachusetts smile.

CHAPTER TWO

Hunter

It's not like I'm not happy for my best friend. I schlepped up here from New York to go to his engagement party, didn't I?

"Can I get another shot?" I ask the bartender. I'm avoiding everyone. I don't know Ed's friends from home, and the only joint friend we have is working in Hong Kong. Making small talk with a bunch of people I don't know is my idea of perfect hell. And everyone's so goddamn happy. I can't take any more "Don't they make an adorable couple" and "Their children are going to be so beautiful." It's all a bleak reminder of my future being flushed down the drain as this party drifts on.

The bartender slides me the tequila bottle. I unscrew the cap and tip a generous pour into the lowball that one of the themed cocktails was served in. It might have been the Something Borrowed . . . No, that was the strawberry one. It was gooood. Maybe it was the Bouquet Toss. No, that was lemon. I know . . . It was definitely the To Have and To Hold. Bit of a spicy kick on that one.

I probably should have asked for a clean glass, but I'm not really tasting the alcohol as it goes down. I just want to obliterate reality for an hour or so until I can go back to my hotel and sleep, then get back to the city to do my job. And Ed's job. Already he's not as focused as he usually is. I swear he spent the entire week booking the honeymoon.

"Hey," Katherine says as she approaches the bar, arm in arm with Ed.

"Looks like you found the bar, dude," Ed says.

"What can I say? Nothing like the ocean air and a slug of tequila."

"So . . . what did you think of Lucy?" he asks.

Katherine playfully slaps him on the arm. "You gotta be more subtle than that!"

I get the feeling I'm missing something.

"Did you two vibe?"

Katherine rolls her eyes and picks a speck of invisible lint off my jacket, the way she always does. It's weird . . . I never spot anything on my clothes, but Katherine always finds something. "We just want the party planning to go smoothly," Katherine says with a smile.

"It will," I say.

"We don't want to end up at a strip club in Vegas," Ed says.

Katherine gives out a slightly hysterical laugh. "No, definitely no strip clubs. You know we want to stay in Massachusetts, don't you?"

"Right," I say, trying to think whether I made any notes when Katherine called me shortly after Ed proposed.

"And it's going to be a joint thing. So you and Lucy will be working together, doing the planning and preparation. That will be super fun, right?"

I nod and take another swig of tequila. "Lucy," I repeat. "Super fun."

On the other side of the lawn, Katherine's mom appears to be sermonizing to a small group of guests. Enraptured? Held hostage? Hard to tell from this distance. Weirdly, I think I hear her say something about Hunter "possessing a good fortune." And also about wanting a wife. Her hands are fluttering in the air, underscoring her words, and then she laughs. At whatever *she's* saying.

I refocus on the middle distance, where I find a woman barreling toward us with fisted hands and a scowl. "Mom's started on *Pride and Prejudice*, Katherine," she says, her jaw tight.

I've definitely been introduced to this woman. I think she's the sister—the one I'm planning the bachelor party with. My mind is fuzzy with tequila, and my brain is stuck in molasses. I don't remember thinking Katherine's sister was hot an hour or so ago when we were introduced, but this woman is beautiful. Bright, big green eyes and hair that's so glossy I wonder whether she put butter or oil or something in it. Is that a thing? And her breasts are mesmerizing. I'm pretty sure she's not wearing a bra, yet they're high and round and . . . Fuck. I might be drunk, but I haven't had enough tequila not to realize I'm staring at my best friend's sister-in-law's chest. At least I'm wearing sunglasses. Hopefully no one noticed.

"There's nothing we can do," Katherine says. "You know what she's like after a white wine spritzer."

"You can't blame the wine. She just needs an audience to start bleating on about Austen." The beauty sighs. "The glass of wine just means Dad's getting lucky tonight."

"Eww," Katherine and Ed chorus.

I watch the happy couple. They're basically the same people but opposite genders. They both have neat hair and a permanent smile. They both like yoga and goddamn kimchi. I bet neither of them has ever been hungover at work the day after a big night out. Goody-goodies. That's what Katherine and Ed are.

I've always known this about Ed. It was one of the reasons why I agreed to go into business with him. I knew I could trust him to tell me the truth. The guy can't lie. But since the engagement, things have shifted. I can tell that his priorities have changed. He's always talking about the wedding and what he and Katherine have planned for this and that. I'm happy for the guy. I just liked it when I knew he was one hundred percent in the game. Because I'm totally committed to our business. I have to be. I can't have another business failure on my balance sheet. I won't let it happen.

"I hope she doesn't start talking all things Austen to your parents," Katherine says to Ed, smoothing her hand up his lapel. "She doesn't realize that channeling Mrs. Bennet isn't a good look."

"What's she going to say?" Ed asks. "*Pride and Prejudice* is Jane Austen's greatest work!"

Maybe I'm drunker than I thought, but I don't have a clue about what's going on. Why are we discussing Jane Austen?

The woman with the great breasts, who must definitely be the sister, holds up her palm to Ed to stop him. "I can't let that one pass. Everyone who hasn't read the books thinks *Pride and Prejudice* is Austen's finest, when it isn't at all . . ." Ed goes to speak, but Lucy isn't having any of it. "And no, not even the miniseries starring Colin Firth makes it acceptable not to have read the books."

Katherine groans at the mention of the miniseries. "Three hundred and twenty-seven minutes."

"Her making us watch that adaptation as often as we did was bordering on traumatic," Lucy says. "I hate it. The only reason I'm so good at math is because I'd do calculus in my head while being forced to sit through it. Lizzy Bennet is a gold digger, and Darcy is a pompous idiot. No, Austen's best book is obviously *Persuasion*. Captain Wentworth is a devoted hottie."

"Captain? Did she write about sailing?" I ask.

Lucy rolls her eyes but doesn't respond. I was only trying to join in the conversation.

She probably hangs out at libraries and has nineteen cats at home. I take a sip of my drink. I didn't need to participate in this conversation anyway.

"*Persuasion* is timeless, and Wentworth is a proper alpha. Not a spoiled guy with a stick up his ass," Lucy says. "It's clear Wentworth is going to know what to do with Anne when he finally gets her naked."

I half choke on my drink when Lucy says "naked," and heat fills my cheeks, like a teenager caught flicking through an underwear catalog.

"'I have loved none but you,'" Katherine and Lucy say in unison.

I'm totally lost. I glance over at Ed, but he's smiling at the two women like he's at a showing of a Hallmark movie. I slide my drink onto the high top table. Maybe I've had one too many.

"She's going to start quoting Austen to the entire party," Katherine says. "And Ed isn't Mr. Bingley." She looks up at Ed. "If you're only earning four thousand a year, I'm not marrying you." She and Ed laugh, but I'm totally confused.

I slide my sunglasses to the top of my head and glance over at Lucy. "Who the hell is Mr. Bingley?" I whisper.

She sighs. "The hero's BFF in *Pride and Prejudice*, who falls in love with the heroine's sister. Mom was determined that Katherine should find her Bingley."

"They sound like side characters. Shouldn't they be the hero and heroine if everyone is so fixated on them?"

"Impossible!" Lucy says, like I've just suggested we throw red ants rather than confetti at the wedding. "Jane and Bingley are perfect. Flawless. Just like Katherine and Ed. Main characters must have flaws, or they're not interesting enough to sustain a reader's attention." She holds my gaze, like she really wants to make sure I understand her. "Anyway, our mother thinks Katherine is the perfect Jane in *Pride and Prejudice* and Ed, here, is the rich BFF who is going to keep her in the manner to which she would like to become accustomed."

"She wants Katherine to marry for money?" I ask. "Like, encouraged her to be a gold digger?"

Lucy pauses for a moment. "Jane and Lizzy married for love." Her tone is resolute. "But their husbands happened to be rich AF."

"Maybe you're Mr. Darcy," Katherine says, grinning at me.

I know I'm missing something, because Lucy gives Katherine a sharp poke in the ribs with her elbow. "Don't be an asshole."

"And you said I wasn't subtle," Ed mumbles.

We're interrupted by someone I haven't been introduced to. Katherine and Ed are swept away by the woman, leaving me with Lucy.

"You're drunk," she says.

I shrug. "You're beautiful."

She doesn't respond, just watches as Ed and Katherine cross the lawn.

Usually telling a woman she's beautiful will change the game. I'm not saying it turns all women to mush, but it usually wins them over a little. And it's no lie—Lucy is most definitely beautiful. She has a smattering of freckles across her nose and green eyes with amber edges. Her hair is long and fans over her shoulders on both sides, catching on the buttons of her dress, like a trickle of water between her breasts. *Shit.* My dick twitches. I stand up from where I was leaning on the table and stumble. Lucy snaps her head around.

"You're *really* drunk. Do you think you should go back to your hotel?" Her eyes flash with panic.

"I'm okay," I say. "Maybe I'll get a glass of water."

"Maybe I'll get you a cab."

"I'm not leaving," I snap. "Ed is my best friend. I'm not going anywhere."

"Yeah, much better to stay and start falling over. Maybe you can feel up his great-aunt Mildred. That would be perfect."

"You're uptight," I say.

"That's funny," she says. "And here I thought I was beautiful."

A surge of nausea hits me square in my stomach, and I grip the table. "I think maybe . . ." I pause, wondering whether I'm going to have to take a seat on the grass rather than fall.

Lucy pulls out her phone. "Where are you staying? Harbor Inn?"

I nod, unable to argue with her. My stomach is churning, and the people at the party have all started to sway. That last glass of tequila has really hit home.

"Come on," she says. "I'll make sure you get into the Uber."

She threads her arm through mine, and I don't object. I can't. I'm clearly way too drunk for a daytime party like this one. I should have given myself a two-drink limit. Lucy smells like rose petals and something I can't quite place. Somehow it settles my stomach a little, and we manage to navigate to the front of the house without me falling on my ass.

"I need to tell Ed," I say.

"I'll say you had to go."

"He's my best friend." He's more than that. He's the guy who saved me from a lifeless career behind a desk, working for someone else. He's my business partner.

"Okay," Lucy says. "I'll make sure to tell him he's your best friend."

Lucy speaks to the Uber driver, who's just pulled up, and bundles me inside.

I hear her shrieking. "Two hundred dollars? He's not going to vomit."

All of a sudden, she's sliding into the seat next to me. "You owe me for this, Hunter. You're going to let me have my way on everything for the bachelor/bachelorette party, you hear me?"

I don't know what's happening, but I just nod.

The Uber proceeds to drive the obstacle course from Katherine's parents' house back to the inn. I swear to God, there weren't potholes the size of Vesuvius and bends like we're racing the Monaco Grand Prix on the way up here.

Lucy leans across me and unwinds the window. I stroke her hair as she stretches over my lap. It's as soft and smooth as it looks.

"Hunter," Lucy snaps. "Get off."

I hold my hands up, realizing she probably doesn't want to be petted like a dog. It's probably a good idea that I left the party. I just don't know why Lucy came with me.

"If you're going to hurl, please do it out the window. There's no way I'm paying the two-hundred-dollar cleanup fee."

I open my mouth to respond, but Lucy squishes her hand against my cheek, trying to press my head toward the window.

"I'm not going to vomit," I yell. "That's all I was going to say."

Lucy shakes her head but removes her hand from my face. "Men are babies."

"I don't need babying," I say. "You didn't have to join me in the car."

"Er, excuse me if I care about my Uber rating. I've spent months building it back up after . . . Never mind. I'm not letting you ruin it for me."

Just as I'm about to ask her what happened to her Uber rating, we pull up outside the inn. "Sorry to take you away from the party."

"At least we all know you're definitely not Mr. Darcy," she says as I stumble out of the Uber. She literally pushes me out of the car with both her feet and slams the door behind me.

I watch the car circle the drive and retrace its steps back toward the party. When the car pulls onto the main road, Lucy turns and we lock eyes. Something hits me in the chest, like a fastball straight to the heart.

CHAPTER THREE

Lucy

I will never forgive Hunter. I missed Ed's speech about how much he loved my sister, and rejoined the party just as my mother was crying about how the academy should have changed the rules to allow Colin Firth to get an Oscar for his portrayal of Darcy. If I'd been there, it would have never escalated to the point of tears. And on top of that, even though I couldn't have been gone for more than twenty minutes, my mother somehow managed to surface from her Colin-induced grief to a) notice I'd left the party, and b) chastise me for not caring about my sister's happiness—or anyone's—other than my own. All I'd been doing was trying to stop the party from being ruined, yet somehow, I'm the problem. I hope Hunter doesn't have the nerve to show for brunch.

I'm carrying a fruit platter to the table when a cab pulls up in front of my parents' house. Surely Hunter will be passed out all day and the Harbor Inn will have to break down the door to get him out when he sleeps through checkout.

But lo and behold, it's Hunter who gets out of the cab, wearing sunglasses and a preppy shorts-and-polo combo that shows off his tan legs and a smattering of chest hair. He's like Ed's hotter, less reliable brother.

But I can't hate Ed like I hate Hunter.

"Here he is," Katherine says excitably as she watches Hunter come up the path. "I'm so pleased you two are getting along."

I pull my mouth into a wide smile. There's no way I can let Katherine know that I think Hunter is a dick. He was at his best friend's engagement party. If he couldn't handle his alcohol, he shouldn't have been drinking. But I want Katherine to think Hunter and I are getting on like a house on fire. That way she'll be reassured the joint party will be flawless . . . unless I can convince her to have the bachelor and bachelorette parties separately. I mean, whoever heard of a joint party?

"I was thinking about the bachelorette party," I say to Katherine. "You know the best spas are in New York. I can ask Amanda about it, because she's bound to get us a great deal somewhere amazing. And then we could go to—"

Katherine's shaking her head before I can even finish the sentence. "Ed wants to fish. There's no way he's going to agree to New York."

I see my opening and dive right in. "Well, he could have his bachelor party here in Massachusetts, and *we* could go to New York. We could still have them the same weekend and everything, so you're not spending too much time apart. That way you could get your perfect party, and Ed could get his."

"My perfect bachelorette is a joint party with Ed in a big house right on the ocean. I can just see us all wrapped up in blankets, toasting marshmallows on the beach before bed . . ." She smiles to herself. "It seems so romantic to be there with all our friends. And so many of our friends are couples. It makes sense to do it together."

"But you're going to have your entire lives together."

Katherine shrugs. "Right. Because we like hanging out together. Marrying Ed isn't a choice between freedom and drudgery. I'm marrying him because life is better with him. And that includes my party."

I sigh. I so badly want to throw Katherine a perfect bachelorette party. If that means a joint party, that's what I'm going to have to give her. I'm locked into preparations with the douche that is Hunter. Well, he owes me from last night. He's going to have to go along with what I want. It has to be perfect. I add *beach bonfire, blankets,* and *marshmallows* to my mental checklist. And that's just the start.

"Then that's what you shall have," I say.

"I know getting a house that big for all of us will be a challenge, especially given how late it is in the season," Katherine says. "People book Cape houses a year in advance."

My stomach churns. I've made a few inquiries already. The combination of the number of us together, the need to be on the beach, and the fact that it's a bachelorette party means no one will rent to us.

"I'll figure it out." I have to.

Katherine looks at me, her big doe eyes making me feel like I have her heart in my hands. "Thank you, Lucy. I have faith in you." My mom calls her name, and she disappears into the kitchen.

I don't know whether I believe her. People say things like "I have faith in you" to Katherine all the time. She's the reliable one. The pretty one. The one who manages to make things work out. I'm not that sister. And although Katherine has always stuck up for me when my parents make comments about how Katherine is . . . more capable, I sometimes wonder whether she really believes it. I have to repay her faith in me and get the perfect house on the beach. Maybe I need to go to the Cape to scope out a rental in person—something not listed on one of the websites.

I've just got to find a place.

I glance over at Hunter. He's the first to sit at the brunch table, and then my father joins him. Hunter's sunglasses are glued over his eyes. The sun isn't even that bright today, and we're underneath an awning. He's being rude. Or he's probably covering his swollen, red eyes after all the booze he had yesterday. Maybe I should make house hunting his problem. We're just weeks away. We need to get something locked in. But I've already looked and come up short.

My dad is called inside, leaving Hunter on his own.

"Hunter," I call. "Can I have a chat?" My voice is all singsong-y, like I don't think he's a dick. It's so completely typical that I'd be paired with a man like Hunter to plan the joint party. Why couldn't I have gotten a lucky break for once? Why couldn't Hunter be an alpha male who will stop at nothing to make his best friend's bachelor party a success?

He stands, shoves his hands in his pockets and rounds the table. I lead him to the edge of the grass, well away from the porch doors and anyone who might overhear us.

When we come to a stop, I pause for a second, waiting for Hunter to say something. I look at him, giving him the chance to apologize for being a sloppy, drunken mess yesterday, to thank me for getting him back to his hotel. Instead, he just stands there, silent, his eyes covered with his damn sunglasses.

"Seriously?" I ask him.

"Seriously what?"

"I don't know, would it kill you to thank me for making sure you got back home? Or thank me for calling you a cab?"

He groans. "Oh my God. Thank you *so* very much for pressing three buttons on your Uber app. Send me your Venmo, and I'll pay you back." Sarcasm drips from every syllable.

"I missed Ed's speech, you asshole."

"You're welcome," he responds.

"I didn't want to miss it. I wanted to hear about how much he loves my sister and—"

"Christ on a bike, speak to Ed on any given day and he'll tell you how much he loves Katherine. And anyway, no doubt you can go to the Instagram of any of Katherine's friends and see it replayed from every angle."

I narrow my eyes at him. He's not wrong. I checked Suzy Wong's IG this morning, and I can hear Ed's speech perfectly through her strangled sobs. "I would like to have been there, taken in the moment. You might like to be completely blotto for all the important moments in life. But I prefer to be present." He doesn't need to know about Mom chastising me for being selfish.

"So you pulled me over here to tell me off?" he asks. "I consider myself spanked. Can I go back to my coffee now?" He takes a step back to the table, and I grab his shirt.

"I'm not done."

He looks down at where I'm pulling on his shirt. "Are we going to have a full physical fight now? Like, is there a ring? Are people placing bets?"

"Sorry," I mumble, dropping the material bunched in my hand. Why am I apologizing? "Look, you don't like me, I don't like you, that's totally fine. But we have to plan this party, and we have to make it perfect. Ed and Katherine deserve nothing less." Hell, *I* deserve nothing less. If I actually manage to pull it off, Mom might cut me a break. And if I don't? It will just be more evidence that I'm the hopeless letdown she's always known I am.

Hunter doesn't respond. He doesn't move. He might have actually fallen asleep standing up.

"And?" he says eventually.

"Oh, good, you're still awake," I bite back. "And so we have to work together to make sure the weekend is perfect and exactly what they want. What they both deserve."

"I'll have my assistant reach out to you." He turns to leave again.

"Don't put yourself out," I respond.

He stops and turns back to me. "What is it you want from me?"

"Well, now that you're asking, I want you to find me a ten-bedroom, ten-bathroom house on the Cape for three weeks from now that will take a party our size. It has to be right on the beach and luxurious as all hell."

"Got it," he says and turns back to the party.

"Hunter," I snap. "Get back here." I chase after him. "Hunter."

"What?" he says as he strides back to the table. "You told me what you want. I'll let you know what I find. Now I need my coffee, and I need you to leave me alone."

I stop and let him go. There's no point in chasing after him. There's no way he's going to help me. I'm on my own.

CHAPTER FOUR

Hunter

I often blow through lunch. I'm either on calls or in meetings. My assistant will leave a salad on my desk, and I won't even get the chance to look at it, let alone eat it, before most people leave for the day. I don't notice the hunger. I'm too busy. Too caught up in making Portis Investments a success. I've always been focused, but seeing a business fail and being at the helm while it sank focuses the mind. If I can add value, I'd rather do that than stand in line for a pastrami on rye.

But today my meeting finished early, everyone in the office keeps going on about what a nice day it is, and my assistant ordered me outside to get my own lunch. She insisted it was her way of supporting my mental health.

She may have been right. Even though I feel slightly guilty about not returning the ten calls I have on my call sheet, it feels good to be out in the daylight. People are everywhere, rushing in every direction. Others are sitting on the bits of walls or steps that have escaped the shadows. They clearly don't have time to make it the five blocks to the park but want to be outside. Cabs are honking. Traffic is at a standstill. It feels so . . . normal. But I don't usually see any of it. I get to the office when it's still dark, and I haven't left before midnight more than twice in the last six weeks. It's ironic that both those times were because of

Ed and Katherine. First, I met the happy couple for dinner when they came down to New York a month ago. Then I had to catch a flight up to Boston for the engagement party on Friday. Their engagement and wedding planning is pulling away my focus as well as Ed's. It's only Portis Investments that's going to suffer. We can't both be mentally checked out at the same time. Someone's got to keep us afloat.

I head to my favorite sandwich shop, Stranger than Fiction. Each sandwich is named after something book related. It's designed for tourists, but move over Holden Caulfield, I love a Swiss cheese sandwich and a malted milk. It isn't much, but you get quite a lot of vitamins in the malted milk.

I take my place in the line, which stretches out the door, and check my phone to see what I'm missing on my email.

The first one is from Ed. The subject is "Sorry bud"—never a good sign. I scan the email and do my best not to swear or put a fist through the nearest wall. He's not coming to the dinner with FMCH tomorrow. He knows how important it is. Landing a client like FMCH could add thirty percent to our revenues next year. What is he thinking? I look more closely at the email. He has an appointment to taste food for the wedding. I reread it to make sure I'm not hallucinating. He can't seriously be skipping an opportunity to sit down with the decision-makers at FMCH to eat fucking chicken.

So far, I haven't said anything to Ed about the way I think his focus has been pulled away. But now? It's gone too far. I can't call him right away. I'm too wound up. I take a steadying breath and glance at the front of the line. Something or someone is taking a long time.

I pull up an email from an old college buddy, Jack. He's from old New York money and has a really nice place on Martha's Vineyard where I stayed one summer back in college. He knows the area, so I emailed him to see whether he knew of a good place for the party. I had my assistant scour all the usual websites, but everything is fully booked or just not big enough.

I'm just opening the email when I hear a shrill voice say, "Shouldn't you be looking for a beach house and not hanging out in the sunshine on a random Tuesday?"

I look up and come face-to-face with Lucy.

I groan inwardly. I thought I'd left her behind in Boston. "What are you doing here?" I ask.

"I work in that building." She points at the mirrored building next to the one Portis Investments is in.

Of course she does.

"I'm getting a sandwich, so shoot me," I say.

"Happily, but I don't own a gun." She shrugs. "And plus, orange isn't my color."

"I suppose that's my fault too?"

She looks at me like she's weighing how difficult it would be to strangle me.

"So have you found anywhere?" she asks, her tone softening a little. "This joint bachelor/ bachelorette party is in three weeks. We need somewhere to stay, and Katherine has her heart set on a beach house on the Cape. We can't let her down."

"We can't keep calling it 'the joint bachelor/bachelorette party.' It's too much of a mouthful."

"Call it whatever the hell you want when you find a house for us."

This woman hates me. I don't understand her problem. Okay, so I was a little drunk the first time we met and a little hungover the second. But it's not like I got drunk to piss her off. Why is she taking it personally?

"I've been reaching out to some contacts to see if I can find anything."

"I don't care about what you're doing. I want results. Don't give me inputs. I want outputs."

The corners of my mouth twitch slightly. She sounds a little like me when I'm looking over people's work and they give me all the background—all the research they've been doing—when I only want to see the conclusion.

"I want a house!" Her voice is growing louder. People in line are starting to side-eye our little tête-à-tête.

"Shouting at me won't make real estate listings magically appear." I look back at my phone to see if the email from Jack says anything that will get Lucy off my back.

Lucy's still talking at me as I read through Jack's response. His family house . . . blah blah, he's just bought a place as an investment . . . blah blah . . . and there's a hyperlink.

"Are you even listening to me?" Lucy snaps at me.

"No. I'm trying to read an email about a rental for this goddamn prewedding party." I squint at the screen. The pictures on the website are beautiful, and it's on Martha's Vineyard. Not the Cape, but near enough. I flip back to the email from Jack to make sure it's available. It's newly refurbished and hasn't been up for rental until last week, which is why it's available for the weekend we need. I just hit the goddamn jackpot.

"Sure you are," Lucy says. "But seriously, get off ESPN or whatever the hell you're messing with on your phone and problem-solve. We need to figure this out."

I groan. Why is she still complaining? I'm not going to tell her I just came up with a solution to our house-rental problem. Let her sweat it out a little longer.

I drop my phone and look directly at Lucy. For a moment, I'm stunned. I'd forgotten how completely mesmerizing her eyes are. She's got a little more makeup on than I saw her in this weekend. She looks kick-ass. I scan her body. She's in a tightly fitted dress and high heels, her hair pulled back into one of those styles that makes her look like a forties movie star.

Something trips in my chest, and I can feel a blush creeping up my neck. How can looking at a girl make me blush? Especially a woman as annoying as Lucy. Does she give everyone a hard time like this, or does she save all her energy for me? For a second, I visualize grabbing her by the wrist, pressing her up against the wall by the sandwich store, and kissing her, just to stop her from talking.

"Hunter!" she says, snapping me out of my thoughts.

"What?" I snap back, irritated by her sniping, irritated by Ed's email, irritated that I've been standing in line for twenty minutes for a goddamn sandwich.

"You are hopeless," she says. "I'm giving you forty-eight hours to find us the best beach house on the Cape. I don't care how much you have to pay or who you have to kill. Just get it done." She turns and heads off, her heels clipping the ground like they're telling me to get. It. Done. Get. It. Done. Get. It. Done.

Does she understand who she's talking to? I run a business of thirty employees and invest assets of over three hundred million dollars. I don't take orders from anyone.

The line starts moving, but I've lost my appetite. Everything feels overwhelming. Not only am I now shouldering Ed's contribution to Portis on top of my own full plate, I'm also party-planning. This isn't how I saw my year going.

CHAPTER FIVE

Lucy

I'm manically chewing the edge of my thumbnail and tapping my toe on the floor of the bar where I'm drowning my sorrows. I just don't know how I'm going to tell Katherine that we didn't find a house on the Cape. Of course, Katherine will be entirely understanding—that's who Katherine is. Understanding. Sweet. Caring. But no matter her reaction, I'm going to feel like the hopeless little sister who can't do anything right compared to her.

"What about something in the Hamptons?" Charlotte suggests.

Charlotte and I have been friends since we were three years old. She's seen me through every lost tooth and broken heart. She knew me when I was a ragbag of lost schoolbooks and stained T-shirts. And she knows me now, when I'm all spreadsheets and patent pumps. Charlotte knows all the versions of me, and most importantly, she accepts them all. She knows I'm not the same scruffy teenager I used to be—the one my mother still thinks I am. Just like I know she's no longer a Belieber.

Times have changed.

"There's just so much more inventory there."

"You know I love the Hamptons, but Katherine wants to be on the Cape. I think being in Massachusetts is the most important factor. Apart from being with Ed." I sigh and tip my head back. "We could look at a hotel, I suppose, but none of the fancy ones have enough rooms—I've already checked. Even if they did, oceanfront rooms for a party our size would be cost prohibitive."

"Katherine will understand," Charlotte says. "It's all very last minute, considering."

Considering Ed and Katherine have been together forever. Ed wanted his business to be more established before they tied the knot, because he knows Katherine wants children as soon as they're married. He wants to be financially stable before they start a family. Once he felt ready, everything started happening in fast-forward. I'm happy for them that they feel ready for this next phase in their lives. I just wish they'd given us all a little more time to plan.

"You're right," I say. "Katherine will understand. But that's not the point. I wanted to be able to give her what she wants. She's such a good person, who does so much for everyone else. She should have an incredible send-off into her marriage."

Charlotte raises an eyebrow.

"What?" I ask defensively. "It's true."

"That might be *part* of the reason you want to throw the perfect bachelorette. But it's not the only reason."

I shrug. "So sue me for wanting people to see I've grown up."

"Your mom's going to be there?"

I nod. "Just for the dinner on Saturday. She's not staying over. Same for my aunt and her two daughters." Charlotte wrinkles her nose. She met my cousins years ago, but they haven't changed. They're terrible snobs, ready and willing to look down their noses at whoever they don't think is good enough. "The only people staying in the house are Katherine and Ed, three of Katherine's friends from college with their boyfriends, me, the best man, and two more of Ed's friends."

"That's a lot of people."

"I know. And we still don't have anywhere to stay. The best man is supposed to have come up with something. I gave him a deadline of lunchtime today, but I've heard absolutely nothing from him, despite me texting him at least nineteen times."

Charlotte laughs. Even though I'm furious with Hunter for not returning any of my texts, I smile. I probably did go a little overboard on the text assault.

"What about glamping?" Charlotte suggests. "Do you think she'd go for it?"

The bachelorette party is so front and center in my mind that when I glance across the bar, I swear I see Hunter. I look back to Charlotte.

"I'm not sure Katherine would love it, but she'd go along with it," I say. "But I don't want Katherine to have to *endure* her bachelorette. She should get what she wants."

"But if it's impossible, it's impossible," Charlotte says, just as the guy I thought was Hunter turns in my direction and we lock eyes.

It *is* Hunter.

Hunter, who blew through my deadline of finding a beach house by today, then ignored each one of my nineteen requests for an update.

He was too busy planning his night out at the bar, by the looks of it.

"I can't believe it," I seethe.

"What?" Charlotte asks.

"It's the drunk best man who's supposed to be finding me a beach house."

"Where?" she asks. "The hot one?"

"He's not hot." That's a lie, but at this precise moment, he could look like Colin Firth had a baby with Matthew Macfadyen and I'd want to rip his face from his body.

I stand. Charlotte pulls at my hand.

"No, Lucy. Sit down. Don't go over there."

"Of course I'm going over there," I say, fisting my hands and looking around for an appropriate weapon. "I can't just sit here and let him get away with . . . with . . . not finding me a beach house." I sigh, trying to tamp down the anger that's started to boil in my veins. "'There's no one so capable as me.'" It's an affliction.

"Are you quoting *Persuasion*? Be reasonable," Charlotte says. "You said yourself finding a beach house was impossible."

My heart is thumping in my chest, and I'm ready for war. How dare he be out socializing when he hasn't fulfilled his basic obligations as best man? As far as I can tell, he hasn't even put in the minimum effort to do his part. "I have no notion of treating him with such respect. That is the way to spoil them."

Charlotte groans and grabs my hand. She knows that if I'm bastardizing quotes from *Northanger Abbey*, it's serious. I pull my hand from her grip and stomp over to where Hunter is happily chatting to his buddies.

"Sir, you are simply being disagreeable, socializing like this!" I blurt out as I approach the table. It's like the cork from the champagne has popped and I've bubbled over, but I have no idea why I'm talking like I'm in a Jane Austen adaptation, just like my mother has the habit of doing when she's trying to impress someone.

Hunter turns to me, his expression thoroughly confused. All at once, the fight leaves my body. I realize his entire group is looking at me. Suddenly, I feel self-conscious. These men are older than Hunter, and it doesn't look like they're out to party. The atmosphere is more formal.

I'm an idiot. This is a business thing.

I want to skip back ten seconds and go back to the bit where Charlotte is tugging at my hand.

Then Hunter laughs. "This is Ed's soon-to-be sister-in-law. Very nice to see you here, Lucy." He's all formality—although he doesn't launch into a Darcy impression—and professionalism. He turns back to the group of five men. "We're organizing the joint bachelorette/bachelor party together." He turns back to me, his eyes wide, urging me to comply. "Perhaps I can call you tomorrow morning?"

I pull my mouth into the perfect grin and nod. "Sure, Hunter. Very nice to meet you all." I find myself doing an inexplicable little bow before I back away from the table.

I head back to Charlotte, defeated and humiliated. Who the hell were those guys? And why am I so unhinged?

"I need a drink," I say.

"I thought you might. I just ordered us both tequilas since my secondhand embarrassment is so strong I want to be unalive right now."

"'Angry people are not always wise,'" I say on a sigh. "Austen was right." I clamp my hand over my mouth. I want to take back every syllable. "Charlotte, I've lost my goddamned mind."

She nods like I just told her I have athlete's foot. She's all sympathy and understanding but doesn't want to get too close.

"Am I becoming my mother?" I ask. I basically morphed into Elizabeth Bennet back there. Without the fine eyes. I think my mom must have passed it down in her DNA or something.

Charlotte gives a shrug that's too close to "maybe" for my comfort.

"I've got to stop accosting people in public spaces. And when I say *people*, I mean Hunter. From now on, I vow to only scream at him in private. And," I add at Charlotte's cutting look, "rather than scream, I'm going to tone it down to a whisper-shout."

"I'd say that's real growth." She tips her head to the side. "From your starting point. But it's probably not your final destination. You could consider that he's having as hard a time as you finding a place. Maybe he dodged your texts because . . . well, first off, there's so many of them, and secondly, because maybe he doesn't want to disappoint you."

I think back to Hunter, drunk at the engagement party. "I don't think Hunter gives a rat's ass about disappointing me. But that doesn't mean I can scream at him in public."

"For no other reason than it doesn't seem to have any effect apart from . . ."

"My own humiliation?" I suggest.

Charlotte holds up one of the shots that's just been placed in front of us. "If the shoe fits . . ."

CHAPTER SIX

Hunter

I slide into the booth at Gardinier, my favorite Midtown restaurant, and allow myself to relax for the first time in a week. Lunch with Ed will be good. I'm going to lay my cards on the table. I'm going to tell him I'm pissed that he canceled only days before the meeting with FMCH. I'm going to say that I don't mind picking up the slack for him while he's busy with wedding stuff, but I can't do it forever. It's unsustainable. I feel like I'm a step away from losing my mind at any moment of the day. If he thinks getting married means this is how things are going to stay, then he better speak now or forever hold his peace. Because if things don't change, I'm out. We need to close down Portis Investments, and I'll go and get myself a job. The alternative is, I lose my mind and Portis goes belly up. I won't let either of those things happen.

But at least I haven't totally lost my mind. Not yet. That honor goes to the absolutely unhinged sister of the bride.

I can't be sure, but I think Lucy called me "sir" in front of FMCH last night. I don't know if she was trying to be polite, but she seemed like she was being all uptight. Victorian, almost. Like maybe she was having some kind of . . . episode or something. Had she tracked me down at the bar? No, I haven't answered her messages, but I've been busy trying to do Ed's job on top of mine. Is she stalking me? I just saw her outside Stranger than Fiction. And then in the bar? I've never run into her before, and now twice in one week. It doesn't make sense. I know we work in offices next door to each other, but there are too many coincidences for my liking. Does Ed know the family he's marrying into? Maybe Katherine's the same as Lucy, but she hides it better.

I might mention it to Ed. I'll just add it to my long list of uncomfortable conversations to have with my best friend.

I watch the door, cell in hand, half expecting Ed to cancel and cite a wedding emergency as an excuse. When I see him walk through the double doors, I exhale in relief.

He didn't cancel.

I'm overthinking.

He's still my best friend and business partner.

And then I see Katherine come through the door behind him, followed by my nemesis of the week: Lucy.

Perfect. This was meant to be a relaxed lunch between two friends to talk about business, not another opportunity to discuss-celebrate-mark Ed and Katherine's wedding.

Ed greets me, all smiles. "Katherine came down with me and was meeting Lucy for lunch. It made sense to make it a foursome."

Made sense to whom? Someone who doesn't know Lucy?

"I do have some things I need to talk to you about regarding Portis," I say.

"Sure. We can talk business, can't we, babe?" he asks Katherine.

She rolls her eyes like all we do is talk business. I *wish* that were the case.

"Come on, babe. We need to go over some stuff. I think. Don't we?" Ed's gaze flits between me and his soon-to-be wife.

Lucy barely meets my eye as we grunt hellos at each other. Ed and Katherine take the seats opposite the booth, and Lucy gets shunted in next to me.

Perfect. Just fucking perfect.

We order our drinks, and Katherine and Lucy talk about the menu and the cocktails, intermittently mentioning names I've never heard of, while I just stare at the menu. I've lost my appetite. I'd rather be back in the office than sitting here listening to Lucy and her sister talk about nothing.

"Everything okay?" Ed asks me.

I glance up at Ed and then at Katherine. I can't have the conversations I need to have here in front of everyone.

"Sure," I say, my head buried back in the menu. I wonder if I can have a work emergency and head back to the office. This is the very last thing I wanted to do this lunchtime. Literally, if you asked me to write a list of all the things I wanted to do today, lunch with Lucy would be right at the bottom after *burn in hell.*

"Are you sure?" Ed asks.

"Yeah. Why wouldn't it be?" I ask.

"You seem stressed."

"Things are really busy," I say. Even though I don't mean it to come out, I hear the resentment in my voice.

"Look, I'm sorry I missed the meeting with FMCH."

I nod, but I can't even look at him.

"Katherine was sick and didn't think she was going to make the tasting thing. I didn't want to be a plane ride away while she wasn't feeling well."

My limbs feel heavy, like I'm disappearing into the floor. It's only Katherine that he has to worry about at the moment. What about when they start having kids? Kids are basically germ machines. There won't be a week that goes by without someone in that house being sick. I'll probably never see Ed again after the wedding. "I'm sorry to hear that," I say. I don't mean it to sound as robotic as it does when it comes out.

"It sounds positive, though," he says. "The meeting with FMCH, I mean."

I nod, and the waitress comes over to take our order. Katherine and Lucy go first. They ask questions about every single dish on the menu, and I'm a second away from grabbing my salad fork and stabbing Lucy through the heart when she finally decides on the chicken Caesar—the same as Katherine. How could it be so difficult?

Ed and I order the Wagyu burger. Because of course we do. Like we knew we were going to the moment we opened the menu. Just like Lucy knew she was going to order the chicken Caesar when she opened the menu, but she had to go through some elaborate facade of considering other options.

"Oh, I meant to order the elderflower mocktail," Katherine says.

"I'll go and ask the waitress," Ed offers. He stands and presses a kiss to Katherine's head, like he's going to struggle being away from her for all of a minute and a half. He heads off toward the server station.

"Or maybe I should go with the Bellini mocktail?" Katherine asks, like either Lucy or I have the answer to what she wants to drink. Katherine stands and goes after Ed, leaving Lucy and me side by side, on our own.

"You haven't replied to my messages," she snipes from the corner of her mouth.

"Which one of the three hundred and fifty messages would you like me to reply to first?" I snark back. Under my breath, I mutter, "Do you think Katherine really wanted the Bellini mocktail, or did she not want to be away from Ed for a single second?"

"Any single one would do," she replies. "And they're in *love*. I think it's cute that they want to be together all the time." She sighs.

We both have our eyes on Ed and Katherine as they stand at the bar and peruse the drinks menu. Ed's arm is around Katherine's waist, and Katherine is resting her head on Ed's arm. It's like they have a need to be physically connected to each other at all times.

"What do you want from me?" I say on an exhausted sigh. "You've stalked me and harassed me in front of potential clients, and now you're acting like you're the injured party."

"I saved you from embarrassing yourself at the engagement party by taking you back to your hotel. I made sure you didn't vomit in the cab.

And when I realized you were holding a serious business meeting in the bar the other night, I left. I don't see you thanking me for any of that."

"Thanking you?" I say through a grin I flash at Ed when he looks over. "For what? For behaving like a deranged psychopath whenever I see you?"

Lucy groans and slumps back in the booth. "You're so dramatic. For God's sake. All I want to do is give my sister the perfect bachelorette party, and you're acting like I'm the one who's got problems. You might not give a shit about your friend, but sue me for caring about my sister. And all your complaining hasn't gotten us anywhere. We still have nowhere to stay and have no prospect of finding anywhere. The bachelor/bachelorette party is just over two weeks away."

"Wrong!" I exclaim smugly.

"Okay, two weeks and one day, you pedantic dick."

"Wrong, we do have a place to stay for the weekend, you hapless harpy."

Lucy narrows her eyes at me. "Hapless harpy? *Hapless harpy?* That's the best you can do. Call me a bitch. Call me a 'deranged psychopath,' but 'hapless harpy'?" She lets out another groan, and for some reason, it vibrates up my thighs and connects to my balls. *"Pathetic."*

"You're right. 'Deranged psychopath' was more accurate. The point is, we have a place to stay. I got us a Friday-to-Monday rental on the Cape. Kinda."

Lucy eyes me suspiciously. "What do you mean, *kinda*?"

"That's what you focus on? Not the fact that I've managed to procure the entire group a house for the weekend, right on the beach. You focus on the fact that I said it was *kinda* on the Cape."

"Yeah, well, being on the Cape is super important to Katherine. So if it's not *exactly* on the Cape, it's not going to fly. Where is this supposed house?"

Ed and Katherine are heading back to the table hand in hand, grinning at each other. They're ridiculous.

"I'll tell you when I next see you," I say through gritted teeth.

Lucy is almost out of her seat, she's so filled with frustration. A part of me is sort of enjoying toying with her. "I've messaged you nineteen times asking you for an update, and you've ignored me. I've tried my best to get you to meet with me, but I get crickets. This celebration is in two weeks. We need to meet and make plans."

Lucy falls silent as Katherine and Ed get to the table.

"You know one of the best things about this joint party?" Katherine asks. In her two hands, she grabs mine and Lucy's hands across the table. "It's seeing the two of you building a relationship and becoming friends. It makes me so happy."

"Seriously," Ed says. "We were saying on the way down that the way Lucy saw you back to the hotel after the engagement party was really nice. It's so great that you're getting on so well. You know you've always felt like family to me, Hunter. And Lucy is going to be actual family. It's so great we can all hang out like this."

"It's perfect!" Katherine says. "I never want to have to worry who to invite to what events. Especially when we're down here in New York."

Lucy gives me a playful punch to my arm. "One big happy family."

"And seriously, you should feel free to talk business," she says. "Some of the time, at least. In fact, now, even. Lucy and I can chat if you two want to talk about something."

Ed looks at me expectantly. But this isn't a business lunch. Not anymore. It's not like we can actually talk.

"I understand how important work is to you both," Katherine says.

Does she, though? Because if she really did, would she even be here? And the thing I was going to talk to Ed about was his focus. Or lack of it. It's not like I can bring that up now. Or maybe if I say a little, Katherine will understand the situation and encourage Ed to get his head in the game?

"Okay," I say, my tone cautious. "We've got a lot going on, as you know. We're all working really long hours, but we're just keeping the wheels on. We need to start automating some of the admin processes we have, and that takes a lot of resources."

"What?" Lucy asks. It takes everything I have not to roll my eyes at the interruption. "Admin processes like KYC and stuff?"

I take a beat. Should I be discussing this in front of Lucy? Why is she so interested?

"Yes, KYC and some of the financial questionnaires. It would be good to have it automated, but doing it takes time—"

"You can get consultancies to come in and do it. That's what we did in our firm. They're industry specific. I had to look into it because I automated all the NDAs. No one had done it because they were all focused on the big documents, but actually it's saved a ton of time because we use them so frequently. It's really worth the investment." She nods enthusiastically, and for a moment I wonder if she's been possessed by a fully functioning human rather than the deranged psycho we both agree she normally is.

"Right," I say, nodding to Ed. "That's what I keep saying. Even though they're short documents, it saves time—"

"And it's more professional these days," Lucy interrupts. "If you're not automating things like KYC while your competitors are, you're wasting money."

"Right," I say, spluttering in agreement. "It's an investment worth making."

"Sounds good," Katherine says.

Ed sighs as if he can't think about another thing. "Maybe we can look into getting a consultancy firm in to do it. We're spread so thin at the moment."

Don't I know it.

"And if we keep growing, it's only going to get worse," I say.

Lucy nods like she's totally in my corner, and it makes me equally terrified and grateful.

"I can give you the name of the firm we used," she says. "We were going to meet up to go through some of the planning for the bachelor and bachelorette weekend, aren't we, Hunter? I can give you more information then."

"Sounds good," I say, trying not to be obvious that the last thing I want to do is meet up with Lucy.

"Remind me when you said that was going to be? Was it tonight? I know you're super eager to arrange everything."

"Well, I've done the hard part and found the perfect beach house," I say. "I don't think we need to overprepare."

"Perfect!" Lucy exclaims. "That's what's so great about Hunter. He's so confident. I'm coming over to your place tonight to plan everything and look at detailed images of this perfect beach house. It's going to be fantastic." She pulls out her phone. "Tell me your address?"

Fuck. I'm in checkmate. I can't refuse to give her my address—it seems shady because we're both playing along with the whole *we get on like besties* vibe. But if I give her my address, I'll have her camped out on my doorstep, demanding this, that, and the other. If Ed wasn't here, I'd just give her a fake address, maybe somewhere way up in the Bronx, so she can have a nice long subway ride to think about her recent actions. But given he's stayed at my place, there's no way I can get away with that.

I should have just messaged her and said I'd found the place. If I'd done that, she probably wouldn't insist we need a meeting. It's my own stupid fault. In fact, if I'd done that, she probably wouldn't have stomped over in the bar and embarrassed us both. Or herself, mainly. I can admit that I've been a bit of a dick, though I'll never confess it out loud. Because she's been . . . a hapless harpy.

"I'm at 222 Lexington. You can come by at eight tonight, and we'll figure everything out."

I deserve my fate, whatever that might be.

CHAPTER SEVEN

Lucy

It's 7:55 p.m. when I press the buzzer for Hunter's apartment. By the time I'm at his door, it will be eight, so technically, I won't be early.

The buzzer crackles and then Hunter speaks over the intercom. "Of course you're early."

"Technically, I won't be—" The door unlocks with a buzz, cutting me off. I balance the Bankers Box on my knee and pull open the door. He could have offered to come down and help me with this.

I arrive at his door and tap it with my foot, as I don't want to put the box down. Hunter is already talking when he abruptly pulls open the door.

"What the actual hell, Lucy? Why are you kicking my . . ." He sees my full hands, and there's a moment when we both silently recognize how quickly he jumped to conclusions. The *wrong* conclusions.

"Add it to the list," I say.

"The . . . what?"

"The list. Of grievances? About me? I'm sure there's a running tab somewhere."

He leans against the doorjamb and crosses his ankles, like it has never once occurred to him to take the heavy box out of my hands. "You forget," Hunter says. "I've met your parents. I've met your sister.

I've even met your great-aunt Mildred. They all seem so . . . *normal.* What happened to you? Dropped on your head as a child? Switched at birth? Alien overlord trapped in a human-skin suit?"

There's an edge to his teasing that makes me feel like he's reached into my rib cage and pulled out my heart. Hunter might be a lot of things—a lot of annoying things—but I didn't realize until just now that he's *mean.*

I glance down at the box in my arms and realize this is pointless. I don't have the energy to go on like this. I can't even be bothered to tell him that Great-Aunt Mildred is Ed's aunt, not mine. I'm never going to be my sister. I'm never going to flit through my perfect life, sprinkling perfection wherever I go. No matter how organized or punctual or put together I am, I'll always just be me. The *other* Jones sister.

I sigh and turn back to the elevators. I'm done. I don't have it in me to fight with someone who doesn't care. At least not tonight.

"Lucy," Hunter calls.

I can't even bring myself to respond.

"Lucy," Hunter calls again as he follows me out of the apartment. "Look, I'm sorry if I overreacted about the door. Let's just go inside." He tugs at the Bankers Box. "What the hell is in here?"

"It doesn't matter," I say.

"It does matter."

My arms are tired from carrying the box, my back is starting to twinge, and I'd give anything to take off my heels. Worst of all, though, is how tired my soul is from constantly trying to prove myself.

"I'm going to head home," I say. "I give up."

Hunter tucks the heavy box under his arm like it's a newspaper and loosely grips my wrist, tugging me back toward his apartment. If I had the energy, I'd chastise him for attempted kidnapping.

"Come in and have a drink at least." His voice is soft, like he's concerned about me. He probably thinks my last few threads of mental health have finally snapped. And he might not be wrong.

I don't fight him because I have no energy left. He leads me back down the corridor and into his apartment.

"Okay, so we can put that there." His tone has shifted. It's not as acidic as normal. It's like he might have realized he's pushed me too far. "Sit here on the couch, so you can see the TV."

I frown. I'm not here to Netflix and chill. We have plans to make. But I don't object when he guides me to my designated spot on the couch. A moment later, he's pressing a cold glass of lemonade into my hands.

"I thought we could start with the house. Does that sound good?" The tone of his voice is the kind used by people who work with the elderly—patient, but wary.

I shrug and take a sip of lemonade. Maybe the sugar will help my mood. Who am I kidding? Nothing's going to help my mood.

Hunter takes the seat next to me and points the remote at the screen affixed to the wall. "Everything looks better on a big screen."

The screen comes to life with images of the most beautiful house I've ever seen. Rising out of a bed of white hydrangeas, with twin gables, a sprawling wraparound porch, dormers, and a rounded turret, it's more Kennedy Compound than cozy beach house. But the authentic gray shingles and clean white window frames make it feel . . . friendly.

I glance at Hunter. Is this an elaborate trick? He can't really have secured this house. There's no way. Then I remember his caveat about the location. I narrow my eyes in suspicion.

"*This* is available?" I ask.

"Yeah. I didn't want to risk losing it, so I already paid the deposit."

"For this house," I say, jabbing my finger toward the screen. "Not the guest house to this house, but *this* house."

"Yes," he says. "This is the house."

"What's the catch?" I ask. "Because I didn't see it on the market. I mean, maybe I wasn't looking in the right price category, because that must cost about a hundred thousand dollars for the weekend. I mean, can we even afford it?"

Hunter shrugs. "I've got it figured out."

"You said it wasn't on the Cape. So where is it? Maine? Canada?" There's no way he managed to secure this house on short notice anywhere near Cape Cod. It's just not possible. There has to be a ginormous catch.

He sighs and pushes his hands through his hair. "Don't lose it," he warns.

I brace myself, sending up a small prayer that the house is located somewhere Cape-adjacent.

"I won't lose it. Where is it?"

"The Vineyard."

I spring to my feet like someone's jabbed a red-hot poker up my ass. "This house." I pause and then go over to the screen and put my finger on the beautiful image on the screen. "This house right here is on Martha's Vineyard."

He nods, panicked, his eyes wide, like he's waiting for me to punch him in the face.

"And it's available for the weekend we need it, and it comes within budget?"

He nods again.

My mind starts to race. What were the other criteria? It had to be on the Cape, but the Vineyard is even better. It had to be big enough . . . Well, this place looks like it could accommodate a marching band. And it had to be on the beach. That's got to be the catch.

"How far away from the beach is it?"

He picks up the remote control and flips to another picture. It shows the side view of the house, complete with silky sand dunes, spiky marram grass, and the foamy surf of the Atlantic.

He's got to be kidding.

If I'd created a house for our weekend, I couldn't have imagined a better one.

I step back from the screen to take in the entire image. "Do you have more pictures?"

He doesn't say anything, just clicks his remote. The picture changes to an image of the porch, which overlooks the water. Mahogany floor, the Star-Spangled Banner, and a porch swing, all surrounded by white hydrangeas. It's the most beautiful thing I've ever seen.

I slump back onto the sofa and cover my face with my hands. I can't stop the tide of emotion welling up in me right now. This house is better than perfect. It's more than Katherine or any of her friends would ever expect.

"If this is a joke, I'm going to kill you." My voice breaks on my threat.

"God, Lucy, are you okay?" Hunter asks. The couch dips as he scoots closer to me. He rests a hand awkwardly on my arm.

"I can't believe it," I say, turning to look at him. Concern fills his bright-blue eyes, and he doesn't look away. "Thank you," I say, my voice soft. "This means everything."

He grabs my drink from the table and pushes it into my hand. I take a small sip and start to feel a bit better. Energy seeps into my limbs, and my breathing comes easier. It feels like I'm recovering from some kind of endurance test, like I've been stranded on an island and finally rescued or just passed the finish line after a twenty-six-mile run. It's relief and gratitude and sheer exhaustion, all mixed up in one.

"Martha's Vineyard will work?" he asks hopefully.

"Absolutely," I say, sliding my glass back onto the coffee table. "It's better than the Cape. More of an adventure to get there. More exclusive. More memorable." And then I realize that all my planning has been around the Cape and not the Vineyard. I'll have to go back to the drawing board. We don't want to waste time going back and forth on the ferry.

"I thought we could even look at getting a helicopter to save time if that's an issue," he says.

I hold Hunter's gaze. He's completely serious. He's thought this through. He cares. And it feels so nice not to be on my own with the burden of planning this weekend.

"Wow," I say. "We should definitely consider it. And fishing. I presume there's fishing around there?"

Hunter shrugs. "I've had a hell of a week. I haven't finalized every detail." A smile curls at the corner of his lips. "But I'm thinking we'll be able to find something."

"Yeah, there's bound to be something, even if you have to get a boat from Hyannis to come and get you."

"Right."

"Right," I reply. We hold each other's gazes for a second. I don't know how to convey how grateful I am. How relieved.

"I hadn't grasped quite how important this is to you," he says, like everything fits into place for him now.

"It is important," I say.

He nods resolutely. "It's going to be great."

My breath hitches in my chest. I really think it is.

He glances to the Bankers Box. "Want to tell me what's in the box?" he asks. "I'm slightly concerned you've got all the equipment needed to murder me and get rid of the evidence."

I can't stop my smile at his comment. It feels like a long time since I've genuinely smiled when it comes to this wedding, even if we are talking about me being a murderer.

"I'm not sure any of it's relevant now," I say.

"Because you've changed your mind about my imminent death?"

I narrow my eyes as if I'm considering whether I'll still murder him. "It's mostly stuff about the Cape. I think we should stick to activities on Martha's Vineyard."

"But what, exactly, is in here?"

I flip open the lid to reveal the papers, printouts, and brochures I've accumulated since Ed and Katherine got engaged.

"Ideas for the bachelorette party. And I put together a spreadsheet to keep track of costs." I hand him a copy. "I printed out a hard copy for you, but I can send you the file in case you want to do a separate one for the guys. The way I see it, some of our costs will be separate—guys are going fishing, for instance, while we're doing other stuff. Other costs will be joint and split evenly. Like the house rental and stuff."

"I've got the house covered," Hunter says.

I go completely still, the box all but forgotten in my lap. "What do you mean?"

"I mean, I'll pay for the house. No need to put it on the spreadsheet."

Is he serious? Katherine didn't say anything about Hunter being rich. I'm sure she would have mentioned it if he was. "You can't do that. We'll split it between all of us."

Hunter shakes his head. "Ed is my best friend. I want to do this."

"Are you sure?"

"Yeah," he says. "I'm sure." He scans my face like he wants to ask me a question. Before he can say anything more, his cell goes off, interrupting the moment. He silences the call and turns back to me.

"What were you going to say?" I ask in challenge.

His phone goes off again, and he cancels the call without even looking at the screen this time. Probably one of a roster of girls wanting his attention. He ignores it and blinks, his long eyelashes sweeping his face. "I know she's your sister and everything." He eyes the Bankers Box. "But this is *so* important to you. I don't get it."

I glance away, slightly irritated at the idea of a woman calling him at this time of night. Which is ridiculous. I have no claim over this guy. "She's my sister. I love her. We've always been close. I just want to do as good a job as she would if it were my bachelorette."

"Is that it? It feels like there's more." He glances between my eyes and lips, and suddenly I'm hot, self-conscious. I need some air. Hunter is poking away at my defenses. But why? And why on earth does he have to look so hot doing it?

"That's it," I say. "I just want everything to be perfect. Just like Katherine."

"You think your sister's perfect?" he asks.

"Of course she's perfect. You've met her."

Hunter shrugs. "Not my type, I guess."

Everyone loves Katherine. There wasn't a boy at our high school who wasn't completely in love with her. Everyone wanted to be her friend. The kind of popularity that Katherine had could have been abused. She could have turned mean and nasty to kids not as blessed in the looks and popularity departments, but, of course, Katherine didn't. Katherine stayed sweet and kind throughout the turbulent teenage years and all through college. She didn't have an ugly-duckling phase, and she didn't have a rebellious one either. She's always been fully herself, and herself is perfect.

I huff out a laugh. "Sure. Of course Katherine's not your type," I say sarcastically. "You'd pass up a Victoria's Secret model, too, huh?"

"Depends," he says. "Maybe."

I roll my eyes, still curious about who called Hunter. Twice. "You don't need to pretend on my account," I say.

"I'm not pretending. I get that you love your sister, but she's not perfect. No one is."

"No one except Katherine," I correct him.

Hunter tilts his head to the side, an *Are you serious?* expression on his face.

"What?" I ask.

"You really think your sister is perfect. She's the one person on this planet who doesn't have a single flaw?"

"I don't know if she's the only one," I say. "But come on. You've met her."

"Yeah, and every time I do, she picks a piece of lint off my jacket, and it irritates the hell out of me."

I clasp my hand over my mouth like he's just confessed to the assassination of JFK. Hunter starts to riffle through my box as if he's just told me the weather forecast.

"You can't find Katherine irritating," I say when I've regained the power of speech.

"Wrong. I can find anyone irritating. You both irritated me at lunch when you couldn't choose what to order, even though I bet you knew as soon as you opened the menu that you were going to order the chicken Caesar salad."

"You get irritated if someone doesn't order quickly? How many dates have you ditched because of that?"

He sighs. "I don't have time to date."

His phone goes off again, perfectly timed to call him a liar. I raise my eyebrows, daring him to tell me again how he's not dating. Hunter's in his early thirties, tall, gainfully employed, and surrounded by millions of beautiful, underserved women. And . . . well, there's no denying he's hot. Not dating? I highly doubt that.

He holds the phone up to me so I can see the screen. "It's my mom."

I don't say anything. He doesn't need to pretend he's not dating on my account. It's not like I care if it's his mom calling, or Veronica with the great ass.

"What's this?" He pulls out an image I printed from the *New England Home Magazine* website. It's a selection of woven throws in seasonal colors.

"Katherine wants to have a fire on the beach and wrap up in blankets and toast marshmallows."

"Yeah, and what's this?" he asks, waving the image like it's a smoking gun.

"Throws I thought I might buy for the beach."

"You're going to buy specific blankets? You can't use what's at the house? Or maybe ask people to bring their own?"

"But then the colors might not go together."

He doesn't respond, but he looks at me like he's examining an exhibit in a museum. "The colors of the blankets. You think Katherine wants them to match?"

"Not match, but *blend.* Otherwise, the pictures we take won't . . . They won't be . . ."

"Don't say 'perfect,'" Hunter says. "Because if you do, I'm picking you up, tucking you under my arm, and taking you to the nearest hospital for a psych evaluation."

I roll my eyes. "You're so dramatic."

"Me?" he says, pulling more papers from the box and dumping them onto his coffee table. "I'm the dramatic one? How long have you been planning this party?"

"What?" I say defensively. "Not long."

He stares, daring me to confess.

"Just a few weeks," I say in a small voice. If no one can hear me, it's not technically lying.

"Liar," he says.

"What? It's just a few weeks."

"Which brand of marshmallows have you selected for toasting?" he asks. But he doesn't wait for a response. "Don't deny you've researched it."

"I have plausible deniability," I say. "Why would I pick out the brand when I don't know what will be available at the store?"

"You'd never source them locally," he says. I feel like he's reached inside my brain and seen every thought. He's right. I'd never leave such a critical detail to chance.

I don't say anything, because what's the point? He'll only tell me I'm a liar. And he'd be right. But it's weird. I've never been called out on my attention to detail before. Certainly never been teased about it. Quite the opposite. Growing up in Katherine's shadow, I was always seen as the messy one. Never prepared, never *right*, next to Katherine's always-prepared, always-perfect self.

"Are you only like this because it's Katherine's bachelorette, or is this you all the time?" He starts to chuckle. "Don't answer that. I know that answer. I bet you were the reason the line at Stranger than Fiction came to a standstill the other day. First of all, you had to decide on your order, and then I bet they had to make it specially."

I sigh. I didn't come here to be picked apart. I can do that to myself easily enough. We've got the house. The rest I can do by myself. Katherine didn't say anything about having to travel together.

"Why don't you plan the meal the night we arrive? I'll do Saturday," I say. "You can arrange the guys' transport. I'll do it for us girls. Then we don't need to plan together. You can be free of me." I pull my mouth into a forced smile and stand, shunting the papers on the coffee table back into the box.

"You're mad. I wasn't trying to be an asshole."

"You don't need to try," I say, sliding the lid onto the box. There's no fight left in my tone. I can't even be bothered to take offense.

"I'm sorry," he says, picking up the box for me. "It wasn't a criticism."

"Sure." I've had a barrage of insults and criticism from Hunter since we met. And I'm done. He's cutting a little too close to the bone. The exhaustion I felt when I first arrived washes back over me in a wave. "Thanks for organizing the house. It really looks wonderful," I say.

"Are you sure you want to leave? We can plan meals and transportation together. It doesn't have to be separated by gender, especially since a lot of the guests are couples traveling together."

"We can email to coordinate."

Something flashes up on the TV, and we both turn to look. It's a FaceTime call coming through. Somehow his cell has connected with the TV. Hunter pulls out his phone, but we've both seen that it isn't his mom calling. It's someone called Debbie, who has red lips and cleavage the size and depth of the Grand Canyon.

Just as I thought: Hunter's a player. And a liar. And he's happy for me to do all the grunt work while he gets kudos for snagging the house. In fairness, it *is* a really nice house. In the end, that's all I needed from him. I can do the rest myself, while Hunter can do whatever it is he's doing with Debbie.

"You should get that." I nod toward the screen. "Looks like Mom really wants to chat."

"That's not my mom, silly. That's my great-aunt Deborah," he says on a laugh. Not even he thinks I'm falling for that one.

I have the urge to take a shower. God knows what I've picked up being in his apartment for as long as I have. I head toward the door, and Hunter follows, carrying my box. "I'll bring it down and put it in the cab for you." He's trying to be nice, but despite finding the Vineyard house, I've seen who he is.

"I'm good," I say, reaching to take it from him. But before I can take it, my cell rings. I pull it out of my pocket. It's Katherine.

"Hi, Katherine," I answer. "I'm just with Hunter, making arrangements for the party weekend."

She squeals. I smile at my sister's excitement. "And you're getting along okay?" she asks.

"Absolutely. We're best buds," I say. Hunter raises his eyebrows in silent accusation.

"I can't tell you how happy that makes me," Katherine says. "When Ed and I have babies, you're going to be the best auntie and uncle of all time." I wonder what Katherine would think if she knew that sometimes Hunter found her irritating.

"Okay, well, call me later. We can catch up when you're back home."

"Totally," I say. "And don't worry. It's all going to be perfect."

Hunter shakes his head ominously. I hang up with Katherine and reach for my box again.

"Let's just call a truce, okay?" I ask. "At least in front of my sister and Ed. Let's agree that to make the most important people in our lives happy, we can pretend to get along."

"Sure, Lucy," he says, and I can't quite read his tone. Maybe he's being genuine. Whether he's faking doesn't really matter. I don't want Katherine stressed that Hunter and I are at each other's throats. She wants us to get along, so that's what she'll get. Even if we have to force it every step of the way.

He releases the box and opens his front door for me. I head back toward the elevator. I glance back at Hunter's apartment. He's got his arms crossed in front of him, leaning on the doorjamb, watching me. The T-shirt he's wearing shows off his muscled arms, and I didn't realize his jeans hung from his hips like that. It's almost obscene. He looks different from how he did in Massachusetts.

Not *Colin Firth had a baby with Matthew Macfadyen* hot, but not bad.

"Thank you for getting me into a cab at the engagement party," he calls out. "I could have really embarrassed myself there."

"No problem," I half shout. It's a little too late to start thanking me for that. He's only done it because he knows this time he's pushed too far. It doesn't matter. I'm going to try my best to fake it with him. It's obviously important to Katherine.

CHAPTER EIGHT

Lucy

Katherine grabs my hand excitedly as we follow our mother into the wedding-dress boutique. I haven't seen her dress yet, and I'm looking forward to getting a preview. Yes, it means I've had to leave Manhattan and come up to Massachusetts again, but Katherine really wanted me here. I get to try on my bridesmaid dress too.

"I really hope you like it," Katherine says. "My dress as well as yours."

"I'm sure I'll love both," I say. "You have fantastic taste."

"It doesn't matter what she thinks," Mom says, bristling. "It's a beautiful dress, and you look like a picture-perfect bride. And the bridesmaid dresses are fine."

Katherine and I share a look. Mom seems a little more tense than usual today.

The air conditioning in the shop is set to arctic, so I rummage around my huge bag for my favorite pink cardigan that I bought three years ago from Zara and still love. One of the shop assistants shows Mom and me to a seating area and offers us champagne, while another takes Katherine off to get changed.

"How's the bachelorette party planning coming along?" Mom asks.

"Good," I reply. Now we have the house sorted, it's been easy to plan around it. I've arranged for logs to be delivered just in case there isn't enough dry driftwood to set a fire on the beach. I've got graham crackers and marshmallows for beachside s'mores, and a chocolate fondue fountain for intermittent snacking through the weekend. After trading messages with Hunter, we've arranged a restaurant for Friday night when we'll have family members joining us, and a private chef to come to the house on Saturday night. We have flights booked into Martha's Vineyard Airport direct, so Hunter's flashy idea of a helicopter wasn't necessary.

Hunter and I have been very civil in our messages. And he's actually been pretty responsive. Our truce is holding.

"I hope it's not going to be tacky," Mom says as she shifts in her seat next to me.

"It's not going to be tacky, Mom," I reply. "It's Martha's Vineyard. It's impossible to be tacky on Martha's Vineyard."

"I'm sure you'd find a way. Katherine and you have very different ideas of what a bachelorette should be."

"No, we don't," I say. If I were going to organize my own bachelorette, I might not have chosen Martha's Vineyard, but there's nothing about the weekend I'm *not* looking forward to. And anyway, I've been completely focused on giving Katherine the weekend she wants. Any conflicting ideas we might have had, I've set aside.

"She said that you wanted everyone to go to New York."

"I just said they have the best spas in case that's what she wanted. It was only because we were having such a difficult time finding a house rental for the weekend."

Mom rolls her eyes like I'm exaggerating how difficult it was to find something. "It's the beginning of June."

"Right, and things are booked up months in advance," I say.

"You're not going to take that cardigan, are you?"

"I don't know," I say. "Why?"

She gives me a look that says, *Do I really have to tell you?*

"It's a really pretty color," I say.

"But it's seen better days. While you're up here, you should go and see Felicity. She's got some beautiful lavender knitwear in for spring/summer."

Felicity is one of Mom's friends. She owns an eponymous clothing boutique local to our childhood home. As much as I like Felicity and admire the way she's had her own business for as long as she has, I wouldn't be caught dead in anything from Felicity's.

Mom must catch the skepticism in my expression. "You ask your sister. She bought a beautiful short-sleeved sweater from there this week."

My stomach lurches at the possibility that my beautiful, perfect sister is shopping at Felicity's. The clothes there are aimed at women over fifty. Katherine might be about to get married, but she doesn't have to completely give up on being young, does she?

Luckily, our conversation about Felicity's is cut short when Katherine emerges from the dressing room.

She's sent me pictures before, but nothing could have prepared me to see her dressed up in her slightly off-white gown and veil. She looks like the fairy princesses we'd dress up as when we were little. Except more beautiful and a thousand times more sophisticated. I jump to my feet, unable to keep my eyes from welling up.

"You look incredible," I gasp. "Perfect."

She grins at me. "I love it." She should love it. It's completely perfect. "I hope Ed likes it."

"Ed would think you look like a goddess in fishing galoshes," I say. "He's going to lose his mind when he sees you in this."

Katherine smiles, her whole face glowing. "Do you think the neckline is too low, Mom?" There's not even a hint of cleavage. Why would she think it was too low?

Mom shakes her head. "Not now they've brought it up a touch. You look beautiful."

The bodice is strapless flat satin with a gathered skirt falling from the waist.

"Do you have the shoes on?" I ask.

Katherine pokes out her toe. "Yes, they always do the fittings with the exact shoes on."

"You'll be able to dance in those," I say. They're not too strappy and the heel isn't too high. Just as well, because Ed is five ten.

"I hope so."

"You haven't practiced?" I ask. "You should wear them around the house."

"Don't be ridiculous," Mom says. "She doesn't want them ruined before the big day."

"She's got a point, Mom. I should break them in. They're not the most uncomfortable shoes, but if I just wear them around the house, it might help me spend the day on my feet."

Mom tuts, but she doesn't argue.

"And what do you think about the veil?" Katherine asks, looking at me. "Do you think I should go longer?"

"Absolutely not," Mom interrupts. "Fingertip is the only acceptable length."

"You're right," Katherine says.

"I like your hair up like that. With the veil on top."

Katherine breaks into a grin. "Me too. It's a bit different for me. But I like it." Her gaze slides to Mom. "Mom's not so keen."

"Katherine has such beautiful hair. I think she should show it off."

"You'll have plenty of time to show it off. There's all the celebrations leading up to the wedding. Not everyone will be at every event, but you'll get to wear your hair down plenty on the other days."

Katherine nods. "Yes. That's a good point."

Mom exhales more loudly than she needs to. "You can't help pushing your opinions on everyone, Lucy. You should let Katherine make her own decisions."

Katherine and I give each other a knowing look. My mother is nothing if not a hypocrite.

"I agree with Lucy," Katherine says. "I want my hair up on the day."

Mom lets out a little huff. "Of course you do."

One of the shop assistants comes through and starts to ask Katherine lots of questions about the fit.

"And have you come up with something to wear for the days leading up to the wedding?" Mom asks me. "You can't just leave it to the last minute and expect to find something."

"Mom, I don't leave things until the last minute," I say. Truth is, I haven't made my mind up about what to wear. I have options, but I haven't bought anything yet. Not that I'll be admitting that to my mom. She'll just take it as proof that I'm as unreliable and flighty as I've always been.

"Just make sure you don't wear that cardigan," she says, nodding at me.

Katherine confirms her choice of veil and tells the tailor she likes the neckline and the length. There's some discussion about the zip, then Katherine heads back into the changing room.

One of the assistants pops her head out from around the corner and beckons me into the changing area, where my bridesmaid dress is hanging. It's a pretty, off-the-shoulder, pale-blue dress. It's understated and elegant, just like my sister.

I change quickly and am pleasantly surprised at how well it fits and how the blue suits my skin tone. I was a little worried I'd look washed out, but of course, Katherine has picked the perfect shade. I turn one way and then the other, trying to see myself from every angle.

"Come out," Katherine calls from the seating area. "I can't wait to see you."

The assistant brings me a pair of silver pumps, and they fit like a glove. I feel like the princess to Katherine's fairy queen. It's like traveling back a quarter of a century and playing dress-up again.

I step into the seating area and glance between Katherine and Mom.

Katherine and I grin at each other. "It's such a pretty color," I say.

"I'm so pleased you like it," Katherine says, her eyes wide and happy. "You look beautiful."

Mom winces. "Is it a little tight?" she asks the tailor. Then she turns to me. "Maybe you should size up."

I glance down. It doesn't feel tight. I check the mirror, but the fabric isn't pulling or bunching anywhere.

"It's not tight," Katherine says. "It fits you just right."

"It's personal preference," the tailor says. "But it's cut on the bias, so it's not meant to be loose. I'd say it fits perfectly."

Mom raises her eyebrows but doesn't say anything else. The excitement I felt when I first saw myself ebbs away. At least the tailor and Katherine like it, though I worry sometimes that my sister's support is just her way of trying to protect me from the sharpest edge of Mom's criticisms.

Katherine stands and we go back into the changing rooms together.

"You really do look beautiful," she says as I go behind the curtain to change. "Just ignore Mom. You know what she's like."

"I know," I say. "She wants me to be you. Sadly for both of us, I've never managed it."

"I get her sniping too," she says. "Just not as badly as you."

"I guess," I say, pulling the curtain open. "I just have to ignore it. It's hard. She's the voice in my head. God knows what she's going to say about dinner at the bachelorette party."

Katherine laughs. "Oh, you don't need to worry about her, then. You know what she's like when she's got an audience. She has to put on the show of being the perfect family."

"Right," I say. "Except we all know we're not."

"You know what I always think?" Katherine asks. "Her parenting is a great manual of how not to bring up two daughters. When it's our turn, we have to embrace our kids' differences."

"And let them grow and change," I insist. "I'm not still the goofy kid I was at fifteen."

"Right," she says. "You have a great job. A great apartment. You're an amazing friend and sister."

Just not the perfect daughter.

"So have you met up with Hunter again since you went to his apartment?" she asks, a mischievous look on her face.

I shake my head. "Just been messaging."

"He's such a great guy, you know. He's the best friend to Ed. He's so loyal and supportive of this wedding and our relationship."

"Does he need to be supportive of your relationship?" I ask. I think back to what Hunter said about Katherine not being perfect, and how he finds her irritating at times. I wonder how supportive he actually is. Sounds to me like Katherine isn't his favorite person. Not that I'm going to say anything to her.

"It helps for your friends to be supportive, doesn't it?" she asks.

"For girls. I don't really understand how it works for guys."

"I know Ed feels like Hunter's been great—stepping in a few times when Ed's been caught up with wedding stuff, that kind of thing." Hunter strikes me as a guy who's focused. When we met, he just . . . wasn't focused on the bachelor party. But he found the house, and he responds to my messages the first time I send them. If he's been filling in for Ed, too, that must add some pressure. Maybe I've been a little hard on him. He's been pretty cooperative since that day at his apartment. That was the last time I actually saw him. He was so . . . kind to me. "He's a good guy," Katherine continues. "And . . . very good looking, don't you think?"

"If you like that kind of thing," I reply.

"Do you?" Katherine asks.

For a second, I wonder if she's asking because Hunter's said something. But it seems out of character for him. Anyway, he hates me.

"He's not my type," I say.

Katherine scrunches up her nose. "Not at all? His body is . . ." Her eyes light up.

"Katherine!" I admonish. "You're getting married in a couple of months."

"Married, not buried. Hunter's a good-looking guy with a great body. I don't know how he does it, because he's a total workaholic.

Maybe he's lifting weights during meetings? Getting his steps in at a walking desk? Or maybe he doesn't sleep."

"Seems more likely," I muse. "I wouldn't rule out him being a vampire."

"Because he's so handsome?" Katherine asks hopefully.

I don't want to burst her bubble and tell her that he's probably itching to give me a neck wound.

"He's not *bad* looking," I concede. I'm sure Debbie agrees with me.

Katherine's eyes go wide. "I knew it. You two have chemistry. I saw it at our engagement party."

I roll my eyes but don't push back. What's the point? If thinking Hunter and me having chemistry makes Katherine happy, then she deserves to stay in her bubble. Only the two of us need to know that our "chemistry" was pure, unadulterated hostility until recently. That's water under the bridge. We've officially entered our truce era.

CHAPTER NINE

Hunter

I hate to admit it, but Lucy being so organized about everything for this weekend has inspired me to put a little bit more effort into things than I would have had she not been breathing down my neck every second of the past two and a half weeks.

We've actually managed to work together collaboratively. And truth be told, she's given me the easy jobs, taking on a lot of the heavy lifting herself. I made a reservation for tonight, but she found the restaurant. I've organized the fishing for Saturday, but the rest of the weekend has been Lucy's doing. As she's reminded me in her near-hourly texts.

I left work early to fly up from New York. As I wheel my suitcase to the gate at Boston Logan, the first person I see is Lucy, looking right at me, slightly separated from the group.

"You're late," she snaps, like I have it within my power to make the flight up from LaGuardia land a little earlier. I thought we'd called a truce. "Did you bring the wigs?"

I wince and my stomach drops because I know I've messed up. I left it late to order the wigs for Lucy's *Pulp Fiction* dress-up surprise. I wouldn't have gotten them in time to bring them up, but I've ordered the wigs to go to the house and paid extra for express delivery. I'm not completely sure whether we'll get them, so I don't want to tell Lucy and get her hopes up. "Sorry."

"Are you kidding? You had, like, two jobs. One of them was to bring the wigs."

"I'm really sorry."

"Now we're going to be all dressed up in clam diggers and white shirts for the bonfire on the second evening, and it's not going to fucking land. We're not going to look like Uma without the wigs." Her hands ball into fists and she stares at the ceiling, like it's taking all her willpower not to punch me in the face. "I knew I couldn't trust you."

"Jesus Christ, Lucy, I'm sorry, okay? I've had a lot to deal with at work. Things can't always be perfect. You can't set the bar so high and just expect everyone to pole-vault over it. People are going to screw up."

"No, *you're* going to screw up. You *always* screw up."

I feel her words come at me like arrows piercing my chest. I can't keep my cool anymore. "Just like *you're* always a demonic witch. I don't know how you and Katherine share the same DNA. You're a—"

"Hey," Katherine calls, interrupting us.

Lucy freezes, staring at me. Her expression is pure panic. It's like she's been caught in enemy territory and is about to get shot. It's hard not to feel sorry for her. Her chest starts to heave, and I step toward her, concerned she's hyperventilating.

Suddenly, Katherine is by our side, looking between us. "Is everything okay?"

Clearly everything is not okay. We're in the middle of a huge argument. I'm this close to turning around and flying right back to Manhattan. Lucy is having a seizure or something. This is not the perfect start to the weekend.

"Everything's amazing," Lucy says, turning and grinning at her sister like nothing's wrong at all. I glance at Lucy, wondering if she's lost her mind or is just biding her time while she plots a way to carve out my heart before boarding our flight.

"Are you sure?" Katherine asks. "Because it looked like the two of you were about to rip each other's heads off. I want you two to be friends."

I don't want to piss Katherine off. She might irritate me sometimes, but my best friend loves her, and I need to get over myself. I go to speak, to make an excuse, but just as I open my mouth, Lucy inexplicably slides her arm around my waist.

I freeze, wondering whether she's going to literally knife me in the back.

"You don't need to worry. We haven't said anything, because it hasn't been very long, but things have taken a turn, a . . . romantic turn . . . between us, and I was just disappointed Hunter didn't make it up on the earlier flight so we could have some time together before the weekend started."

Katherine's gaze flits between me and Lucy. I don't know what my face is doing. I'm too stunned to move. What the actual hell is going on? And why is Lucy still touching me?

Katherine breaks into a grin and clasps her hands together. "Oh my God. Wait until I tell Ed. I knew you two were perfect for each other." She goes to walk away, and Lucy pulls at her arm.

"Don't tell him, Katherine. Please. We want to keep things between ourselves for a little bit. Not put too much pressure on. You know?"

Katherine's face falls a little. "Okay, but you know I'm one hundred percent behind this. You're both . . . feisty. But honestly, two of the kindest hearts I've ever known. I just know this is all going to work out. We're going to be *actual* family, not just chosen family."

I take back everything I've ever said about Katherine being irritating. She's just a sweet, wholesome girl who wants the best for her sister and her soon-to-be-husband's best friend. But she's also lost her mind if she really believes Lucy and I are together.

She hunches up her shoulders and places a finger over her mouth. "I'll do my best to keep your secret." She turns and heads back to the group of friends all waiting for Gate Five to open.

I still haven't moved and neither has Lucy. Her hand is still around my waist.

"Eeek," Lucy says through a gritted smile. "I'm sorry. I panicked when she saw we were fighting."

"So you told her we're . . . *involved*? Is that the most obvious response? Couldn't you just tell the truth and say I forgot the wigs?"

"I don't want her to think we don't get along. She wants us to be besties. You know that."

"So tell her you were telling me a joke? Or regaling me with a story from your journey to the airport or something?"

She exhales and tips her head back. "I'm not good at thinking on my feet. Katherine is so obsessed with the two of us getting along, and she's always telling me how amazing you are—how you're this and that and *so* handsome."

"She tells you I'm handsome? That's weird. She's about to marry my best friend."

Lucy drops her hand from my waist and groans. "Get over yourself. She's not telling me *she* finds you attractive—"

"But you just said—"

"Yes, she says it because she wants *me* to find you attractive."

I'm way past confused.

"If Katherine had it her way, the four of us would be having a double wedding."

I take a half step away from Lucy like she's going to burn me if I get too close. "But that's not happening, is it?"

"No," she hisses. "Of course not. We hate each other. But now—for this weekend—we're pretend-dating."

"What?" I choke out.

Katherine glances up and beckons us over. Lucy smiles the fakest smile I've ever seen and holds her thumb up.

"Did you just give your sister a thumbs-up? Are you a sixty-year-old man?"

Lucy lets out a giggle like I've just told her the most hilarious joke. She's obviously faking it so people think we're being adorable. Then through gritted teeth, she says, "There's no way I can tell Katherine I was lying about us. It will break her heart. I want her to have the best weekend of her life. We'll just have to pretend to like each other for the weekend. How hard could that be? It's not like we have to share a room or give lavish public displays of affection. I've told her we want to keep it a secret. If it's meant to be a secret, we can't act like we're actually dating."

"So we're pretending we're not dating while *actually* not dating, but pretending we're dating, to keep your sister happy?"

"Yeah," Lucy says brightly, as if this is no big deal. "Come on." She lifts her chin toward the group. As we get closer, I can see Katherine talking excitedly to everyone.

Ed breaks from the group to give me a hug. "I hear the best man and the maid of honor are already hooking up. Good call," he says.

My heart sinks into the floor. Is it too late to fake a serious food-poisoning incident? Perhaps I could break my own leg? I'm sure Lucy would help with that if I asked her.

"Ed can read me like a book," Katherine says in explanation. "I'm so sorry, but when he asked me, it all just spilled out. I'm just so excited."

How did I go from being screamed at to pretend-dating the woman beside me, who I low-key hate? We've got to come clean.

Ed and Katherine's engagement has been a curse on me since it was announced.

Before I can pull Lucy to one side, the gate opens and everyone forms a line to board.

This isn't over. We have to tell the truth by the time we land in Martha's Vineyard. There's no way I can pretend to be interested in Lucy. Everyone will see through it immediately.

Thank God they don't allow weapons through airport security, because if I had access to something that could seriously hurt Lucy right now, I'm not sure I'd be able to hold back.

Kill. Me . . . Or her. Now.

Either would be less painful than pretend-dating Lucy Jones.

CHAPTER TEN

Lucy

Everything about this trip so far is excruciating. I can't believe I told Katherine that Hunter and I are involved. What was I thinking? And then everyone made such a fuss about switching seats so we could sit together. I swear Katherine was shushing Ed so she could listen to Hunter and me talking. Neither of us knew what to say.

The journey from Martha's Vineyard Airport seems to be taking four and a half hours. Our party is split between two SUVs, and our driver assured us it was going to take less than fifteen minutes. Our driver is a liar.

We turn off the road and head through gates that have a sign on it with the name Gableview. I try not to be obvious about craning my neck to see the house. Okay, so the images Hunter showed me were incredible, but he's never actually been here. It might have all been bullshit. But as the driveway curves to the left, I let out an audible gasp.

The house is even more beautiful than the pictures. I snap my head at Hunter, but he's buried in his phone. I nudge him and nod toward the house. He narrows his eyes like he's not getting what I'm trying to say. So exaggeratedly, I give a big thumbs-up.

He chuckles, and even I can't help but smile at my ridiculousness.

"Oh, this is gorgeous, Lucy," Katherine says. "How ever did you find it?"

"I didn't," I say. "I can't take any credit. Hunter knew someone who knew someone."

"Jack Alden," Hunter says, as if we're all supposed to know who Jack is.

"This is Jack's place?" Ed asks. I guess Ed knows.

"Sort of. His family has a place on the same stretch of land that they use. This place is an investment property."

The car comes to a standstill outside the beautiful two-story house that looks like something out of a film set. The white siding and gray shingle roof make the house blend into the vast sky above. White hydrangeas surround the front porch, exactly how they were in the pictures—abundant and soft against the crisp lines of the architecture. A Star-Spangled Banner on the side of the house ripples in the breeze. I almost don't want to enter in case the spell is broken.

"I don't think I'll ever want to leave," Katherine says.

I couldn't have said it better.

Ed is the first to take the steps up to the porch and the front door. "Do we have rooms assigned?" he asks. "Or is it a free-for-all?"

Hunter chuckles. I'm not quite sure why.

"I've assigned rooms," I say. "Ed and Hunter are in the second guest bedroom on the third floor. Then we have—"

Katherine interrupts. "I know Ed and Hunter were sharing, and you and I were sharing, but since you and Hunter are a couple now . . . you two can share, and Ed and I can share!" She beams as she talks.

Out of the corner of my eye I can see Hunter shaking his head. Obviously, I don't want to share a room with him. But I can't think of an excuse. Katherine's suggestion has me spiraling. This is not what I had planned.

"It's just silly otherwise," she continues. "And I hate sleeping without Ed now. In fact, a couple of months ago when he stayed in New York for the night, I didn't sleep a wink with him gone."

My insides feel heavy. There's no getting away from this.

"And it means you guys get to hang out a little more," Katherine says, grinning.

I slide on a smile. "Sure," I say. "If that's what you want, Katherine."

Katherine squeals. "Thank you. This is absolutely incredible. I'm so looking forward to this weekend. Wedding planning has been so stressful. It will be good to just kick back and relax."

My fake smile is replaced with a real one when I see Katherine so happy. It's not like we're going to be spending loads of time in our rooms anyway. We're just there to sleep. Hunter and I are adult enough to make it work. I hope. At least I know *I'm* adult enough to make it work.

Hunter follows me into our allocated bedroom, carrying our luggage.

"You know we're only staying two nights," he says, dumping my large suitcase by the bed. The room is done in pale blues and whites, with a view of the ocean. On one wall there's a four-poster bed, white muslin wrapped around the frame gently undulating with the breeze from the ceiling fan. It's like something from a fairy tale. "What have you got in here?" Hunter barks, spoiling the moment. If only I weren't sharing this room with him.

"Plenty of space for a dead body on the way back," I retort.

"Whatever," Hunter replies in the lamest response he's ever given me. "Did you think through what this means? You and I are going to be in a confined space for over forty-eight hours. Why on earth did you say yes?"

"I didn't hear you objecting."

"I was expecting you to make some excuse about how we weren't that far along in our relationship or something. Most guys don't give a shit where they sleep. It's the women who make a big fuss about that kind of thing."

"At least you're not generalizing," I say, unzipping my bag on the floor.

"You want me to lift that onto the bed?" he asks.

"*Eww,* no thank you. That suitcase has been through the airport. You can't put it on that beautiful bed linen."

"Only trying to help," Hunter says.

I sigh, exhausted, partly from the anticipation of this trip and partly from the realization that I'm going to have to spend time and energy fighting with Hunter when all I want to be doing is making sure Katherine has the weekend of her life.

"Well, here we are," I say. "We'll just have to make the best of it. I can take the couch." The navy-and-white couch isn't big, but if I take the cushions and put them on the floor, I can make it work.

"Or we could stage a fight, and I could sleep downstairs," he says.

"No! You can't do that. It will upset Katherine."

Hunter gives a small shake of his head. "We couldn't possibly do that, now, could we?"

"This is her bachelorette party in case you've forgotten. She's going to remember it as one of the best times of her life."

"No pressure, then," Hunter says. "I'm going into the bathroom."

"I'm going to get us some beverages."

"Knock yourself out."

He probably means literally. No doubt he thinks I deserve a good concussion right about now. But he must know that it's not my choice to be sharing a bedroom with him. Not here. Not ever.

I pad downstairs and explore the kitchen. I had a huge order of groceries delivered earlier in the day, and I was told the housekeeper would put them away. I might as well use the time to check that everything came. While I'm doing a mental inventory of the fridge, Katherine comes down.

"Everything okay with your room?" I ask.

"Oh, Lucy, it's just the best. And you put Hershey's Kisses by the bed."

The housekeeper did, at my request.

"I actually have some HARIBO for Ed here somewhere." The housekeeper called to say dry goods were laid out on the counters in the pantry. I just need to find the pantry.

"You're so sweet and thoughtful," Katherine says. Her praise feels so good, like warming cold hands in front of a fire.

"I just want you to have a good time," I say. I open a door and find the pantry just as there's a knock on the door. My stomach plunges. I hope that's not Mom arriving early. I'm absolutely not ready for her. I want to have a shower. Maybe a shot of tequila. But it's hours until she's due. It can't be her.

I cross the kitchen and open the front door. It's a delivery driver.

Two boxes are stacked up beside him on the porch. He hands me his electronic signing pad, and I make an attempt at a signature.

I glance back at Katherine. Does she know what this is all about? She's got her head stuck in the refrigerator and isn't paying any attention.

The driver heads back to his van, and I step out onto the porch to examine the parcels. Both boxes are addressed to "Hunter Bain."

Intrigued, I head back upstairs. Hunter must have finished in the bathroom by now. I pause at the door to our room. Should I just walk in? What if he's still in the bathroom? What if he's naked? My treacherous stomach swoops at the thought. There's no doubt Hunter is objectively attractive. It doesn't mean *I* find him attractive. I nod, agreeing with myself, and turn the knob to our room.

I walk in at the moment the bathroom door opens, steam billowing out, Hunter appearing through the fog.

He's got a small white towel wrapped around his waist. Other than that, he's very naked.

I squeal and cover my eyes.

Hunter's chuckle sets me off.

"Are you laughing at me?" I ask, my hands still over my face.

"Am I laughing at you screaming at the sight of me? Yes, yes I am. Because you're ridiculous."

"You're naked. I wasn't expecting it."

"I just got out of the shower."

"I thought you were . . . doing something else," I say. "I didn't realize you were showering. And I didn't realize you'd be wandering around the room naked, or I would have given you more time."

"Perfect. Well, FYI, I fully intend to be wandering about naked the entire time I'm in here, so maybe you should find another room."

I slump on the sofa and try to focus on the ocean.

I'm overwhelmed.

"I can't fight with you like this the entire weekend," I say, keeping my gaze trained on the horizon. Behind me, I hear a suitcase zipper and the sound of wet terry cloth hitting the floor.

"Then stop fighting," Hunter says.

"I have to get changed and put out the canapés. Then my mom is arriving with my aunt and our two bitchy cousins. I just . . . can't."

The adrenaline that's been racing around my body since this morning is ebbing away. I'm tired. So very tired.

"Then stop fighting, Lucy. I don't know why you're so mad at me in the first place. Maybe you're mad at everyone."

"You forgot the wigs, remember?"

"Right. And nobody died. Everyone still had fun on the plane, and Ed will still think it's cool that you'll all be dressed up like Uma Thurman tomorrow night."

That's true, I suppose. "The wigs just would have made it perfect. But you're right. I overreacted. I've just been so wound up about everything. I took it out on you and I'm sorry. I really am."

The sofa bounces beside me, and I snap my head around. Hunter is sitting next to me. I scan his body quickly to make sure nothing's on display that shouldn't be. He's dressed in a navy polo shirt and khaki shorts, and his hair is still a little wet from the shower. It's sticking up everywhere, and when I glance up at it, he tries to tame the unruly strands with his fingers.

"You're dressed."

"You're forgiven. Tell me about the bitchy cousins," he says.

"They're bitchy and they're our cousins. Not much else to say."

Hunter laughs, and the corners of my mouth twitch at how warm the sound is.

"So Katherine likes them, but they're bitchy to you?"

I shake my head. "Nope. They're bitchy to both of us. But our aunt is here, and it would upset her and my dad if we didn't invite them."

"So the only thing that trumps Katherine's happiness . . . is your mom's," he says knowingly. I feel that gentle poke against my armor again. It's like he's trying to understand me. I'm not sure I deserve him to do anything more than hate me.

"I just want *everyone* to be happy," I say.

"Er, not technically true. I'm not sure you give a rat's ass if I'm happy or not."

"I don't *know* you," I say.

"Well, Lucy, like it or not, you're going to get to know me this weekend." He pats me on my leg. "Come on. Let's call another truce and get on with this weekend. You never know, sharing a room with me could be fun. We might even end up friends."

I raise my eyebrows, and he laughs. That warm feeling in my stomach kindles to life again.

"Well, as long as I'm not the dead body you bring back in that suitcase, I'm going to consider myself a winner. I'm going to head downstairs and give you your privacy so you can . . . do whatever it is that girls spend hours doing before they go out at night."

"That reminds me," I say. "Some boxes were delivered while I was downstairs. They're all addressed to you."

"Oh, great. I was worried the blow-up dolls wouldn't be here in time. Phew." He makes an exaggerated swipe at his brow, like he just dodged a disaster.

"The *what*?" I ask, hyperconscious of not screeching despite the alarm bells going off in my head.

"Is that a problem?" he says.

"Is that a—"

"Calm down, I'm kidding," he interrupts, grinning.

Before I can sputter a reply, he slips out of our bedroom and leaves me to myself. The room feels ten times bigger without Hunter Bain in here. But it also feels significantly more . . . empty.

It's not until I'm halfway through my own shower that I realize he never told me what's in those boxes.

CHAPTER ELEVEN

HUNTER

The guys have been allocated the game room as our gathering space. The girls get the rest of the house, apparently. But we have a pool table, a bar, and a retro pinball machine, so I'd say we're winning.

The beers arrived at the house ready-chilled, and I managed to get everything I ordered unpacked before the guys started to come down.

I clink my bottle against Ed's and take a swig. I pass a beer to Fisher, the only other guy who's arrived.

"You and Lucy," Ed says. "I honestly didn't have that on my bingo card."

"Me neither, brother," I reply. "Me neither."

"She's hot, though," Fisher says.

I nod, not wanting to say too much of anything. Anyway, I can't disagree that Lucy's hot. She is. She's also uptight and annoying. But even so, I know she's tightly wound because of this weekend. She's obviously put so much time and effort into it, and it's really important to her that Katherine has a good time. I can't fault her for that. She's not being a demonic witch because she's selfish and self-centered. She's just focusing on one thing to the exclusion of being nice. If she was a guy, I'd probably shrug it off. What does that make me? An asshole. At least she apologized.

"When did it kick off?" Ed asks.

I groan. I really don't want to start talking about my non-relationship. "Do we have to sit around talking about our feelings?"

"No, but this is Katherine's sister we're talking about. Your track record with women isn't your greatest asset."

"Because my ass is, right?" I turn around and wave my behind at Ed, Fisher, and George, who just joined us.

"I mean it, Hunter," Ed says. "Just don't mess her around."

"I'm not going to." It's not like she could hate me any more than she already does. "At the same time, we're not about to announce our engagement anytime soon. So if you could do your best to manage your fiancée's expectations in that regard, I'd appreciate it."

Ed winces. "I can't promise anything. All I've heard since we arrived is how great it is that the four of us can do things together. How great it will be that our kids can grow up together."

"What?" I try to keep my tone from giving away the hysteria I feel. "Kids? Jesus, man. We only just started dating like a week ago."

"So are you guys exclusive already?" Fisher asks. "That was fast."

I shrug. "It's fine. It's not like I have time to date a whole lot anyway." That's the truth, at least.

"But you must like her a lot," Fisher says as Ed nods enthusiastically behind him.

"Sure," I say. "Want a game of pool?" I glance between Ed and Fisher.

"What do you like about her?" Ed asks.

I reach around the back of my neck. I'm not a great liar. I swear you can see the truth all over my face no matter what my words say. "I don't know," I say. "Like Fisher says, she's hot. And she's caring and has a good heart." None of that's a lie. She's bordering on demonic a lot of the time because she cares so much about her sister. "And I like the fact she's not always . . ." I want to say this without insulting Katherine. I like Katherine. She's nice and Ed loves her. She seems good to my friend. That's all good. But Katherine seems like she's always happy, like life is always sunshine and roses. But that's just not how life is. "She's real, you know? Her smiles are hard won."

Ed huffs out a laugh. "Yeah, that's true enough."

Voices chatter in the hallway, and the rest of the bachelor party appears in the game room. People start talking, and Ed and Fisher play pool. I bet Lucy's stressed about having everything ready before her mom and the rest of her family arrive for the night. Maybe I'll just go out and check on her.

In the kitchen, I find Lucy sporting an apron, setting things out on trays. She glances up at me. "I should have sprung for caterers to do this."

"Can I help?" I ask.

"Would you?"

"What do you need?"

"Just spread this tomato stuff on the toast and pop on an olive. I'll do the blini." She hands me the knife she's been using, and our eyes catch as our fingers brush together.

I set to work, scooping out the tomato mixture from the bowl while Lucy darts around the kitchen. It's like we're in an escape room and the timer's running down.

"I'm sure people would have been happy with chips and dip," I say. "You didn't need to have gone to this much of an effort."

Lucy snorts. "You've met my mother, right? At least we'll only be here forty-five minutes or so before the cars pick us up."

"No doubt everything's on a very strict timetable."

Lucy shoots me a disappointed glance.

"It's not a criticism," I say. "I know you're just trying to make everyone happy."

"Exactly," she says. "And given my mother is in the mix tonight, that's not an easy task."

The doorbell chimes, and Lucy visibly jumps.

"Katherine!" she calls, and Katherine scrambles down the stairs like she was just waiting at the top to be called down.

"Is it Mom?" she asks as she gets to the bottom.

"Crap." Lucy looks down at her apron and quickly pulls it off. "You look beautiful," she says to Katherine.

"So do you," Katherine answers as they both move to the front door.

"Darlings," an older woman in navy says. "So good to finally be celebrating one of your upcoming nuptials."

This must be the aunt. Katherine and Lucy's mother is next through the door and greets her daughters, followed by two younger women—the bitchy cousins, no doubt. Everyone greets each other in a flurry of hugs and air-kisses. It all seems very amicable. Maybe it's because I know Lucy is stressed, but there's something about the scene that doesn't feel quite authentic.

"Oh, I thought you'd be ready for us," Lucy's mom says, scanning her from head to toe. "Do you need more time to get ready?"

"Uh, I'm just organizing some nibbles and drinks," Lucy says, looking visibly flustered.

"Oh, well, let us do that while you go and change for dinner," her mom says. "We don't mind rolling up our sleeves, do we, Gracie?"

I'm not sure if Lucy's mom knows Lucy already changed for dinner and is just being a bitch, or if she's truly insensitive enough not to notice what her words do to Lucy's whole vibe.

"Mom," Katherine says. "Lucy looks gorgeous. She doesn't need to change."

"Sorry, darling! If that's what you want to wear, I'm sure it's fine. I've always erred on the side of caution with lemon yellow, that's all."

Lucy visibly deflates. "I can change. I wasn't sure about this outfit anyway."

"I think it's lovely," Katherine says, and it makes me like her more. It's nice that she's protective of Lucy. I don't remember much of Katherine's mother from the engagement party, but I'm surprised she's so critical of a daughter who tries so hard to make everyone happy.

Lucy darts over to me. "Do you mind if I go change and leave you to get on with this?" she whispers.

"You don't need to change," I say, keeping my focus on the canapés so I can get out of this kitchen as soon as possible. "It's a nice dress."

"But it's yellow. I forgot how much Mom hates yellow."

"It suits you." My jaw is tight, because Lucy is a grown woman who looks great in yellow, and her mom should realize that.

She sucks in a breath. "Thanks, Hunter. I'll just be a few minutes."

"Should we help ourselves to drinks?" Mrs. Jones says. Maybe it's me, and maybe I'm being unkind, but even this question seems to come out as a criticism.

Lucy doubles back to the kitchen and starts pulling out bottles of champagne from the refrigerator.

"I'll do that," I tell her. "Go and get changed if you want to."

She pulls in a breath. "Thank you, Hunter. I owe you."

I've never heard her sound as vulnerable as she does right now. I have the urge to tell Mrs. Jones and her crew that they can help themselves to drinks while I retreat to the game room. But I won't do that, since it will only put more stress on Lucy.

The canapés are all finished. I take a plate in each hand before making my way out to the guests. "Katherine, can you get the door? Drinks on the porch?"

"Great idea, Hunter," Katherine replies. "Mom, do you remember Hunter from the party?"

Mrs. Jones turns and gives me a charming smile. "Oh, you're Ed's business partner. Yes, of course I remember you."

"He managed to get us the house for the weekend."

"It's a beautiful property," Mrs. Jones says, and she touches her hand to my arm. "Very good of you to do this for Ed and Katherine."

"I did the easy part," I say. "Lucy's done everything else. Planned everything to perfection."

Mrs. Jones tilts her head to the side as if to say, *Well, not everything.* "She'll feel better when she's in a different color," she says, not acknowledging what I've said about Lucy's efforts at all.

Lucky for me, Ed and the rest of the bachelor party join us.

I start to pour champagne, and one of the cousins offers to help. "I can be your assistant," she says. "My name's Genny. You're a friend of Ed's?"

"Yeah. We're business partners. And friends. Known each other forever," I say, handing a glass of champagne to Genny's mom.

"But you're based in New York?" she asks.

"That's right," I say, pouring the next glass.

"Yeah, I'm in New York a lot for work. Maybe we should swap numbers. We could grab a drink some time."

My heart starts to thunder in my chest. She's coming on to me. Apart from the fact that I'm not interested—at all—I'm also supposed to be dating her cousin. Except she doesn't know that. Am I supposed to tell her? Well, fuck it, everyone else in the house knows.

"Actually, I'm dating Lucy," I say.

"You are?" she asks, sounding shocked. "Did you know that?" Genny asks her sister. "He's dating Lucy."

I'm not quite sure why she's saying it the way she is.

"Isn't Lucy still a virgin?" her sister says. "No one dates Lucy."

The hairs on the back of my neck stand to attention, and I clench my jaw. Lucy was right, they are the bitchy cousins.

I offer them my fakest of fake smiles. After I finish pouring champagne for everyone, I excuse myself to go check on Lucy.

I steam into the bedroom, but it's dark. Lucy is sitting on the bed, cloaked in shadow. She's changed and has a white dress on. She's looking out of the window.

"Hey, are you okay?" I ask as I slide into the room and shut the room.

"I think I'm coming down with something."

I'm not sure she's sick. More like sick of her own family being so awful to her. "You're right. Your cousins are bitchy."

"Yup," she says.

I want to add that her mother isn't much better, but she doesn't need to hear that.

"I told them we were dating," I say.

Lucy snaps her head around. "You told who?"

"Your cousins. One of them asked me if I wanted to go for a drink, and I told her."

She groans. "Don't tell me what they said."

She knows even without me telling her that her cousins were awful when they heard our "news." It makes my heart ache a little.

"You look really pretty. And you didn't need to change."

She stands, but I can tell it takes effort, like she's weighed down by . . . people's perceptions of her? Her expectations of herself? I don't know what it is, but from here I can feel how it doesn't fit her.

"Thanks. It's easier to put on a white dress than it is to keep the yellow one on and listen to my mother's sniping all evening."

When I first met Lucy, if someone had told me she did anything for an easy life, I wouldn't have believed them. I assumed she did everything in her power to make life more difficult for herself and everyone around her.

Now, I see that's not who she is. I think she's just someone desperately trying to dodge criticism from the people she loves.

"Do you want me to tell people you're not feeling well? Maybe you need an evening in bed?" I don't know why, but I can feel the back of my neck glow hot when I mention her in bed. Maybe it's because we're sharing a room.

"There's no way I'd let Katherine down like that," she says.

Grabbing her purse, she walks over to me by the door. "Thank you." Her hand slides onto my arm and our eyes catch. She lets her hand fall, and I take it in mine.

"Let's go. Make sure you sit next to Katherine or one of her friends. Keep away from . . ." I don't finish the sentence. What do I say? *Keep away from your own mother*. That's what I mean. Who knew I'd feel this protective over a woman I'm not even dating for real?

I can't deny it, my first impressions of Lucy have shifted. I'm not saying we're on the same page, but I understand her better now. And the more I get to know her, the more I see: Her loyalty to her sister. The way she puts up with criticisms from her mother and other family members. The way she puts other people ahead of herself.

It all adds up to someone . . . extraordinary.

CHAPTER TWELVE

Lucy

I grab a packet of marshmallows, bamboo skewers, chocolate, and graham crackers from the pantry and stuff them all in my tote.

I'm really counting on Hunter to deal with the fire aspect of our after-party. I can do s'mores, but fires are above my pay grade.

"Lucy," Katherine calls. "Where did you go? Are you ready?"

"In here," I call. We meet at the door to the pantry. "I'm getting snacks for the beach." I open my tote, and Katherine pokes her head in.

"S'mores?" she says. "You're the best little sister in the world."

"The bar has been lowered tonight," I say, and we both dissolve into giggles. All through dinner, our bitchy cousins directed their bitchiness at each other. Katherine and I placed ourselves at the opposite end of the table from them, Mom, and our aunt, and as a result, we had a great evening. At least twice, Genny, the oldest of the bitchy cousins, flounced off from the table because Gretchen said something unpleasant.

Our side of the table had been nothing but love and great food and way too much wine. Now our family members have left, and I feel a little less tense. The three martinis I've had definitely help.

"What are you two doing in the pantry?" Ed appears from nowhere.

"You're back!" Katherine squeals and loops her hands around Ed's neck. "We're going to do s'mores on the beach. Can you make a fire?"

"I have that covered," Hunter says. My heart lifts in my chest a little at his voice. No doubt due to the fact that I haven't had to nag him three hundred times to organize the fire.

We all make our way down to the beach. The men argue about the best way to make a fire while the women of the group choose throw blankets from the basketful I placed down there earlier. We don't get involved in the fire-making process—not because we couldn't do it, despite having zero experience. No, we watch because there's not a better show on Netflix. These guys trying to assert their dominance by arguing about log arrangement is ridiculous and hilarious, and I'm absolutely here for it.

When the fire is finally going, the flickering flames turn the air a little magical. Everyone is smiling and laughing as I pass around skewers and marshmallows. And it doesn't matter even a little bit that someone gets sand in the bag of marshmallows.

"Did you get me one?" Hunter asks as he comes and takes a seat next to me.

I hand him a skewer with two marshmallows on it. "All prepped and ready for the fire."

I pull my knees up to my chest and hold out my skewer, the flames licking the sugar like they're starved.

Hunter sits close enough that we touch. He's cross-legged, his knee is slotted in under my legs. His shoulder grazes mine.

I glance over at him, shooting him a look that says, *You're taking this couple thing very seriously*, but he just grins.

Fisher pulls a guitar from God knows where and starts playing the chords of a song I can't quite place. He begins to sing.

Everyone's hazy with alcohol and sea air. I feel so . . . comfortable. So free. So relaxed. For the first time since we got here, I feel like I can switch off a little bit. I don't have to field jabs from one of my cousins or my mother. I don't have to fight with Hunter.

The marshmallow goes gooey and golden on the outside. I stack chocolate on a graham cracker, sandwich the marshmallow between the chocolate and another cracker, and pull it off the skewer. It's a nine point two for execution, if I do say so myself.

"That's impressive," Hunter says.

"Thank you for appreciating my s'mores game. It's a lifetime of dedication to my craft."

He chuckles and I offer him the confection. "Wanna swap?" I reach for his skewer.

"Sure," he says. I don't know why, but I like that he agreed. I like that he's not holding grudges. That he's accepting my peace offering. Maybe he's poked a small hole in my armor, and he sees something he can like.

I glance from the fire and his uncooked marshmallow back to Hunter, who's biting into the s'more. I hadn't noticed before how nice his teeth are. How big his mouth is. How masculine his hands are. I suppress a shudder and turn back to my skewer.

I busy myself making my own s'more with the same practiced skill. There's a lot I'm not good at—like wearing yellow—but I can make a s'more like I invented them.

I sink my teeth in and my eyelids flutter shut. Bliss.

I open them to find Hunter looking at me.

"You look like you're enjoying that," he says.

"What can I say? I make the best s'mores."

He reaches over and, for a moment, I think he's going to take my sandwich, but instead he swipes his thumb over the bottom of my lip and holds it in front of me. It has a huge dollop of marshmallow on it.

"Here," he says.

I must flush beet red. He wants me to *lick his thumb*? His eyes narrow slightly, as if he's daring me. I open my mouth a little, and he slips his thumb inside. My insides turn into gooey sugar as I close my lips around him. My heart is thundering in my chest, and Hunter's eyes flare.

Fisher starts to play another tune, and the change in tempo breaks the spell between Hunter and me. We turn back to the fire like we've both been caught doing something we shouldn't.

Hunter's tapping his foot with the music of Fisher's new song, then starts to sing along. The lyrics are about sugar and spice and all things nice. Hunter has a good voice—low and husky—and the vibrations spread between us. Fisher starts strumming more loudly as he and Hunter sing about Sally Cinnamon. It's not a song I've heard before. Hunter turns to me as he sings, and I grin up at him. He smiles around the words, then slides his hand up my back. Our elbows and knees were touching before—parts of our bodies making contact almost by accident. But this isn't an accident. Hunter is touching me like he's my friend, like he's my *boyfriend.* But I don't stop smiling. His large, warm hand spans across my back, keeping me steady.

The song finishes, and we're looking at each other. If this was another time—if we were different people, I can't help thinking—then he'd kiss me about now. He pulls me against him, and I let my body sink into his, like we always do this. Like we know each other. Like he's my boyfriend. He places a kiss on my head, and sparks from the fire fly out like miniature shooting stars. Are we acting? Is he taking his role as my pretend boyfriend to the next level?

"You okay?" he asks so only I can hear. Fisher has put his guitar away, and pockets of low conversations are being held around the fire.

"Yeah," I say, pulling away from him to sit up straight.

He grabs an unused blanket from the basket and wraps it over my shoulders. "Beautifully coordinated blankets, by the way." He shoots me a grin, and I can't even be irritated with him. Maybe I'm desensitized from insults due to spending the evening with my cousins. Or maybe I know he's not being mean. Maybe it's even a compliment. He understands it's important to me, and he accepts that. Warmth spreads in my chest at the realization.

"Thanks," I say. "For the blanket." His gaze dips to my lips and then back up to my eyes. "I didn't know you could sing."

He chuckles. "I can't, really," he says. "I just like that song."

"I've never heard it before."

He nods. "It's pretty obscure. It's from the eighties, by a British band who never made it in America. Fisher's British, so I guess it makes sense he'd know it."

"You like British music?" I ask. We've spent a lot of time texting over the past few weeks. Well, *I've* spent a lot of time texting over the past few weeks, and he started responding at some point. We've also spent a lot of time fighting. But I don't know Hunter very well. And I want to.

"Some of it, I guess. My dad was a big Beatles fan." His expression shifts a bit, and I can't quite place it, but it makes me reach my hand out and curl my finger around his arm.

His gaze falls on my hand and then back up to watch me.

"Are you close?" I ask. "With your parents?"

He shrugs. "Yes. No. Maybe."

I let out a huff of a laugh. I know that feeling. "Life's complicated," I say.

"That yellow dress looked really . . . nice on you," he says.

I let go of his arm and draw a small circle in the sand between us. "Yellow isn't really my color. I think you need to be a goddamn beauty queen to pull it off. I don't know why I tried."

Studiously, Hunter draws his own circle, overlapping the edges with mine, like a Venn diagram. "You pulled it off."

I glance up at him, and he meets my gaze. There's a part of me that wants to dismiss his compliment, to pass it off as him teasing me, but I don't. I can tell he's being sincere. "Thank you," I say.

"It's true. I figure you'd look beautiful in anything, but lemon yellow brings out the amber flecks in your eyes."

I flush with heat, and it has nothing to do with the fire. No one's listening to Hunter talk about my eyes or how I look wearing yellow. But here he is, saying it anyway. Being nice to me, despite me not being so nice to him at times. He's nothing like I thought he was when I first met him. Nothing like the man I assumed he was.

He's so much more.

CHAPTER THIRTEEN

Hunter

I don't know what it is about ocean air, but it relaxes me. I really should think about getting a place in the Hamptons next summer. Between the tourists and the humidity, summer weekends in New York can get stifling. I end up going into the office because there's nothing else to do. Maybe I need more ocean breezes in my life. I turn the light off in the bathroom and open the door to the bedroom. The bedside light is on and the curtains are drawn. But the bed is empty.

"Lucy?" I ask.

"I'm here," she replies in a whisper.

She's laid out a bed in front of the couch, and she's covered in blanket from the bed.

"Oh, no," I say. "I don't think so. Get up off the floor."

"I'm not on the floor. I took the cushions off the couch."

"Yeah, that's not happening," I say. What is she thinking? Like I'd let her sleep on the floor like that.

"It's my fault we're sharing a room. I'm the one who told Katherine we were dating. It's fine. I'll probably have the best night's sleep of my life."

"Lucy, get up right now and get into the bed."

"No! I'm fine." She pulls the blanket up around her neck like a shield.

"No, you're not fine," I say. "Get up." She's the most stubborn woman I've ever met in my life. She makes no move to comply, so I bend down and scoop her up. She flails in my arms, trying to escape, but she's no match for me, and I dump her down onto the bed. "You're sleeping in the bed. If you don't think two adults can share a bed without getting naked, I'll happily take the couch." I glance at the small couch and revise my thought. "I'll be fine on the floor."

Lucy pushes up on the bed so she's sitting. "You can't sleep on the floor." She presses her lips into a thin line. "We'll have to share." She scoots over. "But we need a pillow wall."

I chuckle. "You think I won't be able to resist you?"

She doesn't look at me, and I enjoy her embarrassment a little. We were definitely flirting on the beach. When she's not so uptight, trying to make everything perfect, she's fun and pretty and . . . sensitive. She's all the words I wouldn't have used to describe Lucy when I first met her. She also makes incredible s'mores. I wonder if her mouth still tastes of chocolate. What? Where did that thought come from?

"Just help me with the wall," she says, still avoiding my gaze.

Silently, we put pillows down the center of the bed and then slip under the covers.

"You okay over there?" I call dramatically.

"You're ridiculous," she replies.

I pull the pillow at the top off the bed and toss it behind me so I can see Lucy. She's lying facing me. She doesn't object.

"Maybe I am," I reply.

"The fire worked out," she says. "Just like Katherine wanted."

"Just like Katherine wanted," I reply, searching her gaze. But did *she* enjoy tonight? Surely not everything has to be about Katherine.

"Tomorrow is fishing," she says. "For you guys, anyway."

"Right," I say, just before I remember I haven't brought my seasickness pills. "Shit."

Lucy pushes up on her hands so she's sitting. "What? Did you forget to confirm or something?"

I shake my head. "I didn't bring my seasickness pills."

"You get seasick?" she asks.

"Yeah, I'm not a good boat passenger."

She giggles, and it sounds so young and carefree and fucking intimate I feel it in my balls. It's like this version of Lucy is the real one. The one that doesn't care what people think. The one that can be herself. This is the one I like. I *really* like.

"Why on earth did you arrange a fishing trip for this weekend if you get seasick?"

"Why do you think?"

She shrugs and flops back down on the bed. "I guess because Ed likes fishing so much."

"Exactly. We all do things we don't want to do for people we love."

Her eyes grow wide. "But—"

"But there's a line. Or there should be. You don't need to give up yourself to make everyone happy. There's a line."

Looking back, I took on my father's business because I knew it would make him happy—make him proud of me. And I kept at it—kept administering CPR on the business when I should have called time of death months before. I didn't, because I wanted to make my dad happy. I won't make the same mistake again. I didn't realize until this moment that my biggest mistake was not seeing the line. I didn't necessarily know to look for it then, but experience taught me a hard lesson. It's not one I'll soon forget.

"A line?"

"A line between making someone you love happy and sacrificing everything to make it happen."

Lucy blinks, and blinks again. "You think I cross that line?"

I shrug. "I think you love your sister. You want to make this weekend perfect. I get it. But I think Katherine will be happy to be with her friends and family. I don't think she cares about color-blended blankets."

She sighs. "Yeah. Maybe."

The corners of my mouth twitch. "Maybe?" I can almost see her mind working. "Maybe you look good in yellow, even if your mother doesn't think so."

She looks so fresh and open, I have to stop myself from reaching over and cupping her face. She looks so warm and relaxed.

"Can I ask you a question?" she asks, her hands neatly pressed together under her face as she looks at me.

"Anything," I say.

"Anything?" She grins, a mischievous smile on her face that lights up those green eyes.

"Anything."

"And you'll tell me the truth?"

"Yes," I say before I can poke holes in the idea of being entirely honest with the woman next to me.

"Do you like Katherine?"

She's dropped a grenade over the pillow wall, and we're both waiting for it to explode.

"You're asking me if I like your sister?" I ask, stalling.

"You promised to tell the truth, the whole truth, and nothing but the truth." Her tone isn't the pushy, indignant one I've gotten used to in the run-up to this joint weekend away. It's playful and lacking agenda.

"I do like Katherine."

She holds my gaze, knowing there's more. "But . . ." she coaxes.

"I really like your sister. She's very sweet and a good complement to Ed."

She widens her eyes, urging me to elaborate.

"It wouldn't matter who Ed was marrying, if I'm being honest. I just want to make sure he and I are both equally committed to Portis going forward."

"You think that marrying Katherine will mean he's less committed in the future?"

I groan and roll onto my back. "Please don't tell either of them this. I don't want to get into it."

"It sounds like you *need* to get into it," she says. "If you think Katherine is—"

"This isn't about Katherine," I interrupt. "Like I said, it wouldn't matter who he was marrying. It's a big life change, and big life changes tend to shift priorities."

"And you're concerned that Ed's priorities will shift."

I shrug.

"So it's not that you're jealous? You're not worried about the end of guys' night as you know it?"

I turn back to her. "Jesus Christ, no, I'm not jealous. Did I look jealous tonight?"

Her cheeks pink, but she doesn't answer the question. "So you're worried he's going to mess up the business. Make mistakes and stuff? Or take too much time off?"

I pull in a breath. "Maybe. I've been a part of a business that failed in the past. I don't want another to go down on my watch."

She looks surprised by my confession. "Ed always seems very dedicated to his work."

I smile at the way she defends him. "Yeah. It's just since the wedding planning started, I've picked up a bit of slack. And then if they have kids soon . . ."

"You don't want to be left running things on your own."

That's true enough. I went into this because I wanted to be in business with Ed. I don't want to run the business myself. "I don't want it to be inequitable."

"You should talk to him," she says. "He's your friend, and maybe he knows his eye hasn't been on the ball. Maybe he'll reroute."

"*Hmmm.* That's easy to say. But it's Pandora's box. Once it's open, you can't close it again. If I tell him I'm concerned he's not one hundred percent in, it could undermine our relationship."

"But it's already undermining your relationship," she says. "You're sitting with this problem, and you're not sharing it."

She's right, but something about telling Ed doesn't feel good. At the moment, I'm handling it. He has a lot going on. It's fine. The business is doing well. But I don't want it to be like this forever. "I don't want to say anything yet."

"You want me to say something to Katherine?"

"No!" I snap. "You promised."

She doesn't bite back like she normally does. She doesn't even move. Very gently, she says, "I promised I wouldn't, and I won't."

I believe her. I exhale, feeling better after sharing my worries with her. "Thank you," I reply.

She nods slightly.

"Sweet dreams, Lucy Jones."

She gives me a shy smile that feels like a victory, and I close my eyes. I replay the evening through my head like a film. The fire. The s'mores. The blanket.

Lucy. Lucy. Lucy.

Her mouth around my thumb. My lips on her soft hair that smelled of ocean breezes and woodsmoke. The way her body felt in my arms as I picked her up and laid her in bed.

I open my eyes to find her staring at me.

"Hey," I say.

"Hey," she replies.

"I was just thinking about tonight."

"Me too," she says.

"Did you enjoy yourself?"

"Too much," she says, and then her eyes flutter closed before I can ask her what about the evening she enjoyed so much—and whether they were the same parts I enjoyed best.

CHAPTER FOURTEEN

Lucy

When I wake up, my heart thuds against my ribs as I remember where I am and who I'm sharing a bed with. Except Hunter's not next to me. I pad into the bathroom, and he's not there either.

Fishing.

Of course. They left early. I didn't hear a thing, and I'm usually a light sleeper. I check the time. It's seven thirty. Time for me to organize breakfast.

I pull on a sweatshirt and am about to head downstairs when I practically trip on the two boxes Hunter had delivered yesterday. He's set them right by the door. On top is a scribbled note, signed by Hunter, telling me the boxes are for me.

I'm so confused. I asked him what was in the boxes, but he didn't say anything. Why would he want me to open them now?

I pick up the first box and immediately realize what I'll find inside.

The wigs.

I gave him such a hard time about forgetting the wigs, and he'd already arranged to have them delivered here. Why didn't he tell me? I grin to myself, check that there are the correct number of wigs, then head downstairs. I need to prepare breakfast before people start waking up.

As I get to the bottom of the stairs, I hear someone moving around. I let out a little growl. I wanted to be the first of us girls up so I could set the table and make everything pretty.

But when I round the corner into the kitchen, Katherine's at the counter, scrolling through her phone, a cup of coffee in front of her. She turns and sees me and her eyes light up. "Good morning! I've been awake since Ed left for fishing. I couldn't go back to sleep. I'm too excited about having the entire day in this beautiful place. You couldn't have picked anything better."

I wrap my arms around her in a hug. "I'm so happy you're happy. But I can't take any credit for the house or location. That was all Hunter."

Katherine's eyes sparkle. Instantly, I wish I hadn't mentioned his name. I grab myself a cup of coffee and turn on the oven, like I don't notice how Katherine is just itching to talk about Hunter.

"You seem very comfortable together," Katherine says.

It's not a question and doesn't require an answer. I head to the refrigerator and pull out some fruit to make the fruit salad.

"*Are* you comfortable together?" Katherine asks, noticing her error in not asking me a direct question.

I pull out a chopping board and start to prepare the pineapple. "It's early days," I say. "Very early days and not at all serious. He's busy with Portis. I'm busy with my job. It's probably going to be over next Wednesday—"

"Don't say that. It couldn't be more perfect, having you two date. The four of us—"

"You need to dial back the obsession with the foursome. The four of us aren't a thing. Hunter and I have just been thrown together to organize this weekend. Otherwise, we wouldn't be in each other's lives."

"That's not true," she protests. "You're my sister and he's Ed's best friend. You're both in each other's lives for good."

I smile at Katherine. As much as I want everything perfect so Katherine's happy, Katherine wants my happiness just as much. Was that what Hunter meant last night? Does he think I give everything up for Katherine and she's not appreciative?

"He's very good looking," Katherine says.

"So you said," I remind her.

She rolls her eyes at me and slides off her stool. "Do you want a hand prepping that?"

"Nope. I'm going to put the croissants in when the oven's warm, then set the table. I already have the muffins, but I think some people will want eggs—"

"If they want eggs, they can get them themselves," Katherine replies. "You're not the hired chef." Does Hunter see this side of Katherine? The protective side? The side that doesn't want me to do as much?

"I can't wait for the private chef tonight," I reply.

"Me neither. And during the day today, I just want to walk on the beach, collect shells, maybe a little shopping after lunch with a cocktail."

"Perfect," I reply. "Just to warn you, I brought a couple of glue guns and some other art supplies, along with some ideas from Pinterest for stuff we could do with the shells we collect."

She smiles. "You're always prepared. What's the plan? Gluing them to our asses?"

"If that's your kink, I'm here to support you."

"Is Hunter kinky?" she asks. "I get that vibe from him."

My stomach roils, and I'm sure I'm beet red. "You get the kinky vibe from him? What does that mean?" My mind slides to Hunter in bed next to me last night. The way his T-shirt hugged his body like it was a size too small. The wisps of hair peeking out from the neck. I wonder how his skin would feel against mine.

Hot. Hard. Rough.

"You know," she says. "I can imagine he's quite the domineering type in bed."

I laugh. "Have you been imagining it?"

"Stop!" she says. "No, but I wasn't a virgin when I met Ed. I've had other lovers."

"Lovers?" I ask. "You mean boyfriends?"

"Boyfriends who I slept with." Katherine had precisely two "lovers" before Ed, and one was a one-night stand.

"And the ones like Hunter were kinky?" I ask.

"I'm not saying I slept with anyone like Hunter. It's just [illegible] is he?"

I laugh again. "I don't know. We haven't slept together yet." I don't know why I say it—it just slips out. Maybe the line between what's real and what's fake has faded and I'm just speaking the truth.

We *haven't* slept together.

Yet.

Yet.

Yet.

The word echoes in my head.

"Really?" Katherine shrieks. "Why the hell not?"

He could have made a move last night. We were both lying next to each other without many clothes on. But he didn't even try. Maybe he doesn't like me. Except, I think he does. At least he likes me sometimes.

I shrug. "No particular reason."

"Well, it's not because of the lack of chemistry," she says. "Because we all saw there was plenty of that around the fire last night. I'm surprised the two of you didn't combust."

I bite back a smile. Yeah, I'd felt some of that chemistry. But he didn't make a move.

"And you're sharing a bed. Maybe tonight . . . Do you have condoms?"

I groan. "Katherine, please don't tell Ed about any of this. I know Hunter wouldn't want us all talking about . . ."

"About why the two of you aren't having sex already?"

"We're taking it slow. He's being respectful!" I say, half laughing, half serious.

She shakes her head. "He better get less respectful tonight."

Footsteps on the stairs interrupt our conversation, and I put my finger on my lips. I really don't want my sex life—or lack of one—being the topic of conversation over the fruit salad.

After breakfast, we all shower and head to the beach. Our stretch of sand isn't private, but there aren't many people around—just the odd person walking their dog or running. The breeze keeps it from being too hot, but there isn't a cloud in the sky.

We're all scouring the beach for shells of all sizes. When I show my Pinterest ideas, everyone gets very enthusiastic. It goes up a notch when I suggest a midmorning mimosa to accompany our glue guns.

I brought some cards to stick shells to, along with tissue paper and some string I don't have an identified use for. Yet.

"Isn't it beautiful?" Katherine asks as we trail along the shore.

I stop, and she's looking out to the horizon. "It's a beautiful spot."

"Promise me we can still do things like this after I'm married," she says.

I slide my arm around her waist. "What do you mean? Like scour the beach for shells?"

"I just mean spend time together. I don't want it to be like how it is with Mom when we see her. Like we're going through the motions and we're only there because we have to be. I don't want us to grow apart."

I squeeze her tighter. "We're not going to grow apart."

"But I'm going to be married, and I'll probably get pregnant soon, and everyone says you change after you've had children. I still want to be your sister. I want to hang out and day-drink and talk about boys and stuff." Words tumble out like she's opened a cupboard door that's been filled with a decade's worth of junk she's been trying to hide.

"I'm still going to be your sister," I say.

"But if you get serious with Hunter, you might get married next summer, and then we'll both be on the same trajectory."

I try not to choke at the idea of marrying Hunter at any time, but especially a year from now. "We don't need to be on the same trajectory to be sisters."

"You know I'm going to become a baby bore, and you're going to hate coming to visit. And with a baby attached to my boob, I'm not going to be able to come to New York as often."

"We'll figure out a new normal," I say, trying to be reassuring.

"But I don't want our new normal to be that I never see you. You hate coming to Boston because you have to see Mom, and if I can't come to New York because of babies, it's going to make things difficult."

I think about what Hunter said last night about my mom and pleasing people and lines not to be crossed. "I want us to be the same kind of sisters forever, Katherine. And maybe I'll just come to Boston and not see Mom."

Katherine pulls back and looks at me like she must have misheard what I said.

"I don't have to see her *every* time I'm in Boston."

"You'd really come to Boston and not see her? She'd . . ."

"Combust?" I offer.

"Maybe. Or put a spell on you or something." She goes quiet for a minute, looking out to the sea. "Sounds like Hunter's good for you, if you're all of a sudden willing to stand up to her."

"Why do you think it's got anything to do with Hunter?"

"Well, doesn't it? What else has changed?" Katherine might be right. Our discussion last night about lines in the sand has been turning in my head ever since. Why am I sacrificing for my mother all the time at the expense of my own happiness?

"Maybe I just need to find out exactly what she would do. Anyway, it makes more sense to stay at your place. You have a nicer guest bedroom, and you're—"

Katherine groans. "Ed wants to move."

"Move?"

"Closer to the city. He wants to be able to get to work more quickly and have access to the airport to get to New York. He says he doesn't want to waste time commuting when we have kids, or he won't get to see them during the week. We could afford something nice near good schools, and—"

"Oh, God, Katherine. Why haven't you told me any of this?"

She shakes her head. "Mom's going to be so mad we're moving away from Duxbury. She already talks about how she'll be able to come over and babysit."

"How do you feel about it?"

"Scared. But also excited. I've always wanted to live in Somerville. It's more vibrant than where we live now—where we grew up. I'm ready for something different. I'm ready to give my children a different life than the one we had. I think it's nice for kids to grow up with all that life around them."

I squeeze my sister tightly. Everything's changing. "You're right. Mom's going to go apeshit," I say.

Katherine sighs. "I know. But with Ed in my corner, I'm okay with that."

I'm so proud of Katherine. I'm not sure I've ever deliberately done something I know Mom would disapprove of. Even thinking about coming to Boston and staying with Katherine makes me feel slightly queasy. There's something in me that's like a safety switch that deliberately shorts the circuit if I ever try to do something that doesn't comply with what Mom wants.

"She'll probably try and get you to move back to Massachusetts," Katherine says.

I groan. "You're going to have to help me stand up to her if she does. I don't want to leave New York."

"I won't let you leave New York. Your career is there. Your friends are there. *Hunter* is there." She laughs. She knows she's being ridiculous.

But still, she's right. I have a life in New York. With Katherine moving away from Duxbury and away from Mom and Dad, it might mean Mom turns her attention to my living situation. The last thing I want to do is leave New York City. Like, I can't think of anything worse than moving back to Boston. So why am I dreading the potential conversation? Surely it's a quick *Never going to happen, Mom.* Or, at least, it should be. If I knew where the line was, like Hunter said last night, I wouldn't be wasting time thinking about Mom putting pressure on me to come back to Massachusetts. But I've never seen the line before—never looked for it. Never been able to justify putting myself or my needs before my mother or her needs. But thinking about leaving New York makes the line light up in glowing neon.

There's no way I could ever leave New York City.

CHAPTER FIFTEEN

HUNTER

Nothing about fishing is enjoyable to me. The fucking boat is a problem, for a start. Despite taking motion sickness pills I got from Ed, I don't feel great. My stomach has been churning since my feet touched the jetty. And then there's the stench of fish. How is this meant to be relaxing? All I can smell is fish, and all I can see are glassy-eyed dead bodies while the horizon dances around like it's at Coachella. Super enjoyable.

I glance back to the beach. I swear I could dive off the boat and swim back to shore from here. I'm so tempted. I wonder what Lucy has arranged for the girls this morning. Talking to her last night, things felt so open between us. Like despite our pillow wall, we had none of the emotional walls between us that couples usually do at the beginning of a relationship. Maybe it's because we're not really dating, but I don't think that's it. I think it's because Lucy can't hide her feelings. And knowing who she really is—at her core—makes me feel like I can show her everything too. I don't think I've ever had that with anyone. Maybe that's why I held back from launching myself over the pillow wall between us and kissing her. I don't think I've ever had sex combined with emotional intimacy before, and I don't know where it would lead.

Something begins to tug on my rod, interrupting my thoughts. I sigh and ignore it. I don't actually want to catch a fish. It's gross. Let the damn things just swim around, living their best lives, and let's go have a beer. That's my philosophy on fishing. But no one's interested. Everyone's having the best time. Ed has already caught two small bass. One had to be thrown back. The other was big and is in the bucket behind me.

"Hey, Hunter. Did you catch something?" Ed nods toward my line off the back of the boat.

"Oh," I say, like I'm just noticing. "Maybe?"

The fishing guide, Brice, comes over. "Can you bring her in? Or do you need a hand?"

Despite not liking fishing, I've done it enough to know how to reel in a fish. I set to work, pulling my rod up, keeping tension on the line while reeling and reeling. I can tell by the tug that it's going to be a big one. The fish breaks the water before pulling my rod and going under again. But not before I caught a glimpse. It's a striped bass. "Looks and feels like a cow," I say.

"A cow?" Ed asks.

"Striped bass over twenty-five pounds," Brice says. "You know your fish, son."

Brice grabs one of the larger nets and positions it over the side. I pull up my rod. The fish is thrashing on the line, trying to get free, but my brain is hard-wired to do this. I caught my first fish at five years old. I'm not going to let this fucker go. It's a big one, and I want to be able to tell my dad I caught it before I let it go.

I pull again, and Brice is ready with the net. I wind like mad and bring it clear out of the water. Brice scoops it up in the net.

"That's a nice fish," Brice says. "Haven't seen one landed that big by a tourist in a while."

Brice sets to work getting it out of the net and on the scale. I figure it's got to be at least thirty pounds.

"Is that a fluke?" Ed asks. "Have you fished before?"

I shrug. "A little. With my dad when I was a kid."

"I didn't know that. Honestly, I thought you were a little squeamish about it."

I'm not about to tell Ed I'd be happy if I never held another fishing rod in my life. But I don't want him to feel bad about today's trip. He's clearly having fun, and that's the aim of this weekend, right?

Brad starts to shout. "I got one! It's strong."

Brice leaves my cow on the deck of the boat, flailing around. Everyone's attention goes to Brad.

I should throw my fish back. I just wouldn't mind weighing it first.

Brad loses whatever was stuck on his line, and Brice comes back to my cow. At least it certainly looks big enough.

"Gotta be thirty pounds," he says as he lifts it onto the scale.

Gotta be.

I watch the needle on the scale as it settles. Thirty-six. My biggest-ever catch. I bite back a grin. I shouldn't feel as pleased as I do.

"Grab this mother and I'll take a picture," Brice says.

Why not? I can always delete it. Maybe Lucy would want to see it. I hand him my phone and take the fish. The feel of it—the smell—reminds me of summers spent out on the boat with my dad.

I hold it and look into the camera.

"We can eat that tonight," Ed says. "Great catch, Hunter."

"Nah. We've got a chef booked for tonight." I glance at my watch. It's just over five minutes since I caught this thing. "I better get him back," I say.

"If you're going to do it, do it now," Brice says.

I launch the bass off the side of the boat, watching as it comes to life after hitting the water. I bet it thought it wasn't going to get a second chance. I hope it survives.

Before I can second-guess myself, I type out a message to my dad and send him the shot of me with the bass. We haven't spoken in a few months. That will make his day.

Reluctantly, I retake my spot next to Ed.

"You're a dark horse," Ed says. "First you're secretly dating Lucy, and now you're a fisherman."

I can't help but chuckle. "Not a dark horse. I used to fish with my dad when I was a kid. Haven't done it in years." We would go out every weekend. I loved those weekends, just one-on-one with my dad. I wanted so badly to grow up to be exactly like him. It was why I did finance in college. I wanted to take over the family business. I wanted to become the man he was.

And then everything changed.

"Have you spoken to him?" Ed asks.

"My dad? Sure. A few weeks back." It's a lie. But a small one.

"That's not what I mean. Have you spoken to him about the business?"

I gaze out at the ocean. "Nope. What's the point? He either knew the business was going down and let me take over a sinking ship, or he didn't know, which makes him an idiot. Either way, there's no upside to talking to him about it." Dad finally retired five years after I graduated college. I'd spent those five years learning the business from top to bottom—or so I thought. I knew the clients. I understood the regulatory requirements. I was ready.

Except I wasn't. Dad had kept the financial performance of the business a secret. He'd told me parts, but I never got enough information to get a full picture. I can't help but think that was deliberate. He had to know Bain Insurance was in dire financial straits. The lease on our offices was too expensive and so tightly drafted it was impossible to get out of or move and sublet. The salaries of a lot of the people who'd been there long before me were vastly inflated, but too much valuable company history sat with them, so it was impossible to fire them. And there wasn't any new business coming through.

I tried everything I could to save the business. It was unsalvageable.

"But maybe he has an explanation."

"He's had plenty of time to give it to me. It's been nearly six years since we filed Chapter 7."

I spent a long time blaming myself. My dad had run Bain Insurance for most of his professional life, and he'd provided our family with a good life. We had a vacation home on the lake. A home in one of the nicest suburbs in Philadelphia. We never wanted for anything. It was an idyllic life. One I wanted to replicate for my own family.

"Maybe he's embarrassed."

"So letting his son take the fall is okay?"

"No one thinks Bain failing had anything to do with you."

I let out a cynical laugh. "Of course they do. They all look at the situation and see that Brian Bain ran a successful business his whole life, and then within a couple of years of his son taking over, it was all gone. And he's been a coward all these years and never set anyone straight."

"But the reasons it went into liquidation were because of decisions your father made."

I shrug. "No one sees it that way."

"I see it that way."

"Because I've told you and you're my friend and you believe me."

"So why don't you tell people?"

"And embarrass my dad?" It was bad enough, gradually realizing my dad wasn't the man I thought he was. In the early months when I took over, he'd come into town and we'd have lunch or take a walk. But his visits became less and less frequent. Maybe it was because he was getting older. Maybe he was just bored. Or maybe he saw the complete and utter disappointment in my eyes. First, that he hadn't built the successful business I thought he had. But then, that he'd handed it on to me, and by doing so hung an albatross around my neck. I was doomed to failure. I'd started off enthusiastic and full of energy, and by the time I closed the doors on Bain Insurance, I was broken. I'd lost my confidence, and anyone who might give me a job in Boston had stopped taking my calls. I was a loser.

"I don't know why you're still protecting him," Ed says.

"I don't think I am. He knows what he did."

"But does he?"

"If he doesn't, he's an even worse businessman than I know him to be."

Ed shakes his head. I get that he's angry on my behalf. But he won't convince me to speak to my dad about it. "What really pisses me off," Ed continues, "is that some part of you thinks it's your fault. And that's bullshit."

I'm bored with fishing. I want off this boat. What the hell time is it, anyway?

"You guys ready to pull in your lines?" Brice asks us. I'm grateful for the interruption.

I just want to be back on dry land. And see Lucy. I've been a coward by not kissing her already. There's no way I'm going to continue to be a coward. I'm going to tell her I want to kiss her, and I'm going to be able to tell by her expression whether she wants to kiss me back.

CHAPTER SIXTEEN

Lucy

I scan the deck table, looking at all the shells, cardstock, bits of string, and scissors, then glance back to my creation in front of me. I've arranged my shells on a piece of black card so they form a heart shape. I don't know whether it's the colors of the shells against the unlikely background or the fact that the shells seem to gleam, they're so shiny, but it looks impressive. I'm practically Martha fucking Stewart.

"I love it, Lucy," Katherine says. The rest of the girls *ohh* and *ahh* in agreement and admire their own creations. Katherine has made a wind chime with her shells. Alison has stuck hers on a white background in a circle. Luna abandoned her project in favor of making everyone their second cocktail of the day. "Are you going to give it to Hunter?" she asks.

I snap my head around to check I heard her right. "Of course I'm not. I'm going to get a frame and hang it in my apartment. Maybe in the kitchen."

"Is there room in your kitchen?" Luna asks, setting a tray full of Bellinis on the table.

"Probably not. In the bathroom, then. Or my bedroom."

"Grab a drink," Luna says. "Let's have a toast."

We all abandon our projects, take one of the tall glasses and stand in a circle, ready to say *Cheers*.

"Let's drink," Luna says. "To Katherine and Ed," she says, raising a glass.

Katherine beams, and warmth burrows into my stomach. It's so good to see her happy. This weekend was worth all the planning.

The sound of cars pulling up in the front captures our attention.

"Oh, God," I say. "They're all going to smell like fish."

"I think they showered and changed and then went out for lunch," Katherine says.

"A little more civilized. Which is surprising." I roll my eyes, then remember I'm supposed to be dating Hunter rather than convincing myself that he's gross.

I just hope I don't get those unfamiliar flutters inside when I see him. I don't want to have a crush on a guy like that. Especially one I'm sharing a bed with.

The guys' chatter fills the air. They're noisy and full of life. Maybe lunch included a couple of beers?

As they round the side of the house and see us, they let up a cheer, and I can't help but giggle. They're just being so silly.

Ed runs up the steps to Katherine and lifts her up and out of our circle.

Hunter is next, taking the stairs two at a time and barreling toward me like he's going to walk right through me. I stumble backward, so he doesn't knock into me, but he keeps going, and I back away from him and the group.

"Tell me you missed me," he says, grinning at me like he just won the lottery.

"What?" I say, an answering smile forming on my lips.

"Tell me you've been thinking about me all day." His tone is cocky, and part of me wants to smack it out of him. The other part of me feels my nipples tighten against my shirt.

I narrow my eyes. Is he serious? We're too far away from the rest of our party for him to be hoping for someone to overhear. "Thinking about you?" I clarify.

I slow down, and he's as close to me as he can be without touching me. Our feet are toe-to-toe, and he lowers his head so his face is an inch from mine. "Tell me," he says in challenge.

My heart starts to race, and I can't catch my breath. His body heat warms me. His smile makes me giddy. His scent of freshly washed skin fills my nose. It's all so overwhelming.

"Tell me," he demands.

"You've crossed my mind," I say. "Thinking about how you've tortured me by not telling me you had the wigs."

He grins and slides his hand around my hip to my lower back.

"Why didn't you tell me?" I ask. "You knew I was mad at you."

"I think you kinda like being mad at me."

I roll my eyes. Like anyone enjoys being mad.

"I've been thinking about you," he says. He presses a kiss on my head. Did he hit his head out there on the boat and come back convinced we're actually dating?

"Are you okay? How many beers have you had?" I ask.

"I want to kiss you," he says.

"Oh." I'm too shocked to think of a good answer.

"I've been thinking about how you'll taste. How you'll feel."

"Hunter," I whisper.

"I mean it," he says. "For real."

Our eyes lock, and all I can see is a man who knows what he wants. Determined. Sure and sexy as hell.

I give him a small nod. It's all he needs.

He pushes his hand into my hair and glances down at my lips before leaning in and pressing his soft mouth against mine. My hand tentatively slides up his shirt, and then I almost groan as my palm hits his warm skin. I open my mouth a little, and his tongue slides between my lips, urgent. Pressing. Possessive.

I feel it in my knees, at the base of my spine, between my legs—a low buzz of something. Desire. Yearning. Need.

It's the best kiss I've ever had.

But I want more.

He must feel the same because he pulls me closer. There's no space between us. Our bodies press together tightly as we explore each other. His hand presses on my ass, pushing me closer to him as his other grips my hair.

My thoughts start to blur, and the sound of our friends' chatter ebbs away. It's as if someone's lowering the volume on everything that's not the sensation of Hunter's body against mine. And he's getting louder and louder and louder.

Wow. This guy takes his kissing seriously.

A squeal from behind Hunter interrupts us, and we jump apart.

Hunter spins around, and Katherine comes into view, grinning like she's the happiest bride ever to go on a bachelorette.

"Sorry to interrupt," she says, before pulling Ed back around the corner to the others.

We both watch them leave, and I go to speak, but before I can get my words out, Hunter steps his leg between mine and cups my face. Like the first kiss wasn't enough—like he needs more.

The stubble on his face grazes against my skin, and it's like I'm a match rubbing against the lighting strip on a box. I'm going to combust if he keeps going.

My nipples pinch against the lace of my bra, our breaths mingle, and his mouth is on mine again. He groans, and the sound skirts over my body, calling every hair to stand to attention. His hands shift, sliding down my body, mapping the edge of my breast, the curve of my waist. I want our clothes to dissolve, everyone to disappear, and to be left with his heat, this kiss, and the sound of the waves.

Eventually he pulls back and rests his forehead against mine.

"I've been wanting to do that all day." He sighs. "Well, since last night, actually."

I bite back a smile. "Well, now you've kissed me," I say.

"And now you've kissed me back."

I laugh at our push and pull, fiddling with the neck of his T-shirt.

"You know what I wish?" he asks.

"I couldn't fathom. You've already surprised me today."

He pulls back a bit, resting his arm on the porch post behind me so he's still leaning into me. "Really? You weren't thinking that—"

"Get back to the bit where you were wishing for something," I say to him.

He chuckles. "I wish it was just you and me here. Just for the night. We could hang out on the porch. Watch the waves roll in. You could give me hell for being . . . I don't know—me. I could take no notice. And then I'd pull you onto my lap and kiss you into next week."

I have to look away and over to the ocean. The picture he's painting is far too vivid. Far too tempting for me to look at him as he describes it.

I snake my hand under his shirt and hook my fingers into his waistband. "Huh," I say, mulling over the idea. It's not like I haven't thought about Hunter in this way. In fact, I've thought about him in exactly this way a lot in the past twenty-four hours. I just didn't expect *this*. So soon. So public. And although it feels good to be . . . connected, I'm scared. "Sounds . . . good."

He smiles and takes a step back. "Right. Bachelor and bachelorette duties must take precedence."

I really want Katherine to have the best weekend of her life. But right at this moment, I wish we could press pause on *The Katherine and Ed Show* and maybe disappear, just the two of us, to see if we could act out the exact evening Hunter just described.

CHAPTER SEVENTEEN

Hunter

I grab a tray of drinks from the bar since they were taking way too long to arrive at our table and head back to our party.

"Here's Hunter 'the Tongue' Bain." Ed thinks he's made up the most hilarious nickname, and who am I to spoil his fun? Kissing Lucy Jones was . . . Well, I haven't been able to keep the grin off my face since.

Everyone grabs a tequila from the tray, and Ed holds his bottle up to the guys' *Cheers*. "You know you have to marry her now."

My jaw tightens just a fraction. I know he's joking, but still, it's a lot. I don't want to think about anything but right now.

"There's no way you can ever break up," he continues.

"Why would you?" Fisher says, like it's already been decided by committee that I'm marrying Lucy Jones. "She's hot and looks like she keeps you on your toes."

"Says the committed bachelor," I say.

Fisher just shrugs and grins at me. "Do as I say, not as I do."

"You need to stop getting ahead of yourself," I say to Ed. If only he knew that today was our first . . . crossover into romantic territory. Before today, it had all been faked. Or maybe none of it had been fake? Not the stuff between just the two of us anyway.

"I mean it, though," Ed says. "We're . . . we're a family, you, me, Katherine, and Lucy." There's a vulnerability in his tone that hits me at the back of my throat. "You can't mess this up, Hunter. I don't want to be choosing between inviting you or Lucy to holidays and celebrations."

"You said that," I remind him. "But I'm also serious. You need to behave yourself."

As if to prove a point, someone taps me on the shoulder. When I look around, there's a pretty blond girl standing next to me, smiling.

"I was just wondering if you're single and if you want my number?" She wrinkles up her nose in a way I probably would have found adorable about forty-eight hours ago. "Do I recognize you?" she asks. "Are you famous?"

"Definitely not famous. And not single either. But thanks for asking." Her face drops a little, and I'm not sure if it's because I'm not a celebrity or because I'm not single.

"I have a couple of friends who're very single," I say. "But they're not famous either." She glances around at our group. "Fisher, meet . . ."

"Lindsay," she says, forgetting me instantly. Fisher stands and they go to the bar.

Not only am I officially taken and unofficially not interested in Lindsay but I'm also a matchmaker. Feels pretty good.

"That's what I'm talking about," Ed says. "You're used to beating them off with a stick. You need to get some real good swinging action going, because if you break up with Lucy—which is strictly unacceptable under any circumstances—you definitely can't cheat on her."

"Noted," I reply. I've never cheated on anyone. I've never really understood men who cheat. If you want a woman other than the one you're with, break up and be with the new woman. There's no need to be a dick.

"Consider yourself warned," Ed says.

I get him being concerned. I really do. If I think about it for too long, I'm concerned too. I don't want to mess things up so I see Ed even less than I do now. If I was thinking entirely clearly, I should have stayed away from Lucy. That ship has sailed. And honestly, if I think about it, Lucy and I have been heading in this direction since we first laid eyes on each other. I wasn't immediately attracted to her, but I was immediately interested. She caught my attention, and that says a lot when ninety-nine percent of the time, all my attention is on work.

There's a kerfuffle on the other side of the bar. When I look up, I see Katherine and the rest of the bachelorette party heading in our direction. Katherine makes a beeline right for Ed, and when Lucy walks right past me, I grab her hand and pull her down on my lap.

"Did you think you could walk straight past me?"

She grins at me, her eyes sparkling in the glow from the tea lights on the table. "Why am I sitting on your lap?"

"Is there somewhere else you'd rather be?" I ask.

She tries not to smile, but she's terrible at it. The corners of her mouth twitch and her green eyes twinkle. She glances up and around at our party, but no one is paying attention to us. They're all deep in their own conversations.

"Don't we hate each other?" she whispers in my ear.

"I don't know about you, but I don't hate you," I say, holding her gaze.

"I don't hate you either." She squeezes her eyes shut like it's too much to admit.

I chuckle. "I'm bowled over." Gliding my hands down her legs, I say, "I don't hate this." I sweep my thumb over her lips. "I don't hate this." I trail my fingers down from her collarbone, between her breasts, down, down, down. "I don't hate any of this."

Her cheeks flush pink. "We're supposed to hate each other, though."

I shake my head. "Things change. When you start to dip below the surface, you see things that weren't there before."

"Like?"

"Like the way you love your sister. The way you want your mom to love you."

She frowns at me. "My mom does love me."

"Right," I say. "But you're worried she won't unless everything's perfect." I'm figuring it out as I speak. All the snippets of Lucy are slotting into place, the woman she is coming into focus. She just wants to be loved and accepted. Just like everyone.

She studies me as if I'm a talking dog or something.

"And now I see beneath the admonishments of me," I continue. "The need to control everything and everyone, the desire to please Katherine and your mom and . . . everyone."

"Hunter," she says, her voice quiet and fragile. I'm not sure if she's asking me to stop.

I hold up my hands. "You looked beautiful in the yellow dress. You are lovable. Kind. Generous."

She places her palms against mine, and we lock fingers. She leans forward and places a kiss on my lips. It's soft and light and instantly makes me want more. I want all of her. She pulls back, still studying me.

"I don't think anyone's ever seen me like that," she says. "Me, according to you, is . . ."

"Beautiful?" I suggest. "Self-sacrificing? Thoughtful?"

"I was going to say . . . okay."

Something about her description of herself as just okay hits me right in the middle of my chest. I want to scoop her up and take her somewhere I can protect her from everything. "You're more than okay, Lucy Jones."

Maybe I can see all of her, or at least more than she's ever shown anyone before.

Her cheeks pink and she looks over at my drink on the table, like she's studying a famous painting or something. "What ya drinking?" she asks in a singsong voice.

"Tequila," I say, shifting in my seat. "Let me get you something. What do you want?"

Our gazes meet, and I can't help but wonder what she's like in bed. What she likes in bed.

"I want to stay right here, like this," she says, and she holds out her hand. "Wanna share?"

I shift again, pulling her closer to me. "With you? Anything. Anytime." I scoop up the glass and press it into her hand. I watch as she sips the amber liquid, can't take my eyes from her mouth and her wet lips. I want to lick tequila off every inch of this woman's body.

She hands me back the glass.

I press my lips to the exact spot she drank from and take a swig. Watching her, I slide the glass back onto the table and pull her in for a kiss. This might be the most perfect day ever.

CHAPTER EIGHTEEN

Lucy

The chef cooked a feast, with far too much food that I was too distracted to remember. I do remember Hunter watching me. His hand on my back. On my leg. We're all back on the beach, sporting our Uma Thurman outfits. And I've eaten one more marshmallow than is good for me. Now I'm hazy with alcohol and sea air and sugar. I need to be lying down. Hunter covers the fire with sand, and we all head back to the house.

My heart starts hammering against my chest. What's next? Part of me wants to drag Hunter upstairs as soon as possible, strip him naked, and straddle him. But another part of me doesn't want to break what's been building between us these last few days. It feels new and fragile and precious, and I don't want it all to be about being hot for each other. Although, I'm definitely hot for him. Why wouldn't I be? He's insightful and kind and patient. As well as having rock-hard abs and shoulders I can't stop touching, they're so broad and protective. But I like this guy. It's *more* than lust. Although there's a lot of lust. If we sleep together, doesn't that potentially change everything?

Katherine and I are hugging each other good night at the bottom of the stairs. Out of the corner of my eye, I notice Hunter filling two glasses with water. Is it insane that I really hope one of those glasses is for me? I like the idea that he's thinking of me, looking after me, making sure I'm fully hydrated.

Katherine heads upstairs, and Hunter pads toward me. "I thought you'd want water."

It's like he's given me a dozen roses. I grin up at him. "Thanks. That's kind of you."

The corner of his mouth twitches, and he hands me a glass. "You want me to carry it upstairs?"

Normally this would be my cue to make a joke about how I think I can manage an entire glass of water myself, or that my poor female muscles can just about manage it. But I don't. Instead, I say, "Sure. Thanks."

He gives me a soft smile and gestures for me to go first.

When we get inside the bedroom, he sets the two glasses of water on our respective bed stands, then turns to me. "Do you want to go in the bathroom first?"

I was kinda hoping he'd kiss me again. "Sure," I say and slip inside to take off my wig and change into my PJs. If I'd known things would take the turn they have this weekend, I might have packed something nicer. Something a little sexier. Not that I have sexy lingerie just lying around at home.

I take my makeup off and brush my teeth as quickly as possible, all the time wondering what Hunter is doing next door. Maybe he just fell asleep.

He grins when I go back into the bedroom, and as we pass one another, he tugs on my shorts. "Cute."

I settle into my side of the bed. The pillow wall remains where we left it. I think about dismantling it but decide not to. Everything between us seems so ambiguous. We've kissed, we've told each other we don't hate each other, but Hunter didn't make his move as soon as we were on our own. He didn't even try to kiss me again.

He comes into the bedroom, still grinning at me. He slips between the sheets, partially hidden by the feather wall between us.

"Did you enjoy your day?" he asks, settling down so we're both lying on our sides, facing each other.

I nod, unsure about what's next. Are we going to chitchat? "Yeah, it was super fun."

"What was your favorite part?"

If I were capable of arching an eyebrow, that's exactly what I'd be doing right about now. "My favorite part?"

"Yeah. Which part of the day did you enjoy the most?"

Is he fishing for compliments? Does he want me to tell him how much I enjoyed his kiss? How my favorite part was sitting on his lap, his hands on my body, confessing that we don't actually hate each other?

"I'm not sure I have an order for my favorite parts of today."

"Oh, really?" he says through a smile. His tone is teasing, and I don't get why he's holding back. "Kissing you was definitely my number one. Hearing how you don't hate me was up there too."

I let out a small laugh. "Nope. Don't hate you. Well, not today, anyway. Who knows what tomorrow will bring?"

He holds my gaze for a second, like he wants to say something else, but he seems to change his mind. "Yeah, there's always room for you hating me tomorrow." He reaches for the pillow at the top of our pillow wall and tosses it behind him to the floor. "I don't think we need this."

My stomach swoops as he demolishes the wall between us.

"That's better," he says, sliding his leg over to my side of the bed, his toes touching mine.

At the contact, a thousand thoughts flood my brain. I don't want to rush. I don't want to get hurt by this guy. I don't want to have to deal with the aftermath of not being able to navigate family functions when Hunter and I inevitably fall apart.

I pull my leg away, and he must know what I'm thinking.

"It's a lot," he says. "Their expectations. All the connections between us. It could all go very wrong."

"Yeah," I agree. "It's a lot."

"It's not that I don't want things to . . . go further. I do. You're beautiful and . . . I like you. I feel like you show me a side of yourself that not many people are lucky enough to see . . ."

"Or maybe you see a side of me that not many people *can* see."

"I have my Lucy Jones glasses on, you mean?"

I laugh. "Maybe."

"It feels like we're connected on a level I didn't even know existed."

I roll onto my back because what he's saying is too much. Not because I don't think he's telling the truth. But because I understand his words exactly. He gets me. And I get him. Mentally. Physically. Emotionally. There aren't many people who know me better than I know myself, who see the good in me when they've experienced plenty of the bad.

"At least tomorrow, you'll be free of me. This weekend will be over. We will have both fulfilled our roles, and we can go off into the sunset knowing your best friend and my sister had the bachelor and bachelorette weekend they wanted."

"You'll be free of unreliable me. Forgetting the wigs and my seasickness pills. Not helping organize the groceries or drinks. You can't rely on me, and now you don't have to."

His tone is jovial, like he's in on the joke, but there's something underneath that feels like he's asking me a question.

"I don't think you're unreliable," I say.

He doesn't respond.

"Is that how you see yourself?" I ask.

"Maybe. Sometimes. But I really did have a lot going on these past few weeks, with Ed being so focused on the wedding."

"Yeah," I say. "I didn't realize you were taking on more than you would normally. I just . . . I guess I don't want to mess things up for Katherine, and you're trying not to mess things up in the business. Both our motivations are . . . pure. You know?"

He nods. "I'm going to miss getting my ass handed to me."

"I could record something for you. Just so you could have me chewing your ass out on demand?"

He wiggles his eyebrows. "Sounds kinky."

I roll my eyes. "If kinky's what you're into, then it's just as well that you and I stopped at kissing."

He grins. "The stakes are just too high, right?"

I sigh. It was easy to get caught up with the flirting and the hard body, but if I put my brain in charge rather than my hormones, he's entirely right. There's too much to lose. Too much potential chaos. "Yes. You're probably right."

"Probably means you're going to go down in my personal history as the one who got away."

My stomach twists at the possibility that we're both missing out on something that could be endgame good. "I'll *definitely* be the one who got away. Not probably. Good night, Hunter Bain." I turn to face the window.

I'm so happy that Katherine's had the best weekend. She deserves her happily ever after.

And if I ever get mine, it won't be with Hunter.

CHAPTER NINETEEN

Lucy

I always wear a variation of the same outfit to work: dress and a jacket, mid-heel pumps, hair up and off my face. It's my uniform. My armor. Since the pandemic, business casual has become the new normal, but after lockdown, I came back to work exactly how I'd dressed my last day in the office: ready. I take my job seriously, and I want people to take me seriously. I don't want to be distracted by what I'm going to wear to the office on any given day. I always know. Because it's always the same.

My boss's boss, Sharon, is coming toward me from her office. "Oh, Lucy, there you are. Thanks for that report you sent through. Can I talk to you about it?"

I might have been heading to the bathroom, but I'm sure I can hold it. "Sure." I don't know why she wants to talk to me. It was a straightforward report about the team of paralegals I manage, how many cases we're working on, the WIP, amount billed. It was a standard system report, but I added information about who's working what case and what their rates are.

I follow Sharon into her office and take a seat in front of her desk.

I don't have a notepad, but I pull out my cell from my jacket pocket. I'm pretty strict about using my cell in the office. I don't even pick it up unless it's an emergency. When I swipe it open to get to my notes app, I notice a message each from my sister and Hunter. My stomach roils, and I have to fight the urge to open the messages and find out why Hunter is in contact. Hunter and I haven't seen each other since we shared a cab back into the city from LaGuardia after the Martha's Vineyard trip. He carried my suitcase up the three flights of my Brooklyn walk-up, and we hugged each other goodbye like old friends. For a few days, maybe even a few weeks, I wondered if he'd call or message. I wondered if I should call or message him. But he didn't and neither did I. Every day it's gotten a little easier to stop myself from reaching out.

"Did you want to add to the report?" I ask. "Most things I can get easily from the system."

"No," she says as she takes a seat behind her desk. She's one of the more junior partners, so her office isn't big, but it's still an office, and she has a window. "The report was fine. I wanted to talk to you about something else."

My heart sinks a little bit. I'm always getting pulled onto new projects. I'm seen as a safe pair of hands, and I like that, but it does mean that my workload can spiral a little.

"Did you ever think about being a lawyer?" she asks.

It's the last thing I expected her to say. I've never been asked the question before. People just assume that if you're a paralegal, you're not clever enough to be a lawyer.

I swallow, trying to buy some time to think up a convincing answer. "I guess I did at some point," I say.

"Because you're smart. I brought up your education record. You got good grades in college."

"Right," I say.

"But you never considered law school?"

I smile, trying to keep it together. "I thought about it. But I already had a chunk of student loans, and the job market for law school graduates back then wasn't great. I could get a paralegal job right away, and so . . . it didn't happen."

"I see that happen for a lot of women," she says as if she's talking in code. "I think it comes down to the fact that sometimes, women don't believe in themselves like men do."

The words hang in the air, waiting for a hook.

She doesn't need to know about the conversations I had with my parents about law school. She doesn't need to know my mom told me it would be really expensive, and that most people don't pass the bar, and most of the ones who do don't get jobs and end up working in Starbucks. Sharon doesn't need to know how Mom suggested becoming a paralegal and "seeing how I felt about things in a couple of years."

"Do you know about our program to mentor junior women in the firm so they become senior women in the firm?" she asks.

"I think maybe that's a thing for the lawyers," I say. "Not the paralegals."

"Maybe," she says. "Did you know that fifty-two percent of law school graduates joining our firm are women, yet only eleven percent of those lawyers become partners?"

"Well, I haven't examined the statistics, but that sounds about right to me." You don't need to count heads to see the discrepancy in this and every other firm in New York City.

Sharon smiles. "Yes, well, *we* all see it, because *we* all live it. It takes statistics to convince some of the men of this firm that there's a problem. Anyway, we're trying to address the discrepancy in different ways. I'd like to mentor you, if that's something you'd be interested in."

"To help me . . . progress? Get a raise? That sort of thing?"

"Lucy, you've done really well at this firm. You're clever and organized, and you use initiative. But I think you're capable of more. Much more."

My stomach fizzes with excitement. "Really?"

"Yes, really. I think you've been overlooked. I'm not sure why. But I thought we could work together to help you realize your full potential."

A lump forms at the back of my throat. I can't remember ever feeling so . . . like anything but a number at work. That's how it goes. You're paid a salary and you have to do a job. Talk of potential and mentorship . . . I don't remember ever having had this kind of conversation with anyone before. "I would like that," I manage to croak out.

"Obviously, I don't want to push you onto a path you're not comfortable with," she says. "But my alma mater has an evening program where students can attend law school on a part-time basis. It does mean the whole thing takes longer, but you might want to investigate the program."

"Oh, really? Where did you go to college?"

"Fordham."

My eyes nearly pop out of my head. "Fordham? Well, there's no way I'd ever get into a program at Fordham."

"Why not?" she asks.

"Well, because . . . that's an elite school, and—"

"I've seen your grades. I've seen your work. You'd need to sit for the LSATs, but don't write yourself off. Don't count yourself out before you've even tried."

"Even if I did, in some magical fantasyland, manage to get into Fordham, I could never afford it. No offense, but my salary pays my living costs and not a lot else. Certainly not enough to be able to handle Fordham Law's fees. Or even the repayment plan on those fees."

I expect her to agree with me and accept that I'm not the right person to mentor. She'll understand it would be a waste of time. But she doesn't.

"Like I said, the firm has created this program to enable women to get to more senior positions. We have the financial means to do that. I'm not saying we'd be able to pay for the entire tuition, but depending on your LSAT score and the college you get into, we'd definitely consider paying a portion of it. And, of course, you'd have a job here as a lawyer guaranteed when you graduated."

My jaw hits my knees. "You'd give me a scholarship or something?"

"It depends on the circumstances—as I said, your LSAT and the program you get into would be factors—but we'd consider it. I would advocate for you. And obviously I could help you source other financial aid if I can. I know a lot of people in this city."

It feels like there must be a huge catch. Maybe she's mistaken me for someone else. Maybe my file has been mixed up with one of the other paralegals. "And you know that I went to U-Mass?" I ask, just in case she's confused me with someone else.

"I do. My husband went there. Go Beacons!"

I raise my fists in the air like I'm gripping pom-poms.

"This has come out of the blue," she says. "And you might have other priorities. But maybe it's worth some consideration."

"You're right, it is a surprise. But I'd definitely like to look into it."

"Why don't you do that," she says. "Then get some time in my diary in a couple of weeks, and we can talk about it. There's no pressure, so if you decide that going to law school is not for you, that's fine. I can still support you in your current role, if that's what you want."

"Thank you." I kinda want to hug her. Just the idea that she'd look at me and think I was worth having a meeting with about my career is more than I could have ever hoped for. The fact that she wants to mentor me and thinks I have potential? I can't remember *anyone* ever thinking I had potential. At school, I was constantly compared with Katherine, and I always came up wanting. With my parents it was the same. I'm sure at some point or other they tried to be supportive and encouraging, but I just can't remember. Sharon picking me out of my colleagues and saying I get to be the one feels slightly uncomfortable—like a gorgeous dress you find in the sale that's slightly too small. You know that if you just lost five pounds you'd look like a million bucks. But right now, I want the dress, no matter the extra five pounds. I'm excited-slash-terrified. But my heart is full of hope.

CHAPTER TWENTY

Hunter

It's almost six thirty and I still haven't heard back from Lucy. Does she have me blocked or something? We were on good terms the last time we saw each other. Or so I thought. I've been slammed at work the last few weeks. Not that thoughts of Lucy haven't crossed my mind. They have. Every day. I just haven't acted on them. The stakes haven't changed. We can't start what we can't finish.

As I head down the fire escape stairs of my building, my phone starts to vibrate in my hand, and Lucy's name flashes up. Thank God.

"Lucy! I messaged you hours ago."

"I'm at work. I have actual work to do at work. I don't spend the day playing *Candy Crush Saga* like you."

God, I've missed this girl. I can't shake the grin off my face. "Good to hear your voice, Lucy."

"Anyway," she says, sounding slightly flustered, "I just got the message about Katherine and Ed being in town. Did you know about this?"

"Heard the same time as you. You know we're on a group chat."

"Wait, that's a group chat?"

My smile only grows at her increasingly hysterical tone. I get to the bottom of the stairs and open the door into the heat of the New York afternoon. It's bright, and I have to shield my eyes with my hand, like I'm a mole seeing the sun for the first time.

"They decided to fly down tonight so they could have dinner with us and a full day tomorrow for . . . some wedding-related thing. I glaze over as soon as she starts talking about wedding prep."

"We need a plan," Lucy says. "We should meet before. What time is it?"

I turn around and look up at the building Lucy indicated she worked in when we bumped into each other at Stranger than Fiction. "When are you getting off work?"

"Just now. I'm heading out. We have to meet them at seven, right?"

"And we wouldn't want to be late," I say under my breath. "So what's your plan, Lucy Jones?"

At that moment, I see the woman herself come through the revolving door in the building next to mine. I stand and watch as she raises her face toward the sun, like she's hoping to photosynthesize or something.

"You look cute," I say.

She snaps her head around and sees me immediately. I don't hate the way her smile fills her entire face as we lock eyes.

She wanders over, and I have time to take in her hourglass shape and the way she can make corporate-wear look sexy as hell.

"Hello, stranger. How long have you been standing out here waiting for me?"

"Just three or four hours."

She laughs, and I can only stand and take it all in. She's just beautiful.

"So how often have we seen each other these last few weeks?" she asks.

For a moment I'm stumped, then I realize she wants to create a cover story. "I've been busy at work. You've been busy at work. Maybe we grabbed lunch a couple of times."

"Good," she says. "That works. Katherine's asked me a few times whether I've seen you. I've been pretty vague, but I mentioned lunch, so that tracks."

We grab a cab, and as I slam the door shut, I'm reminded how small these cars are. Lucy and I haven't been this close since Martha's Vineyard.

She sweeps her hand down the skirt of her dress. "So," she says. "How have you been?"

I chuckle at her attempt at small talk. "Like I said, really busy at work. What about you?"

"Yeah," she replies. "Same. And . . ."

"And?"

"I don't know. Something weird happened to me today." I don't respond, wanting her to tell me in her own time. "My boss's boss—one of the junior partners—pulled me into her office and told me she wanted to mentor me."

I try to catch her eye, but she stares out the window, toward the driver, down at her skirt—anywhere but at me.

"That sounds great," I say. "Doesn't it?"

Lucy sighs. "I think so. She was talking about how I have all this potential." She bursts into a laugh, which doesn't have the same unrestrained energy she normally does. "She was even talking about me going to law school—part-time, in the evening."

"Wow," I say.

"Right?" She finally looks at me. "That's a crazy idea."

"Is it? Do you want to go to law school?"

She chews the inside of her cheek. "I don't know. I mean, I haven't thought about it in a long time. Now I'm older. And there's the debt. Potentially." She shakes her head. "We need to be talking about stuff. Like, couple stuff."

"I think that's what we're doing."

She gives me that *don't mess with me* look she wears so well, and I can't help but smile in response. It's good to see her. "Maybe we should meet for lunch for real between now and the wedding. Then we won't have to invent a cover. We'll have a ready-made one."

She starts chewing her cheek again. "Maybe. But we need a cover in the next ten blocks."

"We're taking it slow. We haven't stayed at each other's places—that makes it easier than lying and getting ourselves into trouble. We've met for lunch a couple of times at Stranger than Fiction, and dinner once."

"Or maybe we haven't managed to make a dinner date. We arrange times, but either you're working late, or I am, and we keep having to cancel."

"Sounds good," I say. "Are you mad?" I don't know why I follow it up with the question. I guess I want to know if she would be mad if I canceled dinner because I had to work.

"Mad that you had to cancel? No way. You have your own business. I get how it works. It's a twenty-four-hour job. I like that you're so dedicated."

She fumbles for something in her purse. She must feel me staring, because she glances up. "What?"

"For real that's what you think, or is that part of—"

"For real," she says. "Drive and ambition are attractive, you know?"

I do know.

"What does Katherine think about you going to law school?"

She brings out a tube of lip gloss and expertly applies it in a couple of sweeps. "She doesn't know. I haven't told anyone but you." She smacks her lips together and drops the gloss back into her bag.

My heart inches higher in my chest, and I have the urge to scoop up her hand in mine or smooth my palm over her leg. I want to touch her.

"Here we are," she says as the car pulls in. "Remember, if in doubt, stick as closely as possible to the truth."

"Roger that," I say.

Katherine and Ed are at the table already, and both grin up at us as we arrive.

Katherine squeals as she hugs her sister. "You came together. It's so, so nice to be double dating."

My stomach roils a little. I hate lying to Ed. We've known each other a long time. But everything is changing. Work has taken second place for him since he's gotten serious with Katherine. And I'm feeling that.

"I just ordered the Bellinis," Katherine says. "Those ones we had in Martha's Vineyard were incredible. Didn't we have the best time?"

I sling my arm across the back of Lucy's chair. It was a great weekend.

"I can't believe the size of that striped bass," Ed says. "It was huge."

Lucy turns to me. "You caught a fish? You didn't tell me that." She doesn't say anything, but her expression says, *I thought you didn't like fishing.*

"It was almost forty pounds," Ed says before I can respond.

"Forty pounds?" Lucy says. "That's the weight of a car or something, isn't it?" She turns back to me. "You were okay?" She wants to ask me if I threw up.

I nod and Ed interrupts, "None of us caught anything close to the size Hunter did."

"How interesting," Lucy says.

"So tell us about you two. How's it going?"

"We're here to talk about you," Lucy says. "What are you down here for?"

"Oh, just a suit fitting for Ed. And there's a wedding store downtown that does really cool place settings. It's huge on Insta. I thought I could take a look if I came down too."

"And you don't have to work?" I ask Katherine. I know Ed has plenty to do. But Katherine has a job too.

"I've gone part-time since Christmas," she says, exhaling. "Makes life so much easier. I don't know how I would have coped with all the wedding planning if I'd still been full-time."

My jaw tenses a fraction, and I try not to let my rising stress show in my expression. I know I shouldn't find Katherine's statement irritating, but I do. Even if she's doing more wedding planning than Ed, the fact that she felt the need to go part-time to accommodate speaks to her priorities, and Ed's.

Lucy shifts in her chair and rests her hand on my leg. It's unexpected but comforting. Her warm touch soothes me. I don't know if it's knowing that she gets what I'm thinking, or if it's feeling like I have someone in my corner, but it feels good. My jaw relaxes.

"So is everything set now?" Lucy asks. "There can't be much more to do, can there?"

Katherine laughs. "Oh, I can't wait to say the same thing to you when you get married. It's never-ending. I think because we're having the full four days of dinners and lunches and stuff. It's a lot."

"Yeah, why are you doing that?" I ask.

"There's a contingent coming from Oregon we were going to have to entertain anyway. So then we thought if other people are traveling, we can't not invite them too. And then we figured we might as well just invite everyone to all the things!" Katherine is grinning from ear to ear. It sounds like this is exactly what she wants. But it's a lot.

"It's my idea of a perfect hell," Lucy mumbles, and I tamp down a smile.

"What would you do?" Katherine asks. "Elope? Mom would go insane."

"That's why I'm never getting married," Lucy says.

"Your mom wanted a big wedding?" I ask Katherine.

"Of course. She thinks it's her wedding." Katherine laughs, but I don't think that's funny. If all this ridiculous fuss was what they wanted, fine. But if it's all just to please Mrs. Jones? Not fine.

"As long as I don't have to marry your mother," Ed says.

"Who picked the venue?" I say before I have a chance to realize that it's none of my business and I don't need to get involved.

"Mom has really good taste," Lucy says.

"And there aren't that many places in Boston," Katherine says.

I think I have my answer. I don't understand why their mom gets such a big say in their lives.

"But we love it, don't we?" Katherine says, looking at Ed.

"Yeah, I'm totally fine with it."

Katherine slaps him playfully on the leg. "You're more than fine with it. You said you liked it."

"Yeah," Ed says, scratching his chin. "It's fine. Any of the ones we saw would have been fine. Personally, I would have preferred the hotel on the waterfront."

"But we wouldn't have been able to have as many guests as we wanted. It's still nice being on the Common."

"And as I said at the time, I would have been okay with a smaller guest list. The hotel we got is fine, really."

"Fine?" Katherine says, her voice escalating. "I don't want you to be just *fine* with it."

"He didn't mean fine, did you, Ed?" Lucy asks, looking a little panicked. "I saw the pictures. The ballroom you've got is absolutely gorgeous."

"It is," Ed says. "But I'm not going to go into a marriage pretending that my first choice was anything but the hotel on the waterfront. I'm not going to lie to you so you feel better about going with your mom's choice."

I've never witnessed anything but perfect coupledom from Ed and Katherine. This is all entirely new. Although I might not feel as uncomfortable as Lucy, it feels strange seeing Ed and Katherine fight. They're perfect for each other, as Lucy would say.

"I'm going to the restroom," Katherine says.

Lucy gives Ed a look that says *fix this*, but he ignores her and rearranges the napkin in his lap. "Ed," Lucy says, exasperated, before she goes after Katherine.

"I feel like this is my fault," I say. "I shouldn't have asked who picked the venue."

"It's fine," Ed says. "It's not like she doesn't know her mother is an issue."

I'd noticed the weird dynamic between Lucy and her mom, but I hadn't really thought that Katherine might have the same kind of relationship. "She seems to hold a lot of sway over both of them."

"I really hope what they say about women becoming their mothers isn't true."

I let out a half laugh. "I'm sure it's not true. I don't know the mother well, but Katherine is lovely. She's kind and she really loves you. It's just that her mother has a lot of influence."

"I finally got Katherine to agree to move out of Duxbury. She hasn't told her mom yet, but I'm hoping a little distance between her and her family will help. Especially when we have kids. If we stayed in Duxbury, I think I'd be relegated to third parent, honestly."

I wince. "Sorry, man."

"It's just a lot," he says. "And we're both stressed about the wedding. I'm trying to keep on top of work, but Katherine wants so much attention from me—wants me to go to this meeting and that tasting and another sit-down with the florist. If I don't make the time, her mom will step in, and I won't recognize anything about the wedding. I do want this to be *our* wedding, and not the wedding she organized with her mom."

He looks so stressed. Maybe my focus on my own stress at Portis means I haven't stopped to notice that my friend and partner is feeling the pressure too. I feel bad for the guy. There's obviously a lot going on that I haven't realized. Maybe he's been trying to do the best he can.

He throws his napkin on the table. "Excuse me. I have to go sort this out."

"Absolutely," I say.

As he heads to the restroom, Lucy is coming in the other direction. They have a brief word, then Lucy comes back to me.

"How is she?" I ask.

"Stressed. My mom has been dreaming of Katherine's wedding day since she was born. She's had the place settings picked out since her sixteenth birthday."

"I'm completely lost. Let's not talk about the wedding again tonight. Let's just enjoy dinner. This is my fault. I shouldn't have mentioned your mom."

She slides her hand over my leg. I glance down and back up, to Lucy's eyes. "Sorry," she says. She goes to move her hand away, and I cover it with mine to keep it in place.

"Don't be," I say.

Lucy sighs and is about to say something when we're interrupted by Katherine and Ed's return.

"I think we all need more cocktails," I say. "What do you say to a round of margaritas?"

"Sounds great," Ed says.

Katherine's normal smile is back, and I'm relieved. We order our food and more drinks, and everything has shifted back to normal. Thank God.

"So have you two seen much of each other?" Katherine asks.

We both laugh, and I'm not quite sure why. Because our lie feels like safer territory than Ed and Katherine's truth? Maybe.

"We've had lunch together a few times," Lucy says.

"We keep organizing dinner but having to cancel," I say. "One of us is always stuck in the office."

"You have to make time for each other," Katherine admonishes.

"It's difficult," Lucy says. "I've been really busy, and Hunter has . . . Well, you know what it's like, Ed. When it's your own business, it's always going to be a priority." I don't know if she means it pointedly toward Ed, but that's what I hear. She's telling him how committed I am to Portis.

"Would you ever go part-time?" Katherine asks Lucy.

Lucy frowns. "I couldn't afford to live if I went part-time."

"No, but say you and Hunter got serious—no pressure—or if you met someone else. Would you reduce your hours to take the pressure off?"

Lucy glances at me.

"You love your job," I say to her. "And things are going really well for you there, right?"

Lucy nods. "I do love it." She glances up at Katherine tentatively. "I've had some really good feedback recently."

"That's great," Katherine says. "But—"

"I'm not thinking about scaling back," Lucy says.

This would be a perfect time for Lucy to tell Katherine about what's been going on at work. But she doesn't take the opportunity.

"Just be open to the idea," Katherine says. "Our lives are so much less pressurized since Christmas. It takes away some of the stress."

I wonder whether Lucy and I pretending to be a couple is as much of a lie compared with what Katherine's telling us now. She's presenting a perfect picture, but ten minutes ago, they were having a disagreement. Both of them have confessed to feeling serious pressure, part-time work or not.

"I'm focusing on work," Lucy says, sliding her gaze toward me. She hasn't told her sister about her conversation with the partner at work. I wonder why she's not sharing it now. She should be proud of herself, but instead, she's hiding this from Katherine. It's not just our relationship that Lucy's not being honest about, and I have to wonder how deep the lies go.

CHAPTER TWENTY-ONE

HUNTER

I slide into the Uber and gasp like I'm breathing air for the first time in hours.

"That wasn't fun," Lucy says. "Dinner with Katherine is always fun, but that didn't qualify."

"Yeah, it was a weird vibe tonight. Ed was on edge. But honestly, it was good to hear that he's struggling to stay on top of work. Sometimes I wonder if he notices that he's not as committed."

"Please, God, when we have our fake wedding, let's not make it a four-day affair at the venue of my mother's choosing."

I chuckle. "We can elope."

"Honestly, the weekend on Martha's Vineyard was so perfect, I'd like to do something like that."

"I really think you should go part-time before I propose." I grin at her, and she swipes me playfully on the arm. "You haven't told Katherine about law school."

She straightens in her seat. "Nothing to tell," she says.

"You don't think she would approve?"

"I don't know." She seems to think about it for a minute. "I don't think my mom would like it."

"Does she have to?"

She sighs. "It would be easier if she did. Then I wouldn't have to hear about how I'm too focused on my career and men don't like women who are too independent."

"You think that's what she'd say?"

"Probably."

"Well, for the record, I think ambitious, driven, independent women are hot as all holy hell."

Lucy presses her lips together to stop her smile.

I can't resist: I reach over to cup her face and lean in to press a kiss to her full, soft lips. We're sliding around on the back seat of a car. I just want to get out of here and touch her. The more I get to know her, the more I want her. Properly. I love the way she tries to protect Katherine. She's such a loving sister, but my heart aches that she can't be honest with her. And maybe that keeps her from being honest with herself.

The cab hits a pothole, jolting us apart.

"What are we doing?" she asks. "Why do we keep kissing each other? We know it can't go anywhere."

I have to reach into the far corners of my brain to remember why. Oh, yes, because we don't want to make anything awkward when things between us inevitably end.

"I like kissing you," I confess, reaching across the seat and threading my fingers through hers.

"I like kissing you too. I also like Hershey's Kisses, but I have to resist those or I'll make myself sick."

"No ill health effects from kissing me."

She presses her lips together like she's trying to stop her smile and looks out the window, but she doesn't let go of my hand, and relief washes over me. I don't want her to let go. I'm not sure if I'll ever want her to let go. I like her touching me. I like kissing her. I want more. I want to know her more. Kiss her more. Listen to every last thought in her head. We're heading toward my apartment, which is sort of on the way to her apartment in Brooklyn. I insisted on booking the Uber on my account, so it's paid for. But she doesn't *have* to go across the bridge. She could come back to my place. We could kiss for hours. She could tell me more truths about herself. We could hold hands for the rest of the night.

"You know how we're lying to protect your sister? Or something? And we're not actually dating to protect your sister?"

"Yes," she says suspiciously, like she knows some kind of hare-brained idea is going to follow. She's not wrong.

"Well, I thought that, given we're such good liars—we have Ed and Katherine fooled, after all—if we were to . . . I don't know, actually *have* dinner, and things went wrong, we could lie about it easily. Pretend everything's fine. They wouldn't have to know we hate each other. We'd just be switching the lie."

She narrows her eyes like she's really trying to concentrate on what I'm saying. "You think we should date?"

I pause for a second or two, but only for dramatic effect. The words are right there on the tip of my tongue. "I think about you all the time," I confess. "Even when I haven't seen you in weeks. When I actually do see you, I have a really great time. I like you. I like hanging out with you. I'd like to do that some more."

Her slow smile is interrupted. "You have to promise me something."

She could make me promise just about anything in this moment.

"No lies between us," she continues. "You have to promise we tell each other the exact truth. All the time. No lies of omission, no keeping things from me because you think I'll hate you, or because you don't want to make joint celebrations difficult. If you tell the truth, I'll always respect you, and if I respect you, I can't hate you. I might not like you, but I can't hate you."

"Deal," I say. It's the easiest promise I've ever made.

She grins at me. "Okay, then."

"Okay, then."

"Wanna hang out some more tonight?" she asks.

"One hundred percent."

The Uber pulls up in front of my building with perfect timing, and we clamber out. "I'll have to go home before work. I don't have a change of clothes," she says, practical as ever.

"Let's make that tomorrow's problem," I say.

"Tomorrow's problem? Okay." She laughs. "I'm losing my head around you, Hunter Bain."

I take her hands in mine and back her up against the wall of my building. "Oh, yeah?" I press a kiss on her neck. She smells so good—of roses and, somehow, sea air.

Her hand grips my shoulders, and I burrow my head into her neck. "Yeah."

I pull back and scoop her up, carrying her into my building.

"Just like we're honeymooners," she says, tipping her head back. "Thank goodness I decided to go part-time." Her laughter lights up the space around us.

When we get into my apartment, I set her down, but she doesn't glance away from me. I expected her to want a full tour, to inspect every cupboard and drawer, but I have her full attention. It's like she's drip-feeding me pure testosterone.

"So," she says, gazing up at me. "Now that you have me here, what are your plans?"

I let out a deep rumble that comes from my chest. Oh, the plans I have for this woman.

I pull her closer, pressing my lips to hers. Our tongues meet, and it feels like we've crossed a line. Yes, we've kissed before. But in all the scenarios up to now, we've been around each other because our presence was required by someone else. Right here, right now, she's in my apartment because I want her here and she wants to be here.

Things have changed.

We both know it.

I pull her against me, trying to get closer. I deepen our kiss, needing more from her, my self-control ebbing away. I want to strip her naked and lick her from mouth to pussy, but I know already that I'm going to take my time. She deserves reverence. She deserves the best sex of her life. And something tells me I'm not going to have experienced anything like Lucy Jones before.

I grasp her ass, pressing her against me. I'm hard already, and I want her to know how much I want her. She slides her hand between us. When her palm hits my erection, I groan into her mouth.

I feel the throb of veins pulsing in my neck as I grind against her hand. I can't ever remember wanting a woman as much as I want Lucy. I've wanted her since back in Martha's Vineyard. If Ed wasn't so important to me, I would have never been able to hold back from staking my claim.

And now? Now I'm too far gone to even remember Ed's full name.

She fumbles with the buttons of my shirt. As soon as it's open, she slides her hands up my chest. Her soft heat is everywhere, warming me as she touches me.

She releases me and spins. "My zipper," she says, lifting her hands and fiddling with her hair. I pull down the metal tag just as her hair falls down her back, as if one is chasing the other.

"I love your hair," I say. "I love your back." I tease her dress open wider and trace my knuckle down her spine. She shivers, and I push the dress over her shoulders so it slips down and pools at her feet. She turns to face me, but it's not her eyes I'm looking at. I'm taking in the blue lace. The curves. The black patent heels. I'm taking in the absolute perfection of it all.

"You're gorgeous."

"I don't spend as much time in the gym as you." She nods toward me.

"You. Are. Perfect."

"I showed you mine." She lifts her chin. "Take it all off." She grins. She knows she's being sassy and that I like it. A little too much.

I do as she asks, shrugging off my shirt and taking off my pants and underwear together.

She glances at my cock, swollen and thick against my stomach.

"I hope that's not just for show," she says, tilting her head to the side.

"I'll let you be the judge of that," I say, clasping my fist around my length.

She steps toward me, but as she reaches for me, I wrap my hand around her wrist. "I think we'll start like this." I twirl her around, so her ass grazes my thighs.

My heart is thumping so hard I wonder whether she can feel it against her back. I'm weak. My legs are only just keeping me upright, and my knees could buckle at any time.

I lean back a little and drag my finger up her spine. I stop at the fastening to her bra and unclip. I swallow, pulling the lace down and off.

Thank God I'm not facing her at the moment. I don't think I could take any more. The sight of her breasts might be the end of me.

I smooth my hands around her waist and over her stomach. I inch higher and higher, and she leans into me, her soft back against my chest. I dip and press kiss after kiss to her neck. Her hands slip over mine and guide me up to her breasts. We both groan in unison. They're heavy and firm, and as my fingers find her nipples, I want to shout out loud about how good she feels. How she fits me. How this is better than I ever could have imagined, and we've only just started.

I lower one hand down, fingering the lace at the top of her panties. I'm taking my time because I don't want her to be disappointed. I want her to be soaked—desperate for this. I'm not sure when, exactly, I started wanting to have her in my arms like this, but however long it's been is too long. If the feeling isn't mutual—if I don't find her slippery and needy—I know it will hurt more than it should.

She bucks against my hand, impatient for my touch. I slide my fingers under the lace. My head spins as I reach silky wetness. I tip my head back and exhale.

"Fuck, you're so wet," I gasp out. "Like you've been waiting forever for me."

She pushes against my fingers like she wants more. So I give her what she wants. I push over her clit and through her folds.

"Hunter," she gasps. Her knees buckle, and I wrap my free arm around her waist, keeping her upright. I work my fingers through her folds, rubbing and circling, my fingers coated in her need for me. I've never felt so fucking powerful in my life. My cock presses against her back in response, hard and full and so ready for her.

"Oh, God." She says it like she's never felt anything like my fingers. Like it's new and magic and she's experiencing a whole new reality. "Oh, God, *Hunter.*"

"You feel so fucking blissful. Perfectly wet on my fingers. Perfectly soft. Perfectly ready."

Her breathing is ragged and her body hot and soft, pressed against me in all the right places. "I am," she says. "I want you."

I groan at her admission. Yeah, we've shared things I never thought we would. We've talked, we've kissed, but this—this feels like what we were both born for. Like it's our destiny or something.

"Please," she says. "I want you."

I can't take any more. I just can't hold back. I walk us forward a few steps and place her hands on the wall. "I'm half crazy, I need to be inside you so badly. I've thought about this for so long. Imagined how you'd feel, tight around me. How you'd sound when I pushed into you," I breathe in her ear.

I yank down her panties, grab a condom, rip open the packet, and roll it on in record time.

I need her *now.*

We've been working up to this moment since Martha's Vineyard. Since maybe even before that. And now it's finally time.

I nudge her legs apart and press my cock against her entrance. She whimpers like it's the most glorious thing she's ever felt but she's desperate for more. I have to clench my jaw to stop myself from cursing over and over.

I anchor my hand on her hip, the other on her shoulder, and slide into her.

Holding my breath, I push right up to the hilt, trying not to focus on her heat, the pressure, the way her hair falls down her back.

Her legs buckle, and I grab her hips. "No, baby. You need to be strong. Because I'm going to fuck you hard now. And you gotta stand."

"Hunter. Please." Her tone is sweet and pleading. I know I'll hear her begging me to fuck her in my dreams for the rest of my life.

I'm officially toast.

I pull out slowly, then slam into her, my fingers pressing into skin, trying to keep her in place.

She feels so perfect. So soft. So warm, so incredible on my cock. I glance down and get the perfect image of my cock surrounded by her and her wet pussy. I look away. It's too much. I drive into her over and over. It feels like we're in a bubble of bliss. Like we're under some kind of spell where everything is concentrated. Colors are brighter. Smells more vivid. Her sounds pitch perfect.

I gather her hair and wrap my hand around it, tugging her head back.

"You're so beautiful," I say, thrusting forward. "So fucking tight."

Her head tips like she doesn't have the strength to hold it up anymore.

"Hunter," she cries out. "Hunter."

Oh, God, my name on her lips adds an extra floor of pleasure I've never experienced before. Maybe it's because I know how hard it is to impress this woman. Maybe it's because I know she tried hard to hate me. Whatever it is, knowing she's about two minutes away from coming on my cock, from orgasming because of what I'm doing to her, feels like I've been given the keys to the kingdom. It's a high I've never experienced before.

"Hunter," she screams out. "I can't—"

She's helpless now. I own this woman under me. She can barely talk. Barely stand.

"I'm here," I say. "You can come. I'm here."

She calls out and convulses under me, and I can't help but think how she's giving herself to me in that moment. The thought pushes me over the edge of the cliff, and I thrust into her and release at last.

My arms wrapped around her waist, I pant, trying to catch my breath, trying to keep us both upright.

My God. She. Is. Everything.

I discard the condom, then scoop her up in my arms and carry her into my bedroom.

I set her on the bed. "Do you want water?" I press a kiss on her forehead, and she blushes and shakes her head.

"What we've just done, and it's a kiss on the forehead that makes you blush?"

She shrugs and reaches for me. I scoot in next to her, and we lie in each other's arms while we recover. She draws circles on my arm with her finger, and my cock begins to lengthen. This woman could gut fish on a fishing boat in bad weather, and it would turn me on. There's nothing about her that wouldn't make me want to fuck her.

She eyes my erection like she's a kid in a sweet shop. Then, with me lying next to her, she opens her legs.

I chuckle. "Again? So soon? You ready not to be able to walk tomorrow?"

"I'm ready not to be able to walk ever again if it means you're going to fuck me."

I groan and grab another condom.

I want to enjoy her body, suck and bite and play, but at the moment, I can't see straight. I just need to be inside her. I need to fuck her. It's like we're making up for lost time or something. I have to have her.

I kneel to roll on the condom, and she shifts on the bed. I glance up, and her fingers dip down to her pussy.

I groan at her touching herself. In another lifetime, I'd be happy just to sit here and watch her. But right now, I grab her wrist and feed her fingers into my mouth, suckling them, tasting her delicious wetness.

"I want exclusive rights to make you come tonight," I growl out.

A smile curves at the edge of her mouth. "Yes, sir."

"Fuck, Lucy," I curse, grabbing her thighs and pulling her toward me. "You trying to make me come before I'm even inside you?"

She presses her mouth into a thin line. "You think I could . . . sir?"

I push into her and shift so my body's over hers. "I think you could make me come just by looking at me."

"So I'm not a demonic witch anymore?" she asks.

I thrust into her again, and her fingernails dig into my shoulders. "May you always be a demonic witch, Lucy Jones. You don't see me complaining."

"If I'm a witch, you're the devil himself," she says on a laugh.

"But I'm your devil," I say.

Our gazes lock. We're teasing each other, but at the same time we're telling each other something profound. I accept her exactly as she is. I know her. And I'm hers.

In this moment, it's all true. I feel completely connected to her, completely open to her, and completely dedicated to her.

"Hunter," she says, her tone reverent this time.

I press my lips to hers, and our tongues slip together like we're sealing some kind of promise. Like this became less about urgent fucking, physical need, and desperate release and more about a union. A joining of minds, bodies, and souls.

Pleasure rachets up like a car climbing the summit of a roller coaster. Our kisses turn sloppy and wayward. There's too much to focus on, too much to feel.

She opens her legs wider, and I push deeper, wanting to be closer. Wanting to be a part of her. Her fingers trail down my back, and her breathing comes heavier, her body jerking underneath me.

"Hunter, I'm close."

"Me too," I whisper. "Let me watch you."

Her gaze glazes over, and I press into her, pushing her orgasm to the surface. She's the most beautiful woman I've ever seen in my life.

She opens her eyes as she floats back down, and the connection breaks the last tether of my climax. I push into her, keeping my gaze on her the entire time.

Fuck.

Fuck.

Fuck.

What was that?

She hooks her leg up over my hip and trails her fingers up and down my arm. All I can do is think how I never want this to end. How I want to stay in my bed with her forever.

"You okay?" she asks me.

I mumble an affirmative response, and she lets out a small giggle I haven't heard from her before. I realize I want to hear every type of laugh she has. See every smile, every tear. I want it all.

"For the record, I can confirm that it's not all for show."

I grin at her reference to my cock. "Good to know," I say.

Her fingers wander. Over my shoulder, my collarbone, down my chest.

It's all too good. She feels so good. Everything about her is exceptional.

I reach for her breasts. I've been so caught up with desire for her, I've overlooked each individual part of her. I have no idea how that's possible when she's got the most perfect breasts I've ever seen. They're pressed together as she lies on her side, her nipples jutting out, sharp and pointed, red and luscious.

I smooth my hands over her soft flesh, my thumb circling her nipple as she runs her hands over my neck, my jaw, my arm.

She moans as I play with her nipples. I can feel my cock harden again. I'm not sure how that's possible so soon.

She notices and drags her hand over my balls and up my shaft. Things shift in an instant. Instead of a slow, languishing exploration, everything becomes more urgent. I take a breast in each hand and knead them together and tease and flick her nipples. Her leg is still over my hip, and she bucks, pulling our bodies closer.

"More, baby?"

"Always more," she says.

She doesn't have to ask twice. I reach back for another condom, and she takes it from me.

"It's tight," she says as she rolls it on. "You're almost too big."

She knows exactly what to say to make me hard as fucking steel.

She grips my cock at the shaft and glances up at me. She sighs and shifts. We both move so I'm on my back and she's astride me. She keeps hold of my cock and moves the crown through her folds. I wish I could be bare to feel that. To feel her. I want to be closer. To get more of her, if that's even possible.

She positions the head of my cock at her entrance and pauses, glancing at me before sinking down.

Her eyes flutter shut, like sitting on my cock is the most blissful thing that's ever happened to her. I really hope it is. I want to give her every blissful moment in her goddamn life. I want to be by her side when anything good happens to her so I can see the happiness in her eyes.

Her back arches and her breasts thrust forward and I catch them. Their weight in my hands is perfect. I smooth my hands down to her waist, and she begins to move, flicking her hips forward and back, driving me deeper and deeper into her.

Seeing her on top of me like this, her hair splayed out over her shoulders, her breasts, her stomach, her legs clamped either side of me . . . It doesn't get any better. For a fleeting second, I wonder why we didn't do this earlier. Why didn't we sleep together while we were in Martha's Vineyard? Then I realize it wouldn't have been possible. If we'd done this all night, we would have never wanted to stop. We'd have wanted to stay naked, exploring each other the entire weekend. Being with Lucy is addictive, even without the sex. The more time I spend with her, the more I want from her. I wonder whether that feeling will ever stop.

"Oh, Hunter," Lucy breathes. Her tone is so vulnerable and open. I'm completely aware that not many people see this side of Lucy. She doesn't have time to be vulnerable when she's too busy trying to make everyone happy. She's so concerned with everyone else's happiness that she too often forgets who she is and what she wants.

I reach around to her ass and pull her onto me. Deep. Hard.

She gasps and falls forward, her palms on my chest. As she lifts her hips, I pull her back toward me, driving her back onto my cock. Her tightness is completely hypnotizing. It creates a buzz that zigzags across my body, making me want her more.

"Oh, God," she calls. She's not far from coming again. My chest expands, and I thrust up to meet her tight pussy. Yeah, I'm going to make her come again.

I sit up, wanting to be closer to her. Her knees are either side of my torso, squeezing me, tightening everything. Her breasts press against my chest as she moves, sinking onto my cock over and over.

I wrap my arms around her and press kisses against her collarbone. She's so soft. So good. So tight. So perfect. Everything about her is completely perfect.

Her arms wrap around my neck. We're so close, her movements are smaller, but everything's more intense.

"I love . . . I love fucking you," she whispers into my ear.

"I love fucking you too," I reply. But it's not what I mean. It's not all I mean, at least. There's something more. I just can't quite find the words.

We press our foreheads together and our breaths mix as our orgasms explode between us, and it's like we're sharing the same climax. Her breathy moans prolong mine, make me want to tease it out and make it last for hours.

She clings to me as her breathing comes back to normal. I slump back onto the bed, taking her with me. I keep my arms wrapped around her tightly, wanting us as close as possible for as long as possible. I never want tonight to end. I don't want to have to go to sleep and miss any of her.

I want to savor it. Keep her safe. Keep her mine.

CHAPTER TWENTY-TWO

Lucy

I feel like I've been in one of those IRONMAN competitions I hear the guys at work talking about, only I didn't prepare. Hell, even if I had trained for an IRONMAN, I don't think I would have fared better. The things Hunter did to my body last night . . . He should be arrested. Or maybe I could put him under house arrest.

I left him this morning, reluctantly, but there was no way I was going into work in yesterday's clothes. My heading back to Brooklyn at five in the morning also let us avoid an awkward breakfast or any kind of talk about how we'd better quit while we're ahead, because things could get messy with Ed and Katherine or he's not ready to be exclusive.

Because I will not share him.

I'd rather never see him again. And the latter option is horrifying to me right now.

I don't normally take my phone from my purse until lunchtime, but I've kept it with me all morning on vibrate. Not that I'm expecting him to message. But just in case he was to reach out.

Who am I?

Who have I turned into?

I've been dickmatized.

I attach a marked-up version of an NDA I've been reviewing this morning to an email and press "Send." I literally jump back in my seat when I see Hunter's name in my inbox.

"You okay?" the paralegal opposite me asks.

"Yeah, fine. I just . . . yeah, I'm fine." I give her my best fake grin. Which is still terrible.

What the hell is Hunter doing emailing me at work?

I open the email.

"12:30. Stranger than Fiction."

That's all it says. I'm half irritated that he'd just summon me somewhere, totally assuming I don't have plans or I'm not too busy at work to be able to make it. But the other half of me is delighted.

I check the clock. It's just gone twelve. He hasn't given me any notice at all. Arrogant prick. I delete the email and pull out my phone to text him I might be late.

I reply to a couple of emails, then shoot into the restrooms to check I don't look as tired as I feel. I need at least another pound of concealer under my eyes, I'm sure.

Butterflies dance in my stomach while I take the elevator down to the lobby. I slide on my sunglasses as I take the revolving door out into the sunshine. Outside, I'm faced with a smirking Hunter, his arms folded, waiting for me opposite the door. He looks impossibly handsome in the midday sun, his skin more golden than usual, his smile wider. Did I do that to him? Or maybe I just see him differently now.

"Hey," he says, lifting his chin.

"Hey," I reply, trying to hold back a smile.

He takes a step toward me, slips his hands around my waist, and kisses me on the lips.

"Hi," I say as he pulls back. The man *laughs*, giving sound to the same joy I feel in my own heart.

"Let's go eat. I think we burned off enough calories to order one of everything each."

My cheeks heat at his reference—in public!—to our marathon sex session last night. I don't know why. We're in New York City. No one cares what I did last night, and I'm sure no one can hear us over the beep of horns, the shout of street vendors, and everyone's earbuds.

He scoops up my hand, and I glance across at him as if to say, *Are you actually holding my hand?* He grins back, silently affirming, *Hell yeah, I am. What you gonna do about it?*

I laugh and so does he, and we head to Stranger than Fiction.

Once we're in line, I say, "Probably best to text me at work or message on my personal email."

"What? And have you accuse me of playing *Candy Crush Saga* all day? No way. Lucy Jones, you don't look at your phone during working hours. If I want to have lunch with you, how would I ever do that?"

I shake my head but can't wipe the grin off my face.

"What are you ordering?" I ask.

"One of everything," he answers. "I told you."

"You are not. There's no way."

"Are you *daring* me?" he asks.

"Absolutely not. If I was going to dare you to do something, it wouldn't be to overorder at a deli. It would be something far more . . . exciting."

He raises his eyebrows like only the filthiest thoughts are running through his brain.

"And it wouldn't involve any nakedness," I add, narrowing my eyes.

He brings our hands to his mouth and presses a kiss on my knuckles. It's such a small gesture, but it feels significant. Like all the push and pull between us from before has been forgotten and we're two entirely different people with each other now.

My phone buzzes in my pocket, and I pull it out with my free hand.

"It's just from Katherine," I say. "She's finished at the wedding place, and they're heading back to Boston."

Hunter sighs. "Do you think that's the end of the endless meetings and wedding decisions? It's so time consuming."

"I doubt it's the end of it," I reply. "But the wedding is only weeks away. Then it will be over."

"Then it's the honeymoon. Then the move. Then she'll get pregnant."

"That's life."

"Right," Hunter says. His mood has shifted. He's developed edges that weren't there a few minutes ago.

We get to front of the line. Hunter insists on ordering my sandwich and paying, and we grab a table in the little plaza in front of the store.

He very sweetly unpacks my To Grill a Mockingbird chicken club and opens my can of seltzer.

"You're cute," I say. "Thank you."

"You're cute," he replies. "Thank you." He leans forward and places a kiss on my lips, casually, like he does that all the time. I have to bite back a grin.

"Can we take a picture and send it to Katherine?" I ask. "She gave me a hard time while you were getting drinks last night. Says I need to make more time for you, make more of an effort."

Hunter chuckles. "Sure." I hold up my phone and shift a little closer to him. I lean into him and say, "Smile!"

He does, but at the last second, turns and presses a kiss to my cheek.

I laugh and bring up the picture. It looks so cute. I'm beaming and Hunter looks moody and brooding and . . . kinda into me.

I send it to Katherine with a note saying we're having lunch, then I turn my phone to silent. I know she's going to blow it up, and I don't want to get into it with her. I just want to enjoy this moment.

"It's so weird that we work in buildings next door to each other," he says.

"So weird," I agree.

"Did you always want to move to New York?" he asks.

I think back. "I'm not sure. I just knew I had to get out of Boston. I wanted to go somewhere that people didn't know me."

He narrows his eyes slightly. "You wanted to reinvent yourself?"

"I guess. I love my sister, and she's my best friend and she's amazing. But I just wanted to go somewhere where I could be me rather than Katherine's fuckup of a sister."

He pulls back. "What? How are you a fuckup?"

"You should have seen me in high school." I grin at him, but he doesn't smile back.

"How were you a fuckup? Did you have a drug problem? Did you get into trouble with the police? Did you skip school a lot?"

"No! I never skipped school, and I've never done drugs in my life."

"Oh, so you spent time in the clink?" He knows full well I haven't been to prison.

I burst out laughing. "Of course not."

"Then how were you such a fuckup, Lucy Jones?"

I groan. "You know. Next to Katherine, most people are fuckups. I was a little disorganized. My grades weren't as good as hers. I wasn't as popular. Didn't have any boyfriends in high school."

"That was high school. This is New York. You just got told by a partner that you have a lot of potential and they want you to consider law school. You don't sound like much of a fuckup to me."

I've done some research on the possibility of law school. It all seems so intimidating. The LSAT, then years and years of study if I even get in somewhere. Then the New York bar, which is meant to be close to impossible. I shrug. "It's probably just something they say to fulfill a quota or something. They don't expect me to actually go through with it."

He takes my chin and turns my head so I'm facing him. "You know that's bullshit, right? People don't waste their time blowing smoke. Sounds to me like you might be afraid of law school."

He releases me, and I prod at my sandwich. "Yeah, well, maybe I am a little. Super smart people go to law school."

"Right," he says.

"So that's a lot of pressure, trying to keep up with people like that."

"Maybe *you're* people like that. Ever think about that?"

The fact is, I've never thought of myself as someone who would go to law school. Not since college. I pushed those ideas to the back of my mind and got on with life as a paralegal.

"And anyway," Hunter continues, "you have to apply. It's not like they let anyone in. Take the LSAT so you'll know. If you're not going to keep up, you won't get a place."

"Yeah, so I probably won't get in."

"You won't know until you try."

He seems invested in this, and I'm not sure why.

I sigh. "But I don't want to go through telling my parents and everything and then not get in."

"So don't tell them."

I laugh. "You think I should just make the decision to go to law school and not tell my parents? They probably have to cosign my application."

"I doubt it. You're an adult. And yeah, you can make the decision without telling anyone." He picks up his sandwich. "Why don't you just do it in stages? Start with the LSAT. Study for that, take the test, see whether your score is high enough. Then you can go from there."

I take a bite out of my sandwich as I let his suggestion settle in my brain. He's making it sound so easy. As if someone like me can end up going to law school and that's just how it should be.

He stares at me for a beat, then takes a bite out of his sandwich. He looks so sure of himself. So confident. Even though I know he has worries and concerns, I don't see any of them right now in his expression while he's talking about me.

"I guess I could get a study guide. You know, for the LSAT. I could order one and take a look."

"Right," he says. "In fact, there's a store a couple of blocks over on 46th and 5th. We could take a walk when we're finished here."

I take another bite of my sandwich to buy some time. Do I really want to do this? I haven't talked about this with Katherine or Mom, or even really thought it through properly for myself. But I'm just buying a book, right? It's not like I'm filling in an application form for Fordham.

Hunter is looking at me like he's waiting for an answer. Like he thinks it's perfectly normal for us to go to a bookstore together and buy an LSAT study book. Looking into his blue eyes, I start to think it might be perfectly normal too.

"I've not had time to think about this properly," I say on a sigh. "'But why not seize the pleasure at once?—How often is happiness destroyed by preparation, foolish preparation!' That's what my mom would say. Well, *she* wouldn't. Jane Austen in *Emma* would."

Hunter shakes his head, incredulous. "I've never read any."

"Really?"

"Nope. But she's not wrong. Sometimes you have to jump in without thinking too hard." He wraps up our trash and places it back in the bag our sandwiches came in. "Let's go get you a book."

He dumps our trash in the can, and we head east. "I'm going to be working late tonight. But do you want to get drinks later in the week? Or maybe this weekend?"

"So we can send evidence to Katherine?" I ask, enthusiastic. She'd really like to see us spending more time together.

Hunter rolls his eyes. "No, so we can hang out some more. Talk."

A smile threatens at the corners of my mouth. "Are you asking me out on a date?"

"I guess," he says, scanning the traffic heading north and watching for the crossing to change.

"A real date?" I ask. "Not a fake date."

"No, Lucy. A real date."

"We can do that," I say.

"Good," he replies.

"Good," I tease.

The traffic stops, and he scoops up my hand as we cross the street, on our way to go buy me an LSAT book. I'm not quite sure how Hunter and I got to this point. He's far from the man I first met, drunk at my parents' house. He's kind and supportive and encouraging me to lean into a version of myself that *has potential.* I'm not sure if I've ever been so happy to be out in the New York sunshine. Holding hands with Hunter.

CHAPTER TWENTY-THREE

Hunter

On Saturday night, I offer to go and get Lucy from Brooklyn, but she insists on meeting me at a bar in SoHo. I would have been happy to stay in, order pizza, and watch Netflix, but I don't want her to think I'm only interested in sex. Not that I'm *not* interested in sex—I most definitely am. Specifically, sex with Lucy. But I like hanging out with her too. She's fun. And sweet and thoughtful. She makes me laugh. She makes me think.

I step into the bar and pull my phone from my back pocket. Everyone's dressed as if they're from the 1800s. Did I miss something? I scan the room and lock eyes with Lucy. My heart soars in my chest. She looks astonishing. Even in jeans and a T-shirt, she looks like a goddamn angel. Her hair is loose and wavy and hangs down over her shoulders. Her cheeks are pink and her sea-green eyes are quite simply dazzling.

I stalk over to where she's sitting on a barstool, and her smile widens the nearer I get. When I reach her, I do the only thing I can: I cup her face and press a kiss to her lips. God, I wish it were just the two of us here and the rest of the people in this bar would just disappear.

I only want to be with her. Here, in public, it feels like I have to share her a little.

"Hey," she says on a little sigh as I pull back.

"You look gorgeous."

"Hunter," she says like I'm crazy, "I was studying. I lost track of time. I've been wearing this all day. I let my hair down and that's it."

"I don't think you've ever looked so beautiful."

She smiles, but it's not a confident smile. She smiles like she can't quite believe what I'm saying is true, and the thought tugs at my chest. I really don't understand why she's so down on herself. I know she looks up to Katherine, but she and Katherine are just different. Katherine's a teacher who lives in suburban Boston. Lucy is a paralegal in New York City. They lead opposite lives that are impossible to compare, but Lucy still thinks she's not matching up to Katherine.

"This place is wild," she says, changing the subject.

"Yeah. I've been to speakeasy places where the waitstaff wear costumes, but not a . . . what? Victorian place?" I glance up. "Why is there a wolf on the ceiling?" I slide onto the stool next to her.

"I was wondering the same thing," she says matter-of-factly. "I've come to the conclusion that it must be a hound."

I narrow my eyes, wondering if I've lost time somewhere, which might explain my confusion. "A hound?"

"As in Baskerville. The place is called Baker Street, right? It's a Sherlock Holmes–themed bar. At least, I think it is. The cocktails seem themed after Sherlock Holmes books. Or something. My dad had the books and used to read them on a Sunday after lunch." She grabs a menu from where it's standing upright on the bar. "*Five Orange Pips.* That was a story, right?"

"I defer to you on all things Holmesian."

She puts the menu down and grins at me. "Is it weird that I know this stuff?"

I shake my head. "I like you telling me things. It's . . . sexy."

Her eyes widen. "Really?"

I shrug. "Yeah. You're a badass. You don't take shit from anyone. You protect the people you love. You know things about Victorian literature. It's all *very* sexy."

She leans forward on her barstool. Her T-shirt tightens, showing the outline of her breasts. It's just a simple white T-shirt, but from where I'm sitting, her outfit is bordering on obscene. "I think you're sexy too."

My body starts to vibrate. I skirt my hand over her waist and down her thigh. I just want to be closer to her. No matter how close I get, I want to be closer still.

She links her fingers through mine, and we order a cocktail each. "I'm definitely getting the Sussex Vampire," she says.

"Sounds bloody. I'll take His Last Bow."

"You want to take a picture to send to Katherine?" I ask when our cocktails arrive.

Our eyes snag, and after a beat she shakes her head. "I don't think so. Let's just . . . not."

I take a sip of my drink to stop myself from smiling. We're way past pretending, and we both know it.

"Are you going to grow fangs?" I ask as she sips her red drink that's come in a martini glass topped with white foam.

"Oh, wouldn't that be something?" She waggles her eyebrows mischievously. "Would you want me to bite you?"

I trail my gaze down her body. I want to bite her all over. "Not my thing," I say. "But I think you know that. You know *all* my things."

"Do I?" she asks. "I'm sure there's loads about you I don't know."

I pull in a breath. "It doesn't feel like that." In fact, it feels like the complete opposite. It's like she knows everything without me having to tell her. It feels like I've known Lucy much longer than I have—that we're in a decade-old relationship or something. Maybe it's because we started off hating each other and didn't waste time trying to show carefully curated versions of ourselves to each other. Maybe it's because the people closest to us love each other. Maybe it's because it feels like she sees me. Really sees me.

"You don't talk a lot about your parents. Are you close?"

I shrug. "We were," I say.

"And your dad liked to fish?"

"Yeah. Still goes out."

"But you don't like it? Did you used to like it when you were a kid? You seemed to be pretty good at it, at least according to Ed and the guys."

I chuckle, but it has a cynical tinge. "Lots of things change as you get older. How you see the world can completely turn upside down."

"Can it?" she asks.

"Yeah, like most boys, I idolized my dad. He loved to fish, so I loved to fish. He used to like to grow vegetables, so I tried to grow the biggest carrots and the most potatoes." My best memories of growing up all revolve around spending time with my dad. "He was my hero. I wanted to be just like him."

"So when did he stop being your hero?" she asks.

I don't ever talk about Bain Insurance. I told Ed before we went into business together, but that's it. But something about Lucy makes me want to tell her. I want her to know everything about me. I don't want to hold anything back. "Did I tell you I took over his business?"

She shakes her head but doesn't say anything.

"I went to college to study finance so I could take over his life insurance business. Like I said, I wanted to be just like him. When I left college, I worked in the business for four years before he retired and left me in charge."

"Wow," she says. "You were young when you took over. Was it a big business?"

I nod. "Yeah. It was a lot of responsibility. But I was ready for it. I'd studied for a long time. I made sure that I'd worked in every aspect of the business before I took it over. I thought I was prepared."

I glance up at her. Her expression of concern hits me in the chest.

"And I would have been." I take a breath. "But the business was in debt. It wasn't making any money—our costs were too high. Rent, payroll. Everything, really. We were weeks away from bankruptcy when I finally understood the mess my dad had handed me."

"Hunter," she says and squeezes my hand.

"I tried my best to save it. I really did." I look into her eyes, trying to gauge whether she believes me. I worked so hard—negotiating with the landlord, trying to cut costs, letting people go. It was a brutal time. "Maybe I should have spent more time growing the business. If I'd been better at business development, maybe things would have gone another way. Some people only want to deal with people with more gray hairs. If my dad had still been in charge, then . . ."

"Hunter," Lucy says again, firmer this time, "I know you. I know you worked harder than anyone to save that business. You wanted it to work."

"I really did." I pull in a breath.

"If you start off with high costs and a mountain of debt, you're fighting a losing battle. What did your dad say?"

I pick up my drink. I only meant to take a sip, but I down the rest of it, trying to push away the feeling of failure that swirls in my gut every time I think back to that time.

"My dad didn't say anything."

"What do you mean? He didn't warn you about the debt?"

"No, I mean he didn't say *anything*. Nothing about the financial position of the business at all. As far as I was concerned, when I took over, it was a family business we'd all done well from. I planned to go in and grow it. Offer different products. Focus on high-net-worth individuals. But I couldn't do *anything*. I was fixing leaks as soon as I got there. Just trying to stop the business from sinking was a full-time job."

"And after it sank, what did he say?"

I knew the question was coming, but it doesn't stop it hurting when she asks it. Because admitting that my father didn't take responsibility feels like . . . It feels like I lost a father that day. He stopped being the man who'd stand in front of a bus for me. Stopped being the man I could go to for help and advice. Stopped being a man I could trust. "He told me I shouldn't feel bad and that I should learn from my mistakes."

"Oh, Hunter." She doesn't say more, and I don't need her to. She doesn't make excuses for him or say that it must have been a misunderstanding—rationalizations I've tried to make over the years.

"He abandoned you when you needed him most," she says simply. She slides off her stool and presses her palm on my cheek. It's so comforting. So warm. So completely what I need. Yes, I was an adult when I took over Bain Insurance, but I needed my dad to step up in that moment. Even if he hadn't told me the state of things in advance . . . Maybe he was embarrassed or thought I could fix things. But when everything eventually collapsed, I needed him to tell me it wasn't me who had failed. I needed him to let go of his ego, his pride—whatever it was that stopped him being a father in that moment—and to step up as my dad. To take responsibility.

"I think you're the bravest man I know," she says.

"Don't say that. It's not true."

"It is true. Your dad blamed his lack of business acumen on you and cut you loose. And you took it, shouldered it all. Then you started again. That takes courage."

Her words are like lines on a ship, fixing me to her shore. Keeping me close. Safe.

"No, that was Ed. If it hadn't been for him, I never would have started Portis. I would be working in a bank somewhere."

She looks at me as if she can't quite believe what I just said. "You picked *yourself* up and went and got yourself a job. I would have been in a ditch with a bottle of wine. Ed didn't do you a favor by asking you to go into business with him. Ed is a great guy, but he's no dummy. There's no way he'd have suggested going into business with some worthless dropout who sinks businesses. He knew you were smart, self-motivated, and trustworthy."

"I know, but he took a chance on me," I say.

"Of course he did. But he didn't do it out of pity or charity. He did it because he knew you'd be a good fit for each other. And you know what? You deserve credit for saying yes. Because if what happened to you had happened to me, I don't think I would have trusted anyone enough to make me a Big Mac and fries, let alone run a business with me. Kudos for taking a chance."

Her words echo inside me, filling up all my empty spaces. She sees things through fresh eyes. I've always thought of Ed as someone who saved me. But Lucy is right. I've learned a lot about Ed since going into business with him. He's not a guy who makes business decisions from a place of emotion. I think he did believe in me. Maybe he knew I'd shoulder the burden when he decided to take a step back.

"I like the way you see the world," I say.

"Oh, I don't know. I was ready to write you off the first time I ever saw you. I can jump to conclusions."

Despite all the emotion running through my body, I manage to laugh. "You were protecting your sister's happiness. You're very good at doing that."

She smiles. "Thank you." She slides her hands up my thighs, and the air between us goes electric. "You know what else I'm good at?"

If we weren't in a bar full of people, I'd spin her around, yank down her jeans, and be balls deep into her before she had a chance to tell me.

"Let's get out of here," I say, pulling out my wallet.

"Great idea."

CHAPTER TWENTY-FOUR

Lucy

Every minute I spend with Hunter, I like him more. He's not the man I thought he was when we were first introduced. He's not even the man I thought he was before our date tonight. He's sweet and sensitive and underestimates himself. And I want him all to myself.

"We didn't eat," I say as we tumble into his apartment.

"You're right," he says. "I'm going to have to feast on you."

He has such a dirty mouth, but it's never too much. He always knows exactly what to say when.

He catches my wrist as I walk by him, and he pulls me back to him. "Take off your jeans," he hisses. "Right now. I want to see you in nothing but that white T-shirt that's been driving me wild all night."

I glance down at my plain white tee. "This?" I pull at it. His eyes flare, like I'm in crotchless panties and pasties. I shift from foot to foot under his gaze and get an idea. If he likes the T-shirt, he's going to like it a lot more if I deaccessorize.

"I'll meet you in the bedroom," I say, cocking my head in a way that says, *Please, I'll make it worth your while.*

He holds my gaze, starts to undo the buttons of his shirt, then backs toward the bedroom.

Working quickly, I pull down my jeans, slip off my panties, then unsnap my bra and pull it off while keeping my T-shirt on. The T-shirt is fairly long, and if I were wearing panties, it wouldn't show them.

I scamper across the living space and into the bedroom. Hunter's on the bed, naked. Just how I wanted him.

"Hey," I say, leaning against the doorframe, the T-shirt riding up. I'm not sure if he can see I'm not wearing panties, but he's craning his neck trying to figure it out.

He's left his clothes strewn on the floor, clearly eager to be naked as soon as possible. I spin around so I have my back to him and, keeping my legs straight, I bend to pick up his shirt. "Honey, you dropped something." The cool air against my pussy tells me he can definitely see everything now.

"Fuck, Lucy," Hunter spits. "That T-shirt should be illegal."

I straighten and turn back to face him. "This?" I say, circling my hard nipple. He groans and fists his cock. "I don't wear it very often because you can see right through it."

"Fuuuck!" He grabs me by the waist and pulls me onto the bed. He starts to climb over me, but I sit.

I wag my finger at him. When he pauses, I gather the edges of the front of my shirt and tie them in a knot. All the extra fabric has disappeared so that it fits snugly over my breasts. Instantly he's on top of me, pressing me down, taking my nipple in his mouth through the cotton. The fabric is a barrier between me and Hunter's tongue. If anything, it should reduce the sensations, but instead, they're intensified. He grazes his teeth over the hard nubs, and I arch my back. It's almost overwhelming, feeling him want me like this. He works his mouth, his tongue, his teeth, and I can do nothing but thread my hands through his silky hair. I'm so wet, I must be dripping onto the sheets. I've never felt so sexy, so wanton, so seductive. My orgasm stirs at the core of me, but I don't want to come like this. I want to stay right here for a little longer.

I shift and Hunter moves away. Gently, I push him onto his back and straddle him. He reaches behind him for a condom, and I take the packet from him, but I don't open it right away. I tuck it under the sheet. For now, I'm enjoying the teasing . . . the moments before *the* moment.

I slide my soaked pussy down his cock, not taking my eyes from him. But he's not looking at me. He's looking at two wet patches of T-shirt sticking to my erect nipples.

"Fuck, Lucy. I'm never going to forget this visual for as long as I live."

I flick my hips back and forward, teasing the length of his cock. I could come like this. My entire body is vibrating. Every sense is heightened, every need is merciless, every desire is urgent.

"You're so totally wet."

"You feel that?" I tip my head back. "I don't think I've ever been so wet. Even more than last time with you."

He groans underneath me. I've never been chatty in bed. But he makes me feel so desired that it unleashes something in me. He makes me feel like I could say anything in my head and he'd only want me more.

"I do that to you," he growls.

I nod. "Yeah. You." I lift my chin. No one else. No one ever.

"Fuuuck," he growls, and he grabs the condom packet and rips it open.

My entire body is shaking. I don't think I could get a condom on him if I tried. I watch as he rolls it on and then grasps his cock at the base. We lock eyes and an understanding passes between us: This is sex. It's really good sex. But it's something more too. I've never felt so comfortable, so connected, so completely as one with another person.

I lean forward, and he presses his tip into me and grabs a breast in the other hand. I close my eyes in a lazy blink. He feels so good. So big. So perfect inside me. I never want this to end. I want Hunter to fuck me forever.

His hands slide to my hips, and like he knows I'm caught in some kind of lust-filled haze, he starts to move from under me, thrusting upward. My palms press into his chest, and he pushes up, up, up, so deep inside me, stretching me, filling me, owning me.

I'm floating, my limbs weak, my body vibrating. All I can see, think, and feel is him. Hunter. He presses my hips down to meet his, and I groan at how deep he gets. How full I am. How completely at peace I am with him.

"Hunter," I gasp out. His fingers press just shy of painfully into my hips.

"You're so sexy," he pants, thrusting again. "I want to fuck you all night. All day. Forever."

I twist my hips, trying to give him just a little of what he's giving me. His groan gives me some satisfaction.

His hands slide to my arms, and he holds them tightly against my body so I can't move them, using them as an anchor so he can drive into me relentlessly. Over and over, deeper and deeper.

"Hunter," I cry. It's too much. It's too good. It feels like we were made for each other. I crumble as my orgasm tears through me. He thrusts up, and all I can do is take it as I climax, my body shuddering on his cock. He lets out a roar and thrusts up one final time, both of us reaching the peak at the same time.

I slump forward on his chest. I don't know which racing heartbeat belongs to him and which is mine.

His breath is ragged against my ear, and he wraps his arms around me tightly.

I've never come like that before. Never felt like that before. Never been worshipped the way Hunter worships me.

"You okay?" he asks as our bodies settle.

"I don't know," I say, honestly. "I don't know how I'll . . ." I feel like life has shifted a little. The physical connection I have with Hunter is new and surprising, and I'm already worried that at some point, I won't have it.

I feel vulnerable.

"It feels deep, right?" he asks.

I lift my head to see the expression in his eyes. His bright-blue gaze stares back at me, full of concerns. I nod. "Yeah. It feels . . ."

He exhales slowly. "Let's just . . ."

"Let's just what?" I ask. I shift off him so I'm lying beside him, and he pulls me back so I'm welded to his side.

"I don't know, Lucy. This is new territory for me."

"We said we wouldn't get involved because we'd end up hating each other and have to be cordial during holidays, and—"

"I know," he says. "But I don't think I could ever hate you."

"You gave it a really decent shot there when we first met."

He chuckles and presses a kiss on my head. "I didn't know you. I didn't know how fucking good you looked in a white T-shirt and nothing else." He fiddles with the knot in my T-shirt and works it free, then pulls it over my head.

Is this just sex for him? Because it isn't for me. I don't want to admit that because I don't want to create tension, but he sees parts of me no one else has ever seen.

Proving it, he sweeps the hair off my face and dips to press a kiss on my lips. "And as well as being the sexiest girl that ever lived, you're also smart and funny and driven and so fucking kind it drives me bananas."

I press my mouth into a line so he can't see me smile.

"And when you try not to smile . . ." He sweeps his hand down my legs until his fingers find my folds. "It makes me want to do this." He slips two fingers inside me, his thumb rubbing my clit, while he watches my expression.

"Hunter," I whisper.

"I want to watch you come," he says, and his dick twitches. I move my hand to reach for him, but he shifts, shaking his head. "Let me do this. I want to learn all the ways I can touch you that make you feel good."

I moan at his words and fingers and thumb.

"That feel good? I like exploring your body, your mind. Maybe even your soul from time to time." His fingers start to thrust, and I fist the sheets. I don't know whether it's because he's looking at my body laid out for him like he's inspecting his latest purchase, or whether it's just his fingers or his words, but I'm so turned on I can feel my climax already starting to build again.

"I don't want it to feel too good, though," he says. "Not yet."

He removes his hand, and I whimper at the lost contact. Then he takes the two fingers that have been inside me and slides them between his lips. "Delicious," he says. "I want more of that."

He positions himself between my thighs, and I bring my legs up. He presses my knees wide, exposing me to his stare.

"God, what a beautiful pussy," he says. "I can see how wet you are. How ready you are for more of me."

I whimper as his tongue connects with my clit. His hot breath, his quick tongue, and his sharp teeth all work together to make me throb and pulse. I arch my back, I'm so overwhelmed with the way he seems to know exactly how much pressure to apply, the exact right rhythm.

"Hunter," I scream.

He pulls back, and I feel cool air on my pussy.

"*Fuck*. I have to be inside you." He grabs a condom from the dresser and rips it open. "I'm about to come just from tasting you. Just from hearing your sounds." He rolls on the condom and drives into me, hard and fast. "I can't get enough of you." His arms cage me in as he thrusts into me, and the feeling of fullness is in such a stark contrast to his tongue that it wakes a different part of my climax. I move my body so we're in sync. Sweat sheens his body, making him more god than man as he looms above me.

All I can think about is how I don't want this to end.

"Tell me what you're thinking," he gasps out, barely able to form words.

"You feel so good. I want you to fuck me like this every day." My words are scrambled, but I have no choice but to tell him.

"Like we fit."

Like we're perfect together.

I clench at the thought, and our eyes widen as we both tip over into bliss at the exact same moment.

He collapses on top of me, his sweat-covered torso pinned against mine, panting, exhausted, satiated. The weight of him makes me feel safe and cared for and yes, like he's perfect for me. I wrap my arms and legs around him.

"Fuck, Lucy. If there was an Olympics for sex, we'd take gold for sure."

My stomach makes a gurgling sound, and I laugh.

"Was that you?"

"We skipped dinner, remember?"

"Let me get my phone. We can order something."

I prop my head up on my hand as I watch him locate his phone. He has such a nice ass. A nice back. A really great penis.

He must feel me watching him, because he glances over at me as he picks up his phone. "What?"

I shrug. "Just watching you."

"You want me to fuck you again before the food comes?"

Even though I should be spent and exhausted, somehow, he stokes desire in me again. "Maybe," I say.

"Jesus Christ. Let's order, or we're going to get into it again and you're going to die of hunger before any food actually arrives."

"Sounds good," I say.

"Unless you want to go out," he says, throwing me a look I can't quite place. "I mean, I don't want you to think this is just about . . . You know, we were meant to go to dinner, and we only managed a drink and—"

"I know this isn't just sex," I blurt out. I had to say it. I had to lay my cards on the table, almost like a challenge.

"Right," he says. "It's more than that." He presses a kiss to my head. "But the sex *is* phenomenal."

"Right," I reply. "The sex is great."

I sit up on the bed, my legs crossed so he can see my pussy.

"Let me order something that will take at least forty minutes."

I lean back, watching him as he hits his phone frantically, over and over, then tosses it over his shoulder. "Sustenance is on its way. In the meantime—"

He grabs an ankle and pulls me to the edge of the bed.

His cock rears in front of me, and I'm just at the perfect height. I take his hands and put them on my head. I want him to take what he needs from me.

I circle my tongue at the base of his cock and bring it up to the crown. He groans above me. There's renewed wetness between my legs at the sound of his pleasure. At the sound of my power over him. I want more.

I scoot back on the bed, then flip so I'm on my back, my head tipped back on the edge of the mattress. I glance up at him, and his eyes flare. I bring my knees up and drop them to the side before sliding my hand between my thighs.

"No," he thunders. "That's mine." He grabs my wrist and takes my fingers in his mouth, sucking my wetness off. It's so wanton, dirty, and sexy. I've never had sex like this with someone before, where there are no barriers or embarrassment. There's only what makes each other feel good.

I reach for his cock and feed it into my throat. He leans forward onto the bed, reaching for my pussy. His fingers work through my folds as he slides into my mouth, gentle but unrelenting.

"Fuck, Lucy. Fuck. Fuck. Fuck."

I know what he's thinking. It's too much. It's too good. But all I want is more.

He works his fingers over and over, and his cock slides in and out of my mouth. It gets so deep I don't know if I can take much more, but when he shifts out, I want him back immediately.

I feel crazed with lust for this man. Like I'd do anything he asked of me. My hips twist as the pleasure builds, and I know I'm losing control. There are too many sensations to handle, so many parts of my body responding to his.

And it's as if he knows, because he steps away, sheaths his cock in another condom and rearranges me so I'm lying in front of him again, my legs either side of his.

"Again," he says. I nod in agreement. I'm not sure how long I can survive fucking like this, but I know I can't if we ever stop.

He slides into me, and all the noise, all the overwhelming sensation, all the chaos disappears. It's just Hunter and me, together. And it feels perfect.

CHAPTER TWENTY-FIVE

Lucy

I've taken the entire week off from work to fly up to Boston and help with any last-minute preparations, and to support Katherine in her last few days as my single sister. People have only just started arriving in town for the four days of celebrations.

If I get married, I'm sure Mom won't put herself through the trouble of a four-day carnival. And I can't say I'll be sorry. Katherine seems more stressed than she should be when everyone is gathering to celebrate her and Ed.

"Are you ready?" Katherine asks as she bursts into my room. "You know the car is here in five minutes."

"Yeah, I'm ready." At least I think I am. Usually I wear my hair up for work and down and straight when I go out. Katherine inherited the glossy hair gene, and no matter how hard I try, mine never looks as sleek as hers. But tonight, I've embraced my kink. In my hair, that is. I bought some curl enhancer the other day, and tonight I've scrunched it up and gone big. My hair isn't super curly. It's an in-between kind of wavy that's neither one thing nor another. I'm used to fighting against the texture. Today, for the first time since I discovered straighteners, I'm embracing it.

"Wow, I love your hair," Katherine says. "It's very . . ." My stomach drops as she struggles to find the words. Does she have to work that hard to find a compliment? "Shakira! That's who I was trying to think of. You're a dark-haired Shakira."

Better Shakira than the lead singer in an eighties soft-rock band.

I stand and Katherine gasps. "You look beautiful," she says. "Different from your usual, but sexy."

I glance down at the new dress I bought on a whim this week. It's not normally the kind of thing I'd go for. And frankly, if it were the multigenerational rehearsal dinner, I wouldn't be wearing it tonight. But Mom and Dad are going out with the oldies while we go out with their kids. My dress is nude and tighter than I'd normally wear, with spaghetti straps and a hemline that definitely covers my ass but wouldn't qualify as midthigh. "Too sexy?" I glance up at Katherine, who's wearing white linen trousers and a pretty camisole.

"Absolutely not," she says. "This is the night when it's just our friends hanging out. The young ones." She looks excited. Like the pressure is off for the first time in a while. "Are you looking forward to seeing Hunter?"

My face flushes with heat at her question. Seeing Hunter is all I've been able to think about all day. It's the first time I'll have seen him since we met for lunch before I flew up to Massachusetts. It's the longest I've gone without seeing him since he and I turned into . . . something.

"Sure," I reply, trying to sound nonchalant.

"Do you two actually see each other than at lunchtime?"

"Sure," I repeat. I have to force myself to go home every other night rather than stay at his place. If I'm in his bed, we won't sleep much. I still have to function at work. But even when we're in different apartments, it's like we're never apart. When we aren't together, my head is full of him. My body can still feel him. It's like he's always with me.

"Have you had sex yet?"

"Sure," I say again, grabbing my clutch from my childhood bed. Referring to it as "sex" doesn't seem to give it enough emphasis. I've had sex before, but I haven't had what Hunter and I share.

"You're being very guarded about everything," she says. "Normally you talk to me about your boyfriends."

"Or lack of them," I say as we head out of my room.

"And now that you finally have something to share, you've clammed up." Katherine takes the stairs before me.

"It's not that I've clammed up. It's just . . . we're both busy and not exactly living in each other's pockets." That's not really true. We see each other for lunch as often as we can. On Thursday, Hunter was slammed, but I bought him a sandwich and took it up to him in his office. I pressed a kiss to his head, and he pulled me against him as he continued his conference call. It was only a minute or maybe two, but it was enough. Enough to keep me going until I saw him again. "And anyway, this week is about you, not about me and Hunter."

"Maybe it will be about the two of you soon. You never know. Ed swears Hunter just needs to find the right woman to balance him out."

"Balance him out?"

"Yeah, well, you know how he can be a bit of a grinch." Katherine dips her head to look out the front window. "The car's here," she says to me. "Bye, Mom!"

Mom appears from nowhere. "Don't be too late," she says. "We've got an early start tomorrow morning and . . . Good God, Lucy. What are you wearing?" She looks me up and down. "And your hair!" She scrunches up her nose like I'm week-old trash. Maybe I should change. I have another outfit option.

"She looks great, Mom. See you later." Katherine throws open the door, grabs my hand, and pulls me to the car.

"Do I look slutty?" I ask as we slide into the back seat.

"Sexy," Katherine corrects me.

"Maybe I should change? I have some navy linen pants like yours I could put on."

"I won't let you. You look absolutely phenomenal. Don't listen to Mom." She squeezes my hand. "Fisherman's Quay, please," Katherine says to the Uber driver, who presumably knows exactly where we're going.

We've arranged to arrive a little ahead of everyone so we can check the place settings and put name cards in the correct spots. The restaurant we've chosen is on the water and has a club right next door, so we don't have to worry about walking in heels to get to where we need to be to start dancing. As we pull up, Ed and Hunter are waiting for us outside the restaurant.

"Did you know they'd be here?" I ask.

"No, I expected Ed to be late," she replies, beaming.

Hunter opens my door and takes my hand, helping me out. His blue eyes flare as his gaze starts at my face and then drops to what I'm wearing.

He just nods, skims his hand over my waist and hips, and pulls me in for a kiss. "Are you trying to kill me with that dress?" he whispers in my ear.

Maybe I did choose it to make sure I had Hunter's attention. So far, we've only met for lunch or drinks or dinner before going back to his place. Tonight is the first time I'll have to share his attention, and I can't say I'm looking forward to that part of the evening.

"Wow," Katherine says from behind us. I spin to see her and Ed looking at us. "You two look very"—she frowns—"together."

Hunter slips his hand into mine, and we all head into the restaurant.

"Are you all checked into your hotel?" I ask Hunter as we take our allocated seats next to each other.

"Lucy, do you want to be by me?" Katherine asks. "There's no one here. I can easily swap you."

"I'm fine wherever I'm sitting." I squeeze Hunter's hand. *So long as I'm sitting by Hunter,* I don't say.

"Hunter, do you want to sit next to Ed? Or, as best man, maybe you could be next to me, and Lucy could be next to Ed. Then you're opposite each other."

I love my sister, and I'm so grateful she's met someone like Ed, who I know will always look after her and do everything he can to ensure she's happy. But right at this moment, I hate her. I just want to sit, hip to hip, with Hunter. To enjoy the woodsy masculine scent he wears and know he's doing everything he can to stop himself from sliding his hand up my dress. "That's fine," I say, wearing my best fake smile. Hunter chuckles beside me, and I know he knows that sitting opposite him is the opposite of fine.

"Will you save me a dance later?" he asks as we stand.

"You better not be dancing with anyone else," I say. We separate and arrive opposite each other.

"I think I'm going to move Gary and Melinda as well," Katherine says. "They can go at the end. Right?"

"I don't think it matters where Gary and Melinda sit," I say, stealing glances at Hunter, who hasn't taken his eyes from me since we sat down.

"You don't?" Katherine asks, her voice slightly higher pitched than normal.

"I really don't. Everyone met each other at the engagement party. No one's coming tonight who doesn't know everyone else. Everyone's going to have a great time as long as you have a great time." Hunter's sexy smirk fills my peripheral vision. "Let's all have a cocktail."

"Okay, thanks, Buddha," Katherine says. "Who died and made you Queen of Chill?"

I glance at Hunter, and we're both trying not to laugh. Is he thinking what I'm thinking? That sex as good as we're having would chill anyone out. "You know if I'm relaxed, there's really nothing to worry about."

"You're right," she says. "Nothing to worry about."

CHAPTER TWENTY-SIX

Lucy

Katherine's been sulking since we got in the car. "I just don't know why I can't stay with my fiancé tonight."

"You can," I say. "Do you want me to ask the driver to turn around?"

"But Mom will go crazy. She says she wants to check on the flowers first thing."

I sigh, still feeling the press of Hunter's hands around my waist, his thigh between my legs as we danced together. The things he whispered into my ear. He told me how he wanted to shove my dress up and have me against the wall outside the club. He pushed his erection against me and told me how good it feels when he slides inside me.

"Lucy!" Katherine cries, pulling me from my thoughts.

"Sorry, yes, I know she wants us to check on the flowers."

"And she's probably going to be waiting up for us. She'll just happen to be in the kitchen, making herself a hot cocoa or something when we come in."

"Probably."

"But I want to stay with Ed."

"I know." I'm grateful Hunter didn't ask me to stay. I don't think I would have been able to say no. The last thing I want to do is sleep in my teenage bedroom, staring at the new wallpaper Mom's put in there that is an explosion of lighthouses and seashells. It's truly hideous.

"Why do we do so much to keep Mom happy?" she asks.

"Because we know if Mom's not happy, life is pretty miserable," I say, taking Katherine's hand in mine.

"So we all dance around her, making sure life is just how she wants it."

I'd never thought about it, but Katherine's right. We all capitulate to Mom. Even Dad. "Yeah. I guess it's just easier that way."

"When I'm married, I'll have to put what Ed and I want first. Do you think she'll understand?"

I shrug. Honestly, I don't think Katherine getting married will affect our mother's expectations that she always gets her own way. "I think it will be better when you move. Does she know yet?"

Katherine shakes her head. "No, I want to leave it until after the wedding. I don't want to risk a big argument before. I think I'll drop a few hints while we're on the honeymoon. Maybe even send her a few links to places in the area where we want to live." She tips her head back on the headrest and turns to look at me. "You were smart, running off to New York. You got away."

"I don't feel like I got away. Not really."

A beat of silence passes between us.

"Fuck it," Katherine says. "We're fully grown women. If we want to roll in at three in the morning or even six, that's what we'll do. I want to go and fuck my fiancé. Driver, can you take us to the Harbor Inn?"

CHAPTER TWENTY-SEVEN

Lucy

The rehearsal dinner is being held at Mom's favorite restaurant in Boston. Tonight, my hair and clothes are back to "normal." The fact that Mom came into my bedroom first thing this morning to check on what I was wearing and "casually" inquired about how I'd be styling my hair didn't make me feel better about my choices for the club last night. The fact that Hunter couldn't keep his hands off me definitely did.

"So Lucy, when are you coming back to Boston?" Mom's oldest friend, Yvonne asks. We've all gathered in the small bar at the restaurant before taking our seats. Hunter's across the room with Ed's parents, and I've barely seen him.

"You mean after the wedding?" I ask, confused.

She laughs so loud I swear the entire restaurant turns around to stare at us. "No, silly. I mean for good. You need to find your husband and bring him home to Massachusetts with you. Like your sister."

"Katherine never left Massachusetts."

"Exactly. You'll be hitting thirty before you know it. New York isn't made for people past thirty."

It suddenly strikes me that everyone is expecting me to move back home. It's not just Mom. Everyone's just assuming that's what will happen. The thought hits me in the stomach like a fist. I can't think of anything worse than leaving New York. It's my sanctuary. "I like New York."

"Oh, I love to go for the shows. You can't beat Broadway for the musicals. But to live?" She recoils from her own words. "And the traffic. Where's the green space?"

"We have Central Park."

She laughs like I'm Jerry Seinfeld at his peak. "I'm serious. You don't want to bring up kids without space for them to play."

"Well, I have no plans for children at the moment."

"Yes, dear, but you will one day, and you'll want them to be close to their grandparents, won't you? You'll be able to have weekends on the Cape. You just need the man to make that happen."

Is that what everyone's been waiting for? Me to see sense and move back to Boston?

My dad makes the announcement that our table is ready and we should find our seats. I head to the opposite end from my parents, but everyone finds a place before I do. There are about twenty of us, and eventually, I find a seat in the middle. The chair next to me is free, and I look around for Hunter. I find him heading toward me, but just as I nod at the empty seat next to me, Uncle Ralph plonks himself down.

It's so frustrating, having Hunter so close but not having any time, just the two of us. He takes the seat opposite me, and we trade what feels like a secret smile.

Everyone finds their places, Ed's parents taking up the two chairs at one end of the table and my parents taking up the two chairs at the other. Maybe it's me, but shouldn't Ed and Katherine be at the end of the table? Or maybe it's because the parents are hosting this dinner? It feels like the spotlight should really be on the happy couple.

My dad stands and clinks his fork against his water glass.

"Just a few words before we break bread with each other. It's been a delight to have Ed become a part of the family over the last few years. Katherine is such a sweet and precious daughter, I never thought there'd be a man worthy of her, but she found him in Ed. Congratulations to Mr. and Mrs. Franklin on raising the perfect son for our perfect daughter."

I try not to roll my eyes at my father's description of his perfect daughter. Katherine's the perfect one. I'm the imperfect one. That's how you distinguish the two of us.

Someone nudges my foot under the table. My head snaps up to find Hunter grinning at me.

"Anything you want to say, darling?" Dad says to Mom.

My mom shakes her head but stands just the same. "Just to say that Katherine, we're so happy for you. You've found your Mr. Bingley, darling. And rightly so. You're such a kind, caring, devoted daughter, and I know you'll be a wonderful wife."

Everyone claps. I wonder if it's just me who thinks that toast was . . . off, somehow. It was all about Katherine and how she performs as a daughter and a wife. Not who she is in her heart. Katherine is kind and caring. But she's not just a daughter. Maybe I'm being oversensitive. Being under the same roof as my mother for the last few days is slowly driving me crazy.

Thankfully, Ed's parents pass on the speeches, and the appetizers are served. Hunter is seated next to Uncle Ralph's wife, my Aunt Maude. It's literally my idea of hell. Ralph is almost completely deaf, and his wife more than makes up for his silence.

"Your Ed's friend, I hear," Maude says.

I chase a shrimp around my plate and try to keep my head down in case anyone pulls me into conversation about moving back to Boston again. But obviously I'm listening in to Hunter's conversation with Maude.

"That's right. We've known each other a long time. You're Mrs. Jones's sister?"

"Yes. Two peas in a pod. Not like Katherine and poor Lucy."

I take a breath and stab a shrimp with my fork.

Hunter just nods and takes a sip of his wine.

"Me and my sister did everything together," Maude says. "We even dated brothers one time. And we had the same interests. The same outlook on life. No two sisters have ever been closer."

"But Katherine and Lucy are close," Hunter says.

Maude pauses. "Yes, I suppose so. Like cousins more than sisters. They're so dissimilar. Katherine is such a homebody—a nurturer."

Hunter's gaze slides to mine, and I pretend I haven't heard. Except I have heard, and my cheeks flush bright red. I chew my shrimp like it's made of molasses.

"Is that good?" I ask Uncle Ralph, who seems to have the vegetarian option. I'm trying to distract myself from Aunt Maude's withering verdict on my character.

"Food, yes, of course it's food. You think they'd be serving up bricks?" he barks.

I sigh and turn to my left. It's a member of Ed's family who seems engrossed in conversation with whomever's on his left. I'm left in the middle to listen as Aunt Maude tells the guy I'm sleeping with that I'm not nurturing.

"Lucy's never been . . . Well, she's obviously not as clever as Katherine," Maude says as I continue to shrivel in my chair.

"But she's a paralegal, isn't she?" Hunter asks in the gentlest way.

"Yes, but honestly, I have no idea how. I think those people do a lot of shredding. You know those huge shredding bins? I bet she does a lot of shredding. She was never any good at school."

"Aunt Maude," I say. "You do know that I can hear you, don't you?"

"What?" she asks oblivious. "I'm just saying you were never any good at school."

"I got a 1430 on my SATs."

"Did you?" she asks, looking surprised. "But what did Katherine get?"

I sigh. "1480."

"There you go. Katherine was more academic. But it was bound to be the case. She was more organized that you. You remember that time when you forgot to let the cat out and she ruined your mother's curtains?"

"I was thirteen."

"The cat tore those curtains to shreds." My aunt leans forward and tries to get my mom's attention at the head of the table. "Do you remember when Lucy forgot to let the cat out?"

Mom shrieks. "Oh, God. Those curtains were so expensive, and they were just ruined." She shakes her head. "But I shouldn't have relied on Lucy. It was my own fault."

"I'm keeping a list," my dad says. "Your husband will get a bill when you finally walk down the aisle. All the things you ruined. All the messes we had to clear up." He chuckles, and my mom joins him.

I'm the joke of the family.

"I always said you'd be trouble, Lucy. I knew it when I was giving birth to you."

I groan. I don't want to hear about how I cried coming out of the womb. Not again. Can I leave the table without people thinking I'm making a scene? Sometimes I just tire of being the joke of the family, the runt of the litter, the kid who just can't get it together.

"That's not how I see Lucy at all," Hunter interrupts. "Maybe it's because I didn't know her as a child. But as a woman, she's not the person you describe. Not at all." My heart lifts in my chest at the way he's going to bat for me. Katherine sticks up for me, but Hunter doesn't have skin in this game. He doesn't have to be in my corner like this. "She's incredibly well respected at her job. She's kind and self-sacrificing. Beautiful. Positive. She wants everyone around her to be happy. I think she's . . . wonderful."

Hunter turns to me and smiles. His grin is all warmth and sunshine, and I'm so grateful that he's here, staring at me, sticking up for me, on my side.

"Well, of course she's much better now," Mom says. "But she and Katherine are still like chalk and cheese. Did you even see what she went out wearing on Wednesday night?"

Hunter's eyes flare and he nods. He's answering Mom, but he's staring at me just like he did on Wednesday, his eyes filled with fire and lust.

"Katherine looks lovely," I say, breaking Hunter's gaze. "And I can't wait to see her as a bride."

"Yes," my dad says. "She'll be the perfect bride."

The conversation turns to the wedding. I see my opportunity to leave the table for a few minutes and gather myself. I knew this wedding week was going to be full of comparisons between Katherine and me—comparisons in which I inevitably end up on the losing end. I'd mentally prepared myself. But it's still hard hearing it sometimes.

I head out to the front of the restaurant, so I can watch the water and take a few deep breaths. The next thing I know, Hunter is standing next to me, his hands pushed into the pockets of his linen suit.

"Meeting your family is . . . something," he says as we both lean against the small brick wall in front of the restaurant.

"You're starting to see how much better Katherine is in every way?"

"Absolutely not. But I'm starting to understand why you're so hard on yourself. How could you not be when your parents are even harder on you? Is every family function like this?"

"You mean the jokes about what a mess I am? The unflattering comparisons between me and my sister? The put-downs? The mean comments." I nod. "Pretty much, yeah."

"No wonder you moved to New York." He leans over and presses a kiss to my head. I lean against him.

"Yeah. But now that Katherine's getting married, I'm going to be expected to move back. My mom's best friend literally just asked me when I'm coming home for good."

"Like you're playing at having a life in New York? Just because that's what they expect doesn't mean that's what you should do."

"I know. But it's just another thing I have to fight against. The comparisons to Katherine. The stories about how I ruined things and was a mess when I was a kid. And now it's them all telling me it's time to move back to Boston."

"You want to move back?" he asks.

"Are you kidding me? New York is more a part of me than Boston ever was. And why in the hell do they want me back if I'm such a walking disaster?"

"I think it's just an easy narrative they've fallen into."

"I think they still believe it. Even though I planned the perfect bachelorette weekend. None of it matters. They only see the bad stuff."

Hunter slips his arm around my waist. "Did you tell them about how your boss wants you to go to law school?"

"As if. They'd probably ask whether I misunderstood, or they'd think I was lying to impress them. It's not like I can actually do it anyway. I can't study and work and become a lawyer." I fold my arms in front of myself and lift my head from Hunter's shoulder. "I love my sister, but I can't wait for this wedding to be over."

"Then the pressure will be off you."

"Mom and Dad will go back to whatever it was they were doing, and I can go back to New York. Ed will go back to focusing on work, and—"

"And then Katherine will get pregnant, and Ed will be distracted by Katherine's pregnancy and eventually a baby, and then it will be a second baby and croup and chicken pox and school districts and every possible thing."

I try to take in what Hunter's saying. He's worried about Ed's ongoing distraction. It's not just the wedding he's frustrated about, but the whole idea of what married life will mean for his business.

"Portis is doing well, though, isn't it?"

Hunter nods. "Yeah. For sure. But the Boston office is really Ed's domain."

"Your financials are separate?"

"No, but I don't know what goes on there on a day-to-day basis."

"You mean you don't know the clients in Boston?"

"The big ones I do. Most of them actually. But as we grow, I'm not going to be able to keep track in the same way I do now. I'm not going to be able to cover everything."

"Does Ed need to be covered?" I ask.

"He does if he's going to take his eye off the ball."

"Doesn't sound like Ed."

"No. But people change. Isn't that what you wish your family could see? You've changed for the better. But Ed . . . He missed a client meeting."

His voice isn't resentful—it's full of worry. But why? Ed is the most dependable man on the planet. Then I realize that his concern is buried deep. It's decades old. I turn to him. "Ed's not your father."

He frowns and takes a step back almost as if I've struck him. "I never said he was. But I'm not going to make the mistake of blindly trusting someone again."

I shiver at his words, and my insides drop. Believing in your father and finding out he was a liar must be the worst kind of betrayal. At least my parents have been consistent in their disappointment in me. "You can trust Ed," I say. "And me."

He sighs. "We'll see."

For the first time since Martha's Vineyard, I feel a distance opening up between Hunter and me rather than the horizon closing in.

"We should go back in," I say.

"Yeah." He pushes off the wall to stand. "We don't want you to be the sister that disappears during the rehearsal dinner."

"That will be the story at Thanksgiving, no doubt," I say on a sigh.

Hunter scoops up my hand and presses a kiss to my knuckles, the chilliness between us dissipating like early morning fog. "I'm here for you, Lucy."

"And you can trust me," I say. Except I'm not sure he hears me, because he's already heading back into the restaurant and pulling me behind him. Even if he had been listening, I'm not sure whether he'd believe me. I'm not sure Hunter will ever believe he can trust anyone ever again.

CHAPTER TWENTY-EIGHT

Hunter

Best man duties aren't as onerous as I thought they might be. I had to take care of the rings, give a couple of pep talks when Ed's nerves were at their highest, and dance with Ed's mom and granny. Even my speech was warmly received. People laughed in all the right places. I couldn't help but notice Lucy laughed more loudly than most. From what I can tell, the wedding has been a success. Katherine looked really pretty, and when I told her so, she found no invisible lint to pick from my lapel. No one fluffed their lines at the altar, and I haven't heard Mrs. Jones quote Jane Austen once.

Everything seems to be as perfect as Lucy could have imagined for her sister. I'm happier about that than I'd ever admit to Lucy.

"You're the best friend a guy could ever have," Ed says, slightly slurring his words. I don't think I've ever seen Ed drunk before.

I slap Ed on the back. "You, too, my friend."

"I mean it. I love you so much."

I chuckle. Now we're declaring our love for each other. This is new. "I love our friendship. I love our business."

"And I want you to be godfather to our first child," he splutters.

My stomach falls to the floor. "Katherine's pregnant?"

"Not yet, but when the time comes, tell me you'll say yes?"

He looks up at me like he's proposing and terrified of rejection because he already bought the ring and told his family.

"Yeah, of course I'll be godfather."

"Lucy will be godmother, of course. This is perfect. It's all working out. You two just need to get engaged now."

Lucy and I haven't been ignoring each other. But we haven't seen much of each other today either. This morning we were all busy in our respective hotel suites. Since the ceremony, every time I look around, she's talking to another elderly aunt or uncle. She's keeping everyone happy. I guess that's how it should be at a wedding when she's the maid of honor, but it's clear this is what Lucy is used to. She desperately wants to be the daughter her parents want. And as much as she tries, she'll never live up to Katherine in their eyes. Because she's not Katherine and she shouldn't even have to try to be her. She's enough, even if she doesn't realize that.

"Well, that's not going to happen anytime soon. I want to focus on work. You know that."

"The business is going great, man. You don't need to worry so much."

"One of us has to," I reply.

"You really don't. The place runs itself."

"No, Ed. It doesn't. We need to make sure we're providing our clients with what we say we will. We need to ensure we're compliant with the new regulations coming in, and we—"

"I have a proposal for you," Ed interrupts.

"Hate to break it to you, man, but you're already married."

Ed laughs like I've told the best joke ever. "No, but seriously, I think we need to hire someone. Maybe a couple of people. One person can be in charge of regulatory and compliance. And we need a really good office manager."

"But I lead on regulatory and compliance."

"Right, and you're working around the clock. I know you've picked up the slack for me in the lead-up to the wedding. We need more people. But if we employ them, you need to be prepared to loosen the reins a little."

Loosen the reins? Is that what my dad was doing when he started to go off course in his business? He probably got to a point where he thought the business ran itself and he could sit back a little. I don't want to fall into the same trap.

"Let's talk about this another time." I'm sure when Ed's sober, he'll have a change of heart. He knows you have to keep a tight grip on things in business.

"I mean it, man. You need to have a life. We both do."

"I don't mind working hard," I say.

"Neither do I. But I also want to hang out with my wife, and we're going to have kids soon. I want to work, but I also want to be able to have family vacations and Sunday barbeques."

This is exactly what I was worried about. Ed's priorities have shifted. He's not thinking about work and building a business. He's thinking about vacations and *not* working. And this is before he's even had kids. Maybe I should offer to buy him out of Portis, except I can't afford to and it was his idea in the first place. The back of my neck prickles, and I tip my head from side to side, trying to release the building tension, but it doesn't work.

"Surely you want to hang out with Lucy," Ed continues. "Go antiquing or whatever it is the two of you do when you hang out."

"Antiquing?" I ask, wondering if he's ever met me. I'm not a guy who goes fucking antiquing.

"Or maybe you can take up fishing again," Ed suggests. "We need more of a balance. We need to enjoy life."

The thought of fishing tightens my chest. The heat in the ballroom seems to have gone up ten degrees. I wonder why more men haven't taken off their dinner jackets. The last thing I want to do is to take up fishing again. "Let's talk about it all when you're back from the honeymoon." I pat him on the back. I need some air.

As I head to the exit, the girls are gathered to catch Katherine's bouquet. Lucy has stepped to the side, despite Katherine pleading for her to move to the middle.

Somewhere along the way, I'd started to allow myself to believe that everything was going to turn out okay. It was just a chink of hope. The tiniest sliver of optimism that I wasn't going to be a complete failure, and now this.

Fuck these people. Fuck weddings. Fuck fishing. Fuck everything.

I get to the exit as cheers erupt behind me. Someone's caught the bouquet. I just need to breathe. To get out of here. To escape.

I want to hold off the reality of what Ed's just said a tiny bit longer.

I need to sort through what's going on in my mind. I want to think about what Ed is really saying to me—and what he's not saying. What he's hiding. Does he want out completely? Or maybe he just wants to be a silent partner. We're earning good money from this business, but it's not enough for him to never work again. Especially if he and Katherine are planning to raise a family. Does he have other plans? Maybe he wants to work for a competitor. Or maybe he doesn't want to be his own boss anymore and just wants to work a nine-to-five.

I stumble to the bench underneath the apple tree in front of me and put my head in my hands. The music has started up again, and I wonder whether I can go back to the hotel. Would anyone notice I was gone? I need space to think. I've always known Ed and I are different. He comes from old money in Boston. My family is from good Irish working stock. We're not as polished as Ed. And we expect to work. Maybe Ed has some inheritance I don't know about. My thoughts are all jumbled, and I just wish I could tear off this stupid tux and breathe.

"Hey," she calls.

My head is in my hands, and I don't look up. I know it's Lucy. I don't need to see her to know it.

She sits beside me on the bench. "I caught the bouquet. Well, Katherine passed it to me. I'm not sure it counts." She stops. "Are you okay? I saw you talking to Ed."

I nod, but I can't find the words. She smooths her hand over my back, and I sit back finally.

"What did he say that's sent you spiraling?"

"I need to step back," I blurt.

"From the business?" she asks.

I shake my head. "From everything that isn't the business." I'm going to have to be the one who takes all this on. I can't rely on Ed. I don't want to bring in new people. If he's going to step back from the business, I need to step forward. I need to work harder. Harder than I'm doing at the moment. I need to keep all the plates spinning. I glance over at her, and she looks like I've struck her. I hate myself, but I don't have any other options. I need to refocus.

"What did he say?" Lucy asks.

"He wants to step back from Portis. He wants me to 'loosen the reins.'" My mind is racing, trying to find solutions, to come up with a silver bullet that's going to solve this problem. "Fuck," I spit. I knew this was coming. Why wasn't I more prepared?

"But he's not saying he's leaving, is he?" she asks.

He might as well be. "No," I say. "He wants to have more balance. To have barbeques at the weekends and stuff. I don't know."

"And that's not what you want? You work really hard, Hunter."

"The reason we have a successful business is because I work really hard."

She sighs beside me. "If you say so," she says.

"What?" I ask. I'm caught up by my own thoughts, but it feels like she's imparting some important wisdom that I don't want to miss.

"If you think you're successful because you work a lot of hours, then you're successful because you work a lot of hours."

Is she saying my success doesn't come from working hard? She knows how hard I work. She knows what time I arrive in the office and what time I leave. "Running your own business takes up your whole life. That's just how it is."

"If you believe it, then it's true." She stands and smooths down her dress, like she's done.

"What does that mean?"

"It means that unless you see that your success is more than just the hours you put in, you're never going to work fewer hours."

There's no point in responding. Lucy has never worked for herself. She doesn't get it. She doesn't understand what it's like to be responsible for paying salaries and making sure you don't default on a lease.

"The thing is," she says, fiddling with one of the flowers in the bouquet. "If that were true, there'd be a low ceiling on success. There'd be no Warren Buffett or Steve Jobs. People would have a cap on how much they could achieve because there are only so many hours in the day."

I try to hear what she's saying, but it's like she's spouting quantum physics. I can't make sense of her words, and I've already got too much spinning around in my head. I can't take anything else in.

"I'm going to leave you to take your step back," she says. "From me. And I'm going to go and enjoy the party."

This is my window of opportunity. I could say I didn't mean I wanted to take a step back from her. Because I don't want to lose her. But I don't have a choice. I have to let her go.

She turns and heads back into the marquee. Part of me wants to bury everything I'm feeling about my conversation with Ed and follow her. I want to dance and laugh and hold her close. I want to spend the night naked and tangled up with her breath on my skin and her fingers in my hair.

But I know now's not the time to lose it, not the time to give in to temptation. We're at a tipping point. Ed is stepping back, and I need to step forward. I have to save this business.

I have to save *us*.

CHAPTER TWENTY-NINE

Lucy

I kick my shoes off as soon as I'm through my front door. On the wall ahead of me hangs a gold-edged mirror my mom bought me when I moved into this apartment. I've never liked it. It's old fashioned and not in that cool vintage-y way. Less "granny chic" and more "Granny, no thank you." My mom even chose where to put it. She said it was always good to have a mirror near the front door so you could check your appearance before you left or before you opened the door.

But I hate it, and I'm reminded that I hate it every time I come back to my apartment. It's still there, every day, despite me hating it, even though Mom hasn't visited since she came when I moved in three years ago. I sling my bag on the floor and reach for the mirror. It unhooks easily, and I lift it off the wall. I stand back to look at the blank space where it just was. It looks a little bare, but maybe I could find a picture to go there instead. I set the mirror back onto the hook and pour myself a glass of water.

I'm running up against the deadline to apply to sit for the LSAT if I want to do it before applications close for law school in September. I'm also sitting on an email from Sharon, asking whether I'm interested in her putting me forward for one of the in-house scholarships that will be launched this year. It's an unwritten rule in our law firm that partner emails never have to wait more than an hour—and then only if you're in a meeting or on a call on something else. Sharon's email has been in my inbox since ten fifteen this morning, and I still haven't responded. If I want a law school scholarship, I have to answer her before I go to bed tonight, or I can forget about it.

I take a sip of water. I thought the journey home from the office would clear my head and let me think, help me come to a decision, but it didn't. Neither does the water. Neither does being at home.

I take my laptop and go to my couch. If I tell her I want to be considered, that doesn't mean I've automatically got the scholarship, does it? I might not get accepted into law school. I might not even get a good enough score on the LSAT.

The LSAT study book Hunter and I bought, what seems like months ago now, is sitting on the coffee table. I set my laptop to one side and grab the book, flipping through the pages like they might have the answer to Sharon's email in there somewhere.

I've mentally tried out some of the questions. I haven't committed anything to paper. I haven't even allocated time in my schedule to study. Although I have more time on my hands now that Katherine and Ed are on their honeymoon and Hunter has taken a step back.

A step back from me.

From us.

From life.

Maybe he has the right idea. I certainly have more time on my hands since I haven't taken my lunch breaks this week and I've spent every night at home. The hours I've gained back in my schedule could be totally devoted to the LSAT. It's what Hunter would do, isn't it? No doubt he's still in the office at this very moment. Worrying. Stressing. Taking the weight of the world on his shoulders. I can't blame him. Given what happened with his dad, it's totally understandable why he wouldn't want another business he's in charge of to fail. He doesn't seem to realize that when he took over his father's company, it had already failed. From what I can gather, Hunter was an innocent bystander in that scenario. Nothing he could have done would have protected him from the fallout.

He's still sheltering from the fallout. Even now. Braced. Ready. Waiting for it to happen again. It's all he's got room for. My heart aches because I'm not with him, but also because I know he's in pain and can't see a way out.

I toss the LSAT book to the side and pull my laptop back onto my lap. I reread Sharon's email for the tenth time. What am I going to say?

> Are you sure you haven't mixed me up with someone else?

> My mother thinks I'm not capable of dressing myself, let alone going to law school. How can you be so sure I am?

> Sure, I'll put my name down for a scholarship, but don't worry, you'll never have to pay up because I'll never get in.

My phone buzzes, and I hurry to grab my cell from my purse, which I left in the hallway.

It's pictures on the group chat with Ed, Katherine, Hunter, and me. Katherine in a red bikini, holding up a shell. Katherine and Ed holding up cocktails. Ed with a snorkel and mask on. They look like they're having the time of their lives. It's nice they want to share it with us.

Hunter and I haven't officially split because we weren't officially together. I haven't mentioned anything to Katherine because I don't want anything to interrupt her having a great time on her honeymoon. And maybe part of me is hoping the conversation I had with Hunter will be forgotten now that he's had a chance to process what Ed was saying. Ed loves working with Hunter and doesn't want to step back in any meaningful sense. He just doesn't want to work *all the time*. Then again, he doesn't have the history Hunter does.

As I'm swiping through the photographs, a video call from Katherine comes through.

"Belize looks horrifying," I say dramatically as Katherine comes onto the screen. She's in the hotel room and Ed is behind her.

"It's awful. I miss you. I wish you were here."

"It's our honeymoon," Ed mumbles behind her. "You're not supposed to miss your sister on your honeymoon."

I laugh. "Are you telling me *you* don't miss me, Ed?"

He turns to face the screen and steps closer. "Of course I don't! Belize is awesome and it feels so good to not be wedding planning or worried about . . . anything."

My heart lifts in my chest at seeing them both so happy.

"Have you seen much of Hunter since the wedding?" Katherine asks, her eyes brimming with hope and excitement. I'm so lucky to have Katherine. She's genuinely excited when I'm happy. The feeling is entirely mutual.

The question triggers a low, sonorous pain inside me. "Not really," I say, honestly. "He's really busy. And . . . worried about stuff."

Ed shuffles Katherine so he's now sitting where she was and she's on his lap. "He's really stressed?" he asks.

"Yeah. I think so."

"I remember telling him we need to hire more people so we can enjoy our lives," he says. "It didn't go down well."

I sigh. There's nothing I can say to make this better. I understand why Hunter has taken it so badly. I wish I could make him see that Ed's trying to help them both. He's not about to betray Hunter. I know it. All Hunter can see is history repeating itself.

"Can you reassure him I'm not trying to tank our business?" Ed says. "We've both worked too hard for us to let that happen."

"I don't think he's in the headspace to hear it, Ed." Nothing hopeful has room to grow in him.

"Has it made things tense between the two of you?" Katherine asks.

"A little," I say. "But I've been busy at work too. I have to get back to the partner on whether I want to be considered for a firm scholarship to law school."

"What?" Katherine asks.

I wince inwardly as I've realized I've used my outside voice for my inside thoughts.

"Didn't I tell you that one of the partners offered to mentor me? She mentioned that I should consider going to law school in the evenings." I try to sound casual, but I'm terrible at faking anything.

Katherine's brow is furrowed, and she gets closer to the camera like she's trying to read some small text. "No!" Katherine says. "You didn't tell me that. When did this happen?"

"I don't know. Before the wedding sometime. It was all a blur."

"So what did she say? Do you want to go to law school?"

Now the cat's out of the bag, I may as well come clean. "She thinks I have a lot of potential and that I should apply. But then again, I'm a good paralegal. Do I really want to work for years and not even know if I'm going to become a lawyer? I might be bad at it, or I might not graduate at all. It's such a time commitment, not to mention all that money. I might waste it all, and—"

"This partner approached *you,* though, Lucy. She thinks you can do it."

"Right, but it's for this new program they've started, about encouraging women in the firm to fulfill their potential. They probably have some quota to meet or something."

"It's incredible that they've approached you about this. Why didn't you tell me before? I'm so excited for you!"

"I just wanted you to focus on the wedding. And I'm not even sure that I'm going to go ahead with it."

"I'm really sorry, Lucy," Katherine says. "I've been so caught up with wedding planning. You're going to do it, though. Aren't you? I always thought it was a shame you didn't go to law school."

"You did?" I ask.

"Yeah. Why didn't you end up going?"

"It was too expensive. Too much of a risk. It's a lot to take on if you crash out halfway through."

"I don't think it's a risk. Not for you, anyway. You've always done anything you've set your mind to. You're the most determined person I know."

Ed nods in agreement, and I can't help but smile. Sometimes I doubt Katherine's reassurances that what Mom is saying about me isn't true. I don't know why. She's entirely consistent in the way she sees me.

"But it's crazy, right? I can't actually do it."

"Why is it crazy?" Katherine asks.

"Law school? For me? Mom would say—"

"Mom is ridiculous," Katherine says. "Don't let her dictate what you are and are not. If you want to do it, you should do it." Katherine shrieks and for a split second, I think she's laughing at me. That she's going to say, *Kidding! Of course you can't go to law school. Who do you think you are?* "Have you still got that bowl on your coffee table?"

I glance over at the brown glass bowl Mom bought me as a graduation present.

"Turn the camera around," Katherine says. "I bet you still have it."

"It was a gift!" I say, trying to defend myself.

"It's disgusting. Have you seen it, Ed?" Ed shakes his head. "Show Ed. You'll die when you see how ugly it is. I swear it was such a weird gift. Especially when I got a Tiffany necklace when I graduated."

I'd expected to receive the same exact gift my parents had given Katherine when she'd graduated two years earlier: a silver necklace with a heart hanging from it. When I unwrapped the sludge-colored bowl, I told myself I shouldn't have expected a gift in the first place, and not loving the bowl was ungrateful.

"Did you ask for the bowl?" Katherine asked.

"Did I ask for a *brown* bowl as a graduation gift?" I ask her, wanting her to really listen to the question she's asking me.

"I asked for the Tiffany necklace," Katherine says.

Katherine's statement takes me by surprise. It didn't occur to me to ask for anything. "It wouldn't have mattered if I'd asked. I still would have gotten the bowl." I grab it from the table and hold it up so Ed can see.

He wrinkles his nose.

"Why do you have it out?" Katherine asks. "To torture yourself?"

It's a good question. I hate the bowl. I've always hated it. But Mom picked it out herself. I had to have it out, didn't I?

"What if Mom comes over and it's not out?"

"When's the last time she came to your apartment? Hell, when's the last time she came to New York City?"

I know the exact time. "When I moved in here."

"Oh, God, yeah, and she brought that awful mirror she'd been given by the neighbor across the street who died the next day."

"What?" I ask.

"Was it Betty? Or Beverley? You know, the woman across the street. She gave Mom the mirror, and then Mom gave it to you as a house-warming gift because she didn't want it."

Three years that horrible mirror has been in my hallway because I thought my mom had bought it for me with thought and love, and because she wanted me to look nice when I left my apartment. But it was none of those things. She was basically using my apartment as a recycling center when she gave it to me.

"Don't tell me you still have that up, too?" Katherine hoots with laughter.

But it's not funny. Not to me. The mirror. The bowl. They're symbols of how Mom pretends to care. Pretends to show affection when what's she's doing is exactly the opposite.

"What did you get as a wedding present from Mom and Dad?" I ask.

"Oh, just some cash," Katherine says casually.

"A lot of cash," Ed says. "Too much."

"Paid for the honeymoon. And a bit more," Katherine mumbles. She's seen the different way Mom treats us, and she knows she gets the better end of the bargain. I don't blame her for not rocking the boat.

I happen to know the honeymoon was over twenty-five thousand dollars. I also know Mom and Dad have paid at least the same toward the cost of the wedding, despite Ed saying they were going to cover it themselves. Since when did my parents have money like that sitting around? I'm certain they don't have another twenty-five grand saved for when I get married. My mom will probably raid the local flee market and give me an old shoe or something as my wedding gift.

It's not about the money, of course. It's about the fact Katherine gets treated differently. Like I'm an afterthought. I wouldn't mind if Mom had given me a pebble off the beach for my graduation, if it had been heartfelt. But the brown bowl didn't come from her heart, and neither did the hallway mirror.

"Have you told them you're moving?" I ask, wondering if that will shift the dynamic. My mother might give Katherine more attention, but she's still controlling and overbearing.

"Not yet, but we got an offer accepted on a place," Katherine says.

"That's great," I say. "So you'll be moving soon?"

"Hopefully we'll be in and settled before the holidays."

It's obvious, but it hits me that Katherine will spend the holidays married for the first time this year. She has obligations to Ed during those times now. Of course, Mom might still try her best to get them over to her house, but already I see the pull Mom has over Katherine has loosened.

Katherine has her own family now.

I don't know where that leaves me. I can't bear the thought of spending Thanksgiving back in Boston with a mother whom I know would prefer to be hosting Katherine than me.

A huge urge to clear everything out hits me. I need headspace so that positive things can grow inside me. "I gotta go," I say. "Keep sending the pictures. Love you." I blow a kiss to the screen, and before Katherine can say anything, I end our call. I jump to my feet, swipe my graduation present off the couch and stalk out of my living room. I take my keys and unhook the mirror from the wall again. I'd rather have a blank wall than a mirror from a dead neighbor whose name we can't even remember. I shove my feet back into my shoes, and I head down to the sidewalk. The restaurant two doors down the street is putting out its trash for the day. I don't think twice before I tip the bowl and the mirror into the metal trash can.

I should have done that a long time ago.

Neither of those things meant anything to my mother. And they don't mean anything to me. Nothing good, anyway.

I get back into my apartment, grab my laptop, and hit "Reply" on the email to Sharon. What have I got to lose by saying I'd like to be considered for a scholarship? Okay, so I might not get it, but my mom's never going to know. Katherine doesn't even have to know. I don't have to tell anyone.

Sharon replies immediately, saying she's pleased I've made that choice and she'll be in touch with more details.

It feels good. It feels like I made a decision based on what I want rather than what everyone else thinks about me. Okay, so maybe I'm not entirely confident about going to law school. Hell, I'm not entirely confident about sitting for the LSAT. But one thing I know for sure is that Sharon is smart. Maybe she sees something in me I don't see in myself. I'm learning I can't always trust what I believe about myself, but while I'm figuring that out, I can let myself trust people who see the best in me. It's what my mom should have done my whole life, instead of comparing me with Katherine and putting me down. I can't change her, and I can't change the past. But I can start building a future based on who I am today, instead of the walking disaster Mom seems to want me to be.

I grab the LSAT study book and start at chapter one.

CHAPTER THIRTY

Hunter

The decision between the Then There Were None meatball sub and the Gone with the Wind turkey sub shouldn't be a difficult one, but I've gotten to the front of the line twice before heading to the back because I can't decide between them.

It's the first time I've been outside in daylight hours for . . . I've lost track. A week? Maybe longer. I haven't been sleeping at the office, but I've been working longer hours than normal. I've been getting home at one in the morning, and I've been back by five. I haven't been taking lunch breaks or any other kinds of breaks either. I haven't even made it to the gym.

I'm tired. Really tired. But the only thing that's gotten me outside today is the fact that my assistant is out sick. And maybe I miss seeing daylight just a little.

"Hey," she says. I know it's Lucy before I turn my head. Relief washes through me like a warm rain.

"Hey," I reply. "It's good to see you." We didn't exactly leave on bad terms, but I was clear with her that my priority after the wedding was going to be work. I guess she understood it meant I wouldn't have time for her.

"You look tired," she says. Her eyes soften, and I want to dive into their sea-green comfort.

"I'm fine," I say. But I'm not fine. I'm hungry. And exhausted.

"What are you having? I think I'm going for the Persuasion."

"You usually get the Great Gatsby."

"Right," she says. "But things change. I'm trying new things." She stops herself from saying more, and I can see her mind whirring. "Not all new things. Just new small things. Clearing out stuff in my apartment I don't like. You know, that kind of thing."

"And new sandwich fillings?"

"Right. Yesterday I got a grinder—A Tale of Two Cities, I think it was called."

"Wow," I say, genuinely surprised.

She laughs. "I know. It's not groundbreaking, but I figure we all live our lives in certain patterns, believing certain truths, and sometimes it's good to push a little. Create new patterns and . . . I don't know. Maybe it's just about . . . seeing what's in front of us. Seeing the routines and so-called truths and challenging them a little."

I scan her face, trying to figure out if what she's saying is aimed at me. Is she trying to send me a message? There's nothing in her expression except pure honesty. Pure openness. Because that's who Lucy is.

"I threw out a bowl," she says, like that will answer all the questions I have. "And a mirror. And some awful pants my Mom said looked nice on me. If I were a fifty-six-year-old woman, they probably would look nice, but I'm not there yet. I tossed some faux flowers I bought because I saw them in a magazine and thought they would look nice, but they never really looked good. So they've gone too."

I nod at her, because I'm not quite sure what she wants me to say and I just like to look at her. I like to hear what she has to say. I like being close to her.

I miss her.

"You probably think I'm nuts for keeping all this stuff I don't like. It just made sense to me for a long time. But all of a sudden, I've seen this crazy behavior, and I can't unsee it, you know?"

She nods ahead, and I realize the line has moved forward and we're nearing the front. Except I don't want it to be our turn, because then she'll have to go back to her office and I'll have to go back to mine.

"Did you decide?" she asks. "You usually get the Jane Eyre, don't you?"

Yeah. I always get the pastrami. I don't know why I've gotten to the front of the line twice and still been undecided. It's always the same answer.

"I want to hear more about you," I blurt. "Can you stay? Eat lunch with me?"

Her face breaks into an enormous smile, and it's so infectious the corners of my mouth turn up. It aches slightly, like my mouth is out of practice. "Sure," she says. "If you have time."

We pay for our sandwiches and try to find a table. When we've eaten here before, we always head for the shade, but the only table available is in the sun. "Are you okay in the sun?" I ask.

"Yeah," she sighs. "I really am."

We take a seat and unwrap our sandwiches in silence. I don't mind that it's a little bit awkward, just so long as she's close. I get a faint whiff of roses, and I feel the muscles in my jaw unlock. Lucy is just what I needed today. She's who I've needed these last weeks. She's light and sunny and exactly the opposite of who I thought she was when I first met her.

"Did you see the pictures of Ed and Katherine?" she asks, filling the silence. "They look like they're having the most fantastic time."

I pull out my phone. I don't think I've bothered to look at the photos.

"It's on our group chat," she explains, as if she knows I won't have seen it.

I bring up the pictures. Sunshine. Sand. Smiles. "You're right. They look happy."

As soon as I say the words, I'm aware of how *not* happy I am. I'm not happy at all. The last few weeks, I've just been surviving. Is this my life now? Is this all I'm going to have? A snatched lunch every few weeks with the woman who's meant more to me than anyone I can ever remember? A few precious moments of sunshine before the shadows of the surrounding buildings cast me into darkness again? Is this the price I have to pay to keep the business Ed and I have built afloat?

"I'm going up to Massachusetts this weekend." She pauses, and I realize she's waiting for me to say whether I'm going.

"Oh, yeah. Ed invited me, but I can't make it. It's my mom's birthday, so I'm going back to Pennsylvania."

"Isn't it strange how you came from one side of New York, and I came from the other, and here's where we ended up?"

"New York takes us all in," I say. "Gives us all second chances. A chance to reinvent ourselves."

She sighs. "Wow, I like that. A chance to reinvent ourselves. Yes."

I watch her as she's focused on the city to my left. The skin on her cheeks looks so smooth, I long to reach out and run my knuckles down her face. She lifts her sunglasses up and sets them on top of her head. "I did that the first time for sure. I moved away, and for the first time in my life, I wasn't living in Katherine's shadow. I came here as a paralegal. No one back in Boston would ever have thought I would end up as a paralegal. Katherine was the smart one. The organized one. But you know what?"

I'm rapt. I want to hear it. "What?"

"I'm a great paralegal. And you know what else?"

"Tell me." I love the way the bridge of her nose wrinkles a little when she's talking passionately. She's so expressive. Her heart is out there, showing everyone who she is.

"I'm smart. And organized. And I'm a good sister. A good daughter. I'm just not Katherine, and I'm never going to be Katherine, and I'm okay with that."

"I'm okay with that too," I say.

She laughs. "I'm probably not making much sense. And I'm not looking for you to agree—"

"But I do agree." I miss her so much. I want to pull her into my lap and bury my face in her neck. I know holding her will make me feel better. "You're a good person, Lucy. And of course you're smart and organized and all those other good things. I've never doubted it."

As we stare at each other, both of us grin. I'm not sure what we're smiling about. The New York summer? The sandwiches? The happiness that comes from being in each other's company? I know that since I moved to New York, I haven't been happier than I am when I'm with Lucy.

"How are you?" she asks, her voice tinged with concern. "Are you taking care of yourself?"

"Things are going well," I reply and take another bite of sandwich to avoid getting into the nitty-gritty. I don't need to hear about how I should be sleeping more or taking better care of myself. What's important is the business is doing well. Clients are happy. Employees are productive. That's what's important.

Doesn't mean I don't miss her.

She smiles at me, watching me chew. "Tell me."

I finish my bite, and Lucy seems happy to wait in silence. She shoots me a look like she knows I'm trying to avoid talking and she's not going to let me get away with it. Our eyes lock as we both chew, and I chuckle at the ridiculousness of the situation.

Eventually, what seems like an hour and a half later, I swallow. I take a swig of my drink, but Lucy is already taking another bite. She's not going to fill this silence for me.

She always was the most stubborn woman.

"The business is going well," I say. "Our revenues are up ten percent year on year. I've got a pitch for a new client coming up this week. I'm all prepped for it. I've kind of honed those things now. Plus we have a track record that makes things easier."

"That's great," she says, finally breaking her silence. "Sounds like you haven't missed Ed at all. I always believed in you."

Her words hang on my shoulders, heavy and unmoving.

She always believed in me? Of course she did. How could I have doubted it?

"I've tried not to disturb him on his honeymoon," I say. The fact is, I haven't needed to disturb him. We work closely together. I usually know what's going on in his office and vice versa. There have been no surprises. Nothing crawling out of the woodwork that I didn't expect. She nods, urging me to say more. "It's not been as bad . . . like, things didn't collapse when he left."

Her smile doesn't exactly say *I told you so*. It's sympathetic. Caring. I've missed it.

"Maybe we're both learning that how it was doesn't mean it always has to be that way," she says.

It's been two weeks. It's not like Ed has retired. "Maybe," I say. "Anyway, Ed's back on Monday."

"You heard they got an offer accepted on a house?"

"Yeah. So they'll be caught up with that soon," I reply. I just gotta keep on as I'm going. All the plates are spinning in the air. I've proven to myself, if I work hard enough, I can keep them spinning. I don't want to give them an opportunity to drop. I can't afford to take my eye off anything.

"Life is moving on," Lucy says on a sigh.

I'm not sure life *is* moving on. Not for me, anyway. I feel like I'm on a treadmill and I'm having to run faster and faster just to stay in the same spot. Ed's life is moving on. Katherine with him. Even Lucy's moving on. I won't get to see her as she blooms. Now she's gained a little confidence, there'll be no stopping her, but I won't be there to witness it. The thought slices through me like a broken shard of glass. Everyone's moving on. But I'm still in this one spot. Stuck.

CHAPTER THIRTY-ONE

Lucy

I actually wish there were *more* lighthouses on the wallpaper in my old childhood bedroom. The repeat on the pattern means there are only three versions. Three lighthouses is just not enough in a room this size. It's the way to madness. I hate it.

I hate everything at the moment. I hate being here at Mom and Dad's, but for the first time ever, I also hate being in New York. I hate half hoping, half worrying that I'm going to run into Hunter. I hate being without him. I hate that I'm missing him.

I usually unpack my bag when I arrive. Mom usually insists. But not today. I'm only staying overnight. I want to see my sister and *ooh* and *ahh* over her honeymoon photos. I want to hug her, then I want to be here for her when she tells Mom she and Ed are moving. Then after lunch tomorrow, I'm going right back to New York. I've brought my LSAT study book with me so I can go through it on the plane. I need to reprioritize. Put myself first. I want to pass this exam.

There's a timid knock on my door, and I know it's Katherine. She comes in, grinning, and without saying anything, we pull each other into the biggest hug. It hasn't been long since I saw her, but it feels like forever.

"I'm so nervous," she whispers.

"You're doing this for all the right reasons," I say. "This is the best decision for you and Ed."

"Mom's not going to see it like that."

I nod. There's no denying it. Katherine is the golden child. I can't imagine moving away is going to change that, but Mom's not going to be happy.

"Are you going to tell her right away? Or leave it until you're about to go home?"

Katherine bites the inside of her cheek. "I don't know. Ed wants to get it over with. We just accepted an offer on our house. Someone came yesterday to see the place. We still had suitcases laid out in the laundry room, but they loved it and want to move as soon as possible. They want to close in thirty days."

My eyes go wide. "Wow. Will the Somerville place be ready by then?"

"Yeah. It's ready as soon as we're ready."

"I can't wait for you to be on that side of the city. You know I'm going to be staying with you when I come into town. It will get me away from this god-awful wallpaper!"

Katherine gasps. "You don't love these lighthouses? I was thinking about putting the exact same paper up in the guest bedroom."

I narrow my eyes at her. "Liar."

"You can help choose everything that's going into the guest bedroom. I want you and Hunter to feel really comfortable in there."

My heart twinges when she mentions Hunter, but I don't say anything. Hunter and I have agreed not to make any big announcements about our relationship to Katherine and Ed. I hope things will feel a little better when our split is out in the open. Maybe it's the lies that are taking up all the space in my chest and making my heart feel like it's pushed into my ribs. I'm hoping then I'll be able to sleep better, and I won't constantly wonder what Hunter is doing, how he's feeling, whether he's thinking about me.

"Because you're going to be coming up to see your nieces and nephews every other weekend, right? I'm counting on you babysitting. A lot."

"I'd love to help you decorate. I bet Mom will too. When she's had a chance to get used to the idea of you moving."

Katherine squeals. "No way am I letting her help. I'll end up with wallpaper like this."

"Come on," I say, scooping up her hand. "Ed's right. You need to bite the bullet and get this over with."

Katherine pulls in a long breath and we head downstairs.

"What are you two giggling about?" Mom says as we enter the sunny kitchen.

"Mom, we don't giggle. We are fully grown adults," I say.

"You were giggling. Your father and Ed are outside. Help me carry this tray, Lucy. If you had come this morning, I would have made us lunch. As it is, there are some snacks in the yard."

"I was busy this morning," I say.

"Busy!" she says as if it's the most ludicrous thing she's ever heard. "Have children and then tell me you're busy."

"So we have some news!" Ed says as the three of us enter the patio area. "Don't we, Katherine?"

"Sure." Katherine picks up her iced tea and takes a sip.

My mother's eyes light up, and I realize she thinks Katherine is going to tell them she's pregnant. "News?"

Katherine looks nervously at Ed.

"We've sold the house," Ed says.

Mom looks confused.

"I didn't know it was for sale," Dad says. "Looking for a place with more bedrooms?"

"Not exactly," Ed says.

Mom keeps looking at Katherine. Her gaze flits to her stomach and then back to Ed and then to Katherine. "Where are you moving?"

"Closer to town," Katherine says and swallows audibly.

"I want a shorter commute," Ed says. "Especially if we're lucky enough to have children. I want to be able to put them to bed."

"You're moving away from Duxbury?" Mom snaps. "Where are you going?"

"Somerville," Ed says. Ed's always the most relaxed guy in the room, but even he looks a little nervous right now.

"Somerville?" Mom screams. "Why on earth would you want to move there? That's forty minutes to an hour from here."

"It puts me a lot closer to the office. I could walk to work if I wanted. And we're closer to the airport. I need to be in New York a lot, as you know. It makes sense for us as a family."

My mom puts her hand on her chest dramatically, as if only her hand is holding her heart inside her body. "But it doesn't make sense for *us* as a family. When am I going to see my grandchildren?"

"You're not going to be far away, Mom," Katherine says.

She huffs. "But I'm not going to be around the corner either. Am I? I'm not going to be able to pop in whenever I like. I won't be able to come around with a pie or groceries when you're too exhausted to do anything. You're going to need the help. And what about as your father and I get older?"

"We're not going to be that far away," Ed repeats as my dad pats my mom on the leg, trying to get her to calm down.

"Do you hear this, Jerry? They're moving."

"I heard them," Dad says. "They have to do what makes sense for them."

"But it doesn't make sense to raise children close to the city. You'll have less green space. You'll be caught up in all the traffic."

"You'll love the place," Ed says, cutting off Mom's objections. "It's an old-fashioned Cape Cod with a big backyard. It's perfect for kids."

Mom turns to Katherine. "And this is what you want? Or is Ed pushing you into it?"

"Mom!" I say.

"I'm sorry, Mom," Katherine says. "This is what *we* want. It's a beautiful house, and Ed works so hard. He wants to be a hands-on father, and that's hard with his job. This makes it easier."

We, we, we. Katherine's a *we* with Ed now. She and I used to be a *we*. Maybe we still are. But I can't help thinking that I need my own partner to be the other half of my *we*. My mind is still so full of Hunter. I can't think about it being anyone but him.

"So you just expect us to drive across the city every day when you have children?" Mom says. "It's selfish, Katherine. That's what this is. Pure selfishness."

But it's not selfish. It's just not what Mom wants. She's the one being selfish. She's only seeing this from her perspective. But it's not her life. It's Katherine and Ed's life. I've never seen my mother's self-serving behavior so clearly. Her love is entirely conditional upon Katherine and me doing what she wants. Katherine has always been happy to go along with Mom's demands. She went to the college Mom wanted her to go to, became a teacher because Mom thought it was a good idea. Now, for the first time ever, Katherine is doing something Mom doesn't approve of. I've never seen it so starkly. I was always the black sheep of the family because I wasn't playing Mom's game. I moved to New York City, away from her interference. She had less power over me there. And she didn't like it. So she made me feel bad.

Thank God I moved. She's still had more control over me than she should have. She was always *there*, even when she wasn't. The mirror in the hallway, the bowl on my coffee table, the voice in my head telling me I wasn't good enough.

It's so clear to me.

"What about your job?" Mom says, her voice trembling.

"I'll have a commute this semester while I look for something a little closer to where we live. But it's not that far."

"I suppose you'll be pregnant by then. You can resign."

"I'm not going to resign if I get pregnant. I want to work. It's another reason we want to go to the city. There are more opportunities.

I want our kids to be surrounded by more of the world," Katherine says. "I want them to wake up and be surrounded by possibility."

Mom rolls her eyes. "You'll be back, mark my words. You'll need our help and you'll be back."

Except I don't think they will move back. Katherine's married now, and she has a life outside my parents. Outside Mom. She's tasted freedom. There will be no going back now.

There's a sudden burst of energy within me. I haven't lived here for years now, but Mom's been right on my shoulder everywhere I go. I've been trapped, worried I'm not good enough, for what? For whom? A mother who's trying to control her daughters by withdrawing her approval when they want different things from her.

It's as if a thousand strings have snapped all at once. Now that I can see it, I'm finally free. I'm only going to get my mom's approval when I'm doing what she wants.

Well, I want different things than she does. I want more for myself than she believes I can have.

"I'm studying for my LSAT," I announce. I want to take the pressure off Katherine. She's not used to Mom's disapproval like I am. I can handle it. I've had plenty of practice.

"What?" Mom hisses.

"That's great," Ed says. Katherine beams at me.

"I'm going to sit for the LSAT," I say. "And if I get a good score, I might go to law school." I take a strawberry off the pile of fruit in the middle of the table and sink my teeth into it. It's the sweetest strawberry I've ever tasted.

"Law school? Where are you going to get the money for law school?" Mom asks.

I figure they've given Katherine about fifty thousand dollars if you take into account the contribution to the wedding and the honeymoon. And they don't know that my law firm is offering to sponsor me.

"I'll figure it out," I say. I don't need to explain myself to my mom anymore. I don't need to justify it. If I'd announced this a couple of months ago, I would have felt sick to my stomach that I didn't have their support. But now, I accept it. And I'll do what I want.

"Figure it out?" Mom asks. "How do you think you'll just figure it out? Don't think your father and I are going to be cosigning anything. We have to think of our retirement."

"I'm not expecting anything more than I'd usually get from you, Mom." Finally, I've realized, it doesn't matter what I do or how hard I try to be better for my mom, it's never going to be enough. She's never going to stop wanting more from me. Nothing's ever going to make her happy as far as I'm concerned.

"Well, what does that mean?" she asks snippily.

"It means that I'm done hoping for more, Mom. I'm through with trying to do better so you'll be nicer to me, so you'll stop with the criticisms and the put-downs. I get it. You're always going to think I'm not good enough."

"Don't be ridiculous. I don't know what you mean, I'm—"

"There's no point in pretending it's not happening, Mom. And you know what? You're never going to change, and that's fine. I accept it. But I'm going to do things differently from here on out. I'm going to want better for myself. And maybe I'm going to stay with Katherine and Ed when I come to Boston." If nothing else it will mean I don't have to put up with the stupid lighthouse wallpaper. "And honestly, I think I'll stay at the Harbor Inn tonight."

"The Harbor Inn?" Mom's voice is bordering on a shriek. "What on earth do you mean, you'll stay at the Harbor Inn?" For a second, I think Mom's actually upset at the idea of losing me. And then she says, "Janine might be working. Whatever will she think?"

It doesn't surprise me that my mother is more concerned about what her hairdresser—who does a couple of shifts on reception at the Harbor Inn—will think than the fact that her daughter doesn't want to stay under her roof. I wish I was less disappointed. Maybe there will always be a part of me that wants my mom's approval, but it's never been clearer to me that I won't get it.

I head up to my old bedroom and grab my suitcase. At least I didn't unpack.

There's a quiet knock at the door. I look up and my dad pokes his head in. "Come on, now," he says. "There's no need for you to go anywhere."

I sigh and set my case onto its wheels. "Actually, Dad, I think there is. I'm miserable when I'm around her."

"She's not that bad," he says, his forehead furrowed and his eyes sad.

"Not to you, maybe. I'm done being her punching bag. What mother reacts to their daughter wanting to go to law school like that?"

"You know she doesn't like change. That's all this is. When she's had a chance to think about it, I'm sure she'll come around. You know how she is—she's just worried about money."

I huff out a laugh. "Not so worried that you didn't spend a fortune on Katherine's wedding. And the gift."

Dad has the good sense to look embarrassed.

"I'm not prepared to do this dance we do anymore, Dad. I love you. But honestly, you've watched this for years and you've never said anything. You've never defended me or told her to tone it down. I'm done."

Then I pick up my bag, press a kiss to his cheek, and leave.

CHAPTER THIRTY-TWO

Hunter

I drop my overnight bag at the bottom of the stairs and go into the kitchen to say goodbye to my mom. Her birthday lunch yesterday with my aunt and uncle and two of her closest friends was fine. My dad and I stayed at the opposite ends of the table and avoided any conversation that wasn't about Mom. That's how it is now. That's how it's been since Bain Insurance went bankrupt. Even so, I'm still pleased I made the trip.

"I'm going to head out," I say. "There's stuff I need to catch up with at the office." I'm not going into the office today, but I want to clear out my emails to make sure I'm ready for my early start tomorrow. Ed will be back, and I need to spend a chunk of time on the phone to update him. I need to be ready.

"Thanks for coming, sweetie," Mom says, turning to face me. She holds my hands in hers. "It was lovely to see you. But I'm worried you're working too hard. You look tired."

"I'm fine, Mom," I say.

"Are you?" she asks. "You seem . . . like you're missing out."

Missing out. It's an interesting way of describing what I'm feeling. "Everyone's missing out on something," I say. All I can think about is

Lucy. I'm definitely missing out on seeing her. Missing out on spending our nights curled up together, limbs entangled . . . together. "But owning your own business requires sacrifices. There's no one else to make sure everything is working."

She holds my gaze, and I'm not sure whether she's holding herself back from saying something or she's waiting for me to say more.

"Go talk to your father," she says. "He's outside deadheading my roses. Then come back and say goodbye."

I head out and down the steps of the back porch. Dad has on a baseball hat and Mom's gardening gloves, which are too small for him. "Hey, Dad, I'm just heading back into the city."

"Already?" he asks, focused on the roses. "But this is your mother's birthday weekend."

"I came up for the lunch yesterday, Dad. Her birthday was on Thursday."

"Yes, and this is her birthday weekend." He throws some dead roses in the wheelbarrow and dives back into the bushes with the pruning shears. If I didn't hear him speak, I would have thought he didn't realize I was standing right next to him.

"I have some work to catch up on."

He doesn't say anything.

I haven't brought up the demise of the family firm for a long time now. It's been years. Whenever I've raised the issue in the past, I feel worse afterward, because Dad never takes any responsibility. So what's the point? But something about his tone irritates me. Like he disapproves of me working so hard. Maybe if he'd worked a bit harder, I'd still be working in the family business. I wouldn't be making up for the failure that came so early in my life.

"It takes a lot to run a successful company," I say.

"You don't need to tell me," he replies gruffly. "But you have to prioritize the things that matter."

"Like keeping the business afloat," I say. "That's a priority for me."

"Rightly so. But your mother only has one birthday a year."

"Yes, and I was here for her lunch yesterday. Now I'm going back into town to make sure I have a business that doesn't go bankrupt."

Without saying a word, he shuffles a few feet to his right, away from me, to the next rosebush.

Normally, I'd just turn and walk away, but Mom saying I was missing out has lit a fire in my belly.

I *am* missing out.

And it's because I'm so full of fear.

Fear of repeating my mistakes.

Fear of trusting Ed.

Fear of failing.

"I don't want what happened to you to happen to me." As soon as the words are out of my mouth, I want to scoop them up and put them back in. My heart is racing, and I freeze, wondering whether he'll react or if he even heard me. When I've hinted at the dire financial straits the business was in when I took it over, he always acts like he doesn't know what I'm talking about. But he *does* know. He *has* to know. For years I've tried to excuse his disavowal. I've tried to explain the way he's failed to take accountability.

I'm done.

"What do you mean, son?" he asks, finally standing tall and turning to face me.

"I mean, I don't want Portis to go under like Bain Insurance did."

"Well, I'm sure you've learned your lesson. Out of failure, we build success. I've said that to you before."

He has said it. Many times. Every time I've ever tried to talk to him about the failure of Bain Insurance. Except I'm sick of wearing the failure like I wove the cloth and made the suit. It came off the rack.

"You're right, Dad. I learned a lot from that situation. I learned not to take on a long lease for too much money—like you did. I learned not to keep on staff who were overpaid and underutilized—like you did. I learned that when important decisions are put off, a once-successful business can go downhill—like Bain Insurance did."

He holds my gaze, and I don't look away. My heart is pounding against my rib cage, but I try to keep my breathing steady. This is my chance. If I don't say everything I need to right now, the time will have passed and I never will.

It's now or never.

I don't want to regret not telling him that I know exactly what happened. He should know why our relationship has suffered over these last years. He deserves to hear it, even if he knows it in his heart.

And I deserve to say it.

"I learned that I would never hand a business over to my son when it was racing toward failure, and make him think that failure was his fault."

He looks away and goes back to the roses.

"I guess your reputation as a successful businessman was more important to you than your relationship with your son. I guess it was more important for you to feel like a success than it was to not have me see myself as a failure."

"I don't know what you're talking about. You're not a failure."

"I know," I say. I don't think I've ever believed it until this moment. We've always danced around this subject, and it's allowed me to doubt the reasons for the downfall of Bain Insurance. I've never said it in so many words, that it failed because of him, which has allowed me to think that part of it was my fault. "I tried my best to find a way to sustain it, Dad, but it was dead before I took over."

Dad inhales but doesn't look at me.

"It lost money every month," I continue. "The sales team wasn't bringing in enough to sustain the staffing levels. People weren't renewing."

"The business had its challenges. I'll give you that."

"You'll *give* me that?" I ask. "It's just a fact. You're not *giving* me anything. The business was failing, and had been for some time, but you handed it over and let me take the blame."

He mumbles under his breath and throws more dead roses into the wheelbarrow behind him.

"I'm going back to the city, because when I have a son, I don't want to hand him a business doomed to fail."

Dad sighs and dumps some dead leaves and his shears on top of the pile in the wheelbarrow. "You could have turned that business around."

"Then why didn't you?"

"Life isn't as simple as you make it out to be," he says. "There are no guarantees in business."

I huff out a laugh. "You're right. No guarantees. Except if your costs exceed your revenue, you're losing money. That's a guarantee."

"What do you want from me?" he says. "You're back in the game. A little failure is good for you."

I nod slowly. Nothing good will come from this conversation. He knows what he did. He just doesn't want to say the words out loud. He doesn't want to be the monster that would hand his son a failing business and let him take the blame. No one wants to believe they're a monster. He's made excuses for himself so he can be a hero instead.

"I know what you did, Dad. I know who you are. And that's not the man I want to be. Live with that."

I don't wait for a response. I turn and head back inside for a final goodbye to my mom. I don't look back. I'm leaving my past in the yard, like the dead heads of the roses piled high in the wheelbarrow. I'm done waiting for answers I'm never going to get. I'm done wanting to know why my father would set me up for a fall.

I'm done living my life in the shadow of someone else's failure.

CHAPTER THIRTY-THREE

Hunter

The last place I expected to be on a Monday morning was Boston. But here I am. I need to be here today. I want to see Ed through the fresh eyes I've been able to view the world with since visiting my parents and speaking to my father. Having my father try to dismiss what happened to my face rewrote the ending on every last story I've told myself about how I'd been responsible for the failure of our family business. Even though I knew my father handed me a business that couldn't survive, I couldn't lay the blame fully at his feet.

Not until I watched him try to so blatantly shirk any responsibility.

"Hunter?" Ed stands when he sees me walk into his office. "I was just about to call you. What are you doing here?"

I smile at my friend and business partner. It's really good to see him. "What can I say? I missed you!" I pull him in for a hug. "Nice tan, buddy."

"Belize, man. It was fantastic."

"Yeah?" I say. "Tell me all about it." Normally, I'd be down to business immediately, but my best friend just got back from his honeymoon, and I want to hear all the details.

"Wanna catch me up on what's been going on in the office?"

I shrug. "That will wait. Let's go grab a coffee, and you can tell me about Belize."

Ed grins like I just handed him a cheesecake and a fork. "I could use a coffee. I've been in the office since five."

I laugh at his early arrival in the office. How could I have been worried that Ed was going to slack off? He's just as much of a workaholic as I am. We're cut from the same cloth. He knew that when he suggested we go into business together. I've known it deep down from the start. I just didn't trust that knowledge. My self-doubt has clouded my vision for too long. But I'm free now. Free to trust Ed. Free to trust myself. Free to let go a little. It may take some practice. My training wheels—my long-held beliefs about myself—have come off, but I'm still wobbly. But I know the more I live in this new reality, the easier it will become. My father's fantasy of me being the son who failed his family is just that. A fantasy. He's a father who failed his son.

I don't know if I'll ever be okay with what my father did. But the knowledge is more good than bad. I'm more positive and invigorated about the future of my relationship with Ed, and about our business, than I ever have been. I just need to be open with him today. That's why I'm here.

We head out into the crisp Boston morning, looking for coffee.

"How was the food?" I ask.

"Incredible. And the beaches? Two weeks away is like . . . medicine or something. I feel like a new man. I'm so pumped about this quarter. And now with the move, I'm going to make it in earlier." He's full of energy. Full of life.

"I was thinking about your idea for recruiting more staff," I say. "You're right, our quarter is showing huge growth again. And we need more hands on deck if we're going to be able to keep growing at this rate. Let's get ahead of it and not wait until we're creaking at the seams to bring in more people."

"Exactly!" Ed says. "That's what I was thinking. Let's recruit in advance and be ready for our next phase of growth."

He pauses, then looks at me carefully before he opens the door of the coffee shop. "Are you okay? You seem . . ."

"Let's get coffee." Once we do, I suggest we take a seat rather than walk back to the office right away. "I went to see my parents this weekend," I say as we sit.

"You don't go back very much, do you?"

"It's been awkward for a long time now. I feel all this resentment toward my dad for what happened with Bain because we've never spoken about it openly. You know he's never acknowledged what happened or the fact the business was dying when he handed it over to me."

A look of disappointment crosses Ed's face. Not long ago, I would have interpreted his expression as disappointment in me, but now I recognize he's disappointed *for* me. Disappointed that I had a father who would do that to me.

"This weekend . . . something changed. I couldn't not say something."

Ed's eyebrows lift practically to his hairline, and he shifts forward in his chair. "You confronted him?"

I nod. "I did. I told him I knew what he did."

"What did he say? Did he admit it?"

I pull in a breath. "No. He got defensive. Told me failure was 'the making of me.' But no, he didn't take responsibility."

Ed shakes his head. "God, I'm sorry, man."

"Don't be," I say. "I feel like I've been carrying around a sack of rocks, and telling my dad what I knew and who I knew him to be . . . It's like I set that sack down. I feel lighter. I feel like this is fresh start. I know it's not. We're in the middle of a business relationship, and Portis is far from new, but . . . I feel different. I want a chance to start again."

"What do you mean start again? You're not leaving, are you?" Panic flickers in Ed's eyes.

I shake my head to reassure him. "Absolutely not. But I want to do things differently. I feel like I *can* finally do things differently. The first thing I want to do is apologize to you."

"Me?" Ed says. "You've got nothing to apologize to me for."

"I do," I reply. "I haven't trusted you. I've thought the worst of you. I've almost been expecting you to make a mistake, or to let me down. You've never given me any reason to doubt you, but that's what I've done. I've doubted you and you didn't deserve it." Saying it makes me realize how true it's been. I haven't trusted Ed. I've been waiting for him to fail. When your own father lets you down, you expect the rest of the world to as well.

"I don't know what to say," Ed says.

"There's nothing you need to say. I'm sorry. I want to tell you that I do trust you. With my life."

Ed nods. "That's how I feel about you. That's why I asked you to go into business with me. I knew I could trust you with my life."

I take a sip of coffee, trying to swallow down the lump in my throat.

"You can trust me," I say. "I want to embrace our partnership. I trust it—trust us." It's not just Ed I've put my faith in. After this weekend, I finally trust myself too.

We smile at each other, and Ed nods. "It's really good to see you," he says. "Katherine's going to be excited too."

I wince. "Actually, I'm booked on a flight back to New York this afternoon. I have some stuff to do in the city."

"*Stuff?* That sounds ominous."

"Yeah. I got pretty stressed when you went on your honeymoon." I didn't see my stress for what it was until the conversation with my father. I didn't see that it wasn't Ed I didn't trust. It was myself. "I don't think I trusted that I could run the business for two weeks without you so I . . . I pushed Lucy away." My heart aches at the thought of hurting Lucy. I've taken my self-doubt out on those who mean the most to me. Ed. Lucy. Neither of them have deserved the way I treated them.

"Ahh," Ed says sagely.

"Ahh?"

"Well, I can't say I'm surprised. You're going to try and get her back?"

"I don't know if she'll have me."

"The Jones sisters are pretty stubborn," Ed says.

I know that about Lucy. She's so strong and resilient. It's part of what makes me . . . *love* her.

I exhale at the realization of how strong my feelings really are.

"How long had you and Katherine been dating before you knew it was serious?" I ask. Lucy and I haven't really been dating at all, but I know I can't walk away from her. Maybe the thought of losing her was what gave me the courage to say what I needed to say to my dad. I knew if I kept going the way I had been, I'd never be able to be with her. I thought I had to give everything I had to the job.

A grin unfurls on Ed's face. "Pretty early. Like maybe even our first date. I knew she wasn't just some girl I just wanted to take home once and never see again. She was so kind and so fucking sweet. I could imagine what our lives would be like. I had this super clear vision of how it would be in our future."

I nod. I can see my future with Lucy. We'll live in New York our entire lives. There'll be no moving out to the suburbs. We'll get brunch every Sunday and meet for lunch every weekday. She'll kick ass at law school and be a baller at a white-shoe firm. We'll double date whenever Ed and Katherine are in town, and we'll argue about whether Katherine is perfect. I'll tell her that it's always been Lucy who's perfect. For me. She'll lift me up when I doubt myself, and I'll try to do the same for her. And eventually, she'll look stunning pregnant, in a white dress, standing underneath the AC, wondering whether we should move to Boston. I'll know she won't mean it, but I'll tell her we can move if that's what she wants—because I'd follow her anywhere.

"Yeah," I say. "I see it too."

I just hope she does.

CHAPTER THIRTY-FOUR

HUNTER

I've been standing outside Stranger than Fiction since eleven forty-five. Normally, Lucy gets her lunch around twelve thirty. But it's nearly two now, and she definitely hasn't left her building. I'm really tempted to grab her some lunch and take it up to her building, but I don't want to get her in trouble. That's the last thing I want to do. I want to make things better between us. Not worse.

And then I spot her. She's wearing that navy dress I last saw her in, but her hair is down. Her hair is never down for work. I stand at the edge of the plaza, watching as she crosses the street and heads toward me.

When she's about fifteen yards away, she spots me. She smiles, then draws her eyebrows together, like she doesn't know why I'm standing in the middle of the street watching her.

It probably looks a little creepy.

She has to pass me to get to the sandwich place, so I don't take my eyes off her as she comes toward me. Her gaze darts between me and whatever is going on around me. She slows as she approaches me.

"Hey," I say. "You look . . . hungry." I was going to start with "beautiful," but I don't want this to be confusing for her. Although telling her she looks hungry probably wasn't the best start.

"Yeah, I'm going to get some lunch."

I hold up the paper bag with the sandwich in it. "I got you lunch. It's the special. I thought we could try it together." Her gaze slides from me to what I'm holding up and then back again.

"How long have you been out here?"

"Oh, I only got this fifteen minutes ago." I'd called my assistant down and gotten them to go get another lunch for us both. I didn't want to take my eyes off Lucy's building. I couldn't risk missing her. My assistant thought I'd gone completely nuts. Just getting me out of the building for ten minutes would usually be almost impossible. I'd been standing out here for two hours. But it's worth it.

"Okay," Lucy says suspiciously. "Thanks. I think."

"Want to eat together?" I ask. It occurs to me that Lucy's late for lunch because she's busy and she'll need to get back immediately. If that's the case, I'll have to wait. She's worth it, even if every minute without her feels like a month.

She looks around at the tables. "Sure. I'm trying to only have a thirty-minute lunch break so I can spend the other thirty minutes studying."

"Studying?" I ask. "The LSAT?" I let her lead the way to an empty table.

"Yeah," she says as she sits down. "I'm at least going to try."

"Right," I say. "You have to try. Because if you don't, you'll never know if you could have had something."

She frowns and looks at me like I've lost my mind.

I empty the brown bag onto the table. "'I am half agony, half hope,'" I mumble to myself.

"What was that?" she asks with a smile. "Did you just quote Jane Austen at me?"

"Might have," I say. "There was a big Jane Austen display at the airport bookstore yesterday. I remember you saying *Persuasion* was your favorite. I picked it up. And then there was no internet on the plane on the way back to New York."

"Where did you go?"

"Boston. Back to the beginning."

"Back to the beginning?"

"I needed to say a few things to Ed," I say. "Things that needed to be said face-to-face."

She takes a bite of her sandwich and watches me as she chews, waiting for more information.

"I wanted to apologize to him. I haven't been the best business partner."

Lucy nods like she knows what I'm saying is the truth.

"Because of what happened with me and my dad." It's good to say it out loud. Like saying it dilutes the feelings.

She swallows. "You were worried Ed was going to abandon you, betray you, like your father did."

I nod. Of course, she's always known. Lucy knows me better than anyone ever has. "One of the lines from the book really stuck with me. I mean, a lot stuck with me, but when Anne is talking to Captain Harville—"

"When Wentworth is writing Anne the letter?"

"Yeah, she says, 'If the change be not from outward circumstances, it must be from within.' It stuck with me. Not because of what he's saying about Benwick, but because it finally made me see that my dad's never going to admit what he did. I just need to accept that and know within myself what happened. Trust myself that I know the truth."

She breaks into a grin. "That's my favorite scene of any Austen book."

"Wentworth is half crazy, needing to know if Anne has given up on him," I say, wondering whether Lucy will give me a sign. "We find out what we've always suspected—that he never stopped loving her."

Our gazes meet, so much unsaid.

"My mom's not wrong about Austen," she says, shaking her head. "Just most other things."

"We both have . . ." I can't imagine how Lucy turned out like she did, given her mother. "Things we are letting go of. Things inside we've had to shift and change."

"I think you're right, Hunter Bain."

"I pulled away from you, and I'm sorry," I say. "I was scared. I didn't think I could have a successful business and . . . and you. The woman I love. I didn't think I deserved it."

She's holding the sandwich at her mouth, but doesn't take a bite. Then she lowers it and sets it back on the paper wrapping. "What was that you said?"

I hold her gaze and swallow. I've said it now. There's no taking it back. "I said I love you. I've always loved you. But I understand if you can't forgive me for pushing you away . . ."

I can't interpret her expression. I'm not sure if she's about to laugh in my face or jump into my arms.

"Huh," she says, sitting back in her chair. "Not what I had on my bingo card for today."

Okay, so maybe she's not laughing *or* jumping.

"I get this is a bit . . . unexpected, maybe . . ."

"Why would you think that? The fact that you called me a demonic witch when we first met? Or maybe it's the part where you dumped me two weeks ago, just as I realized that *I* love *you*?"

The metal of my chair scrapes as I shift my seat so I can lean closer to Lucy. "I was a dick. Running scared. Running from failure, from my father, from my future. But I'm done running. I want to live in the present. With you."

Lucy breaks my gaze and glances down at her lap.

"If you love me, Lucy, and I love you, then . . ."

"Then the stakes just got really high," she says. "You showing up in the plaza with a chicken Caesar on whole grain doesn't mean we just sail off into the sunset. What happens if something happens and you want to run again? What happens if business is bad for a year or two? I can't . . . my heart . . . I won't survive it." She looks up into my eyes with such fragility, such vulnerability, that my heart surges in my chest. I don't want to be the man causing her pain. I want to be the man who's making it better. I want to be her shield against the bad things in this world.

"You won't have to survive it," I say softly. "I'm never going to run from you."

"How can you be sure?" She shakes her head like the entire idea is futile and she's given up already.

But I won't let her give up.

"I'll prove it to you."

"That's impossible," she says. "How could you ever prove to me that you'll never leave me? You got scared and you ran. But times will get tough at some point, and you'll get scared again. I don't want to be worried all the time that you're going to bolt."

"You're right. There will be times when things get difficult. But what I've learned since we've been apart is I don't want anything more than I want you."

Her expression is full of hope and tenderness.

"This isn't a book, Lucy. This is the real world. My entire life changed when you walked into it. I've been struggling with the failure of Bain Insurance since it happened. I've been willing my dad to take responsibility, to apologize—something. I've wanted him to do literally anything to tell me it wasn't my fault. Guess what?" She searches my face. "It's never going to happen. I've been circling the runway, in a holding pattern, waiting for someone to tell me to land. Meanwhile, I'm running outta fuel. I was five seconds away from blowing things up with Ed. I already blew stuff up with you. And I don't know if it's losing something I knew was good—because what we had was so, so good—but I finally realized I would lose *everything* good in my life if I didn't make a change within. I looked my dad in the eye, and I told him what I knew. That he gave me a failing business. That he tanked Bain Insurance and left me to take the blame. I told him I don't want to be the father he was." I exhale, sitting back in my chair. "And that's what it took to change something within me. I've broken out of the holding pattern. I've landed. I have clarity and I know what I want." I lift her chin. "'I have loved none but you.' From the moment I saw you and forever. There will be no one for me but you."

She narrows her eyes. "From the moment you saw me? I'm pretty sure that's not true."

"You're wrong. I just didn't realize it at the beginning. I thought you were a pain in my ass, just like I thought Ed was slacking off. Neither could be further from the truth, but the lens I'd been viewing the world through was muddy. Not anymore."

She sighs, and I try to think what else I can do to convince her. "There's no certainty. Life's about chances," I say. "What was that thing you said to me about foolish preparation?" I ask.

A smile spreads across her face. "'How often is happiness destroyed by preparation, foolish preparation!'"

"Right. Maybe you don't need to overthink this."

Her breath hitches in her chest and she exhales shakily. "We were only a few weeks in and . . ."

"I don't know about you, but it hurt like hell, losing you only a few weeks in. I get it. I feel exactly the same. I want you back and I won't let you go again. How can you be sure? Nothing's ever sure. But you'll never know if you don't take a chance."

"I've committed to the scholarship program," she says. "I might not get it, but if I do, I can't turn it down . . ."

"I don't want you to turn it down. What the hell, Lucy? You going to law school would be incredible. You deserve to do that. You're more than worth it."

"But it won't leave much time—"

"You think *I'm* going to have much time? I told you I don't think Ed's about to drop me in it, not that I'm retiring. I'm always going to work hard. It's who I am. But I'm driven by a desire to succeed now. Not by a fear of failure."

"So you wouldn't get grumpy if I'm in bed, studying for my LSAT or the bar exam or something?"

"Grumpy? No. Especially if you wear a really stern, serious look on your face, and maybe wear some glasses."

She rolls her eyes. "Pervert."

"You can't have everything. I can't promise that I'm not going to want to get you naked every minute of the day. And that's probably going to last forever. So if that's a deal-breaker for you . . ." I hold up my hands in mock surrender.

"Three days a month I'm unbearable. Like, I'm a hormonal monster."

"Only three days a month?"

She grins. "I'm serious. It might be too much for you."

"You're entirely too good for me, but never too much. You're a perfect amount. For me."

She bites back a smile, but she looks nervous. "I've spent my entire life a little bit broken. Mom chipping away bit by bit . . . But I've never felt so breakable as I did when you said you wanted to take a step back. I can't do that again." She reaches for me.

"I promise you won't have to." I cup her face in my hands and bring my forehead to hers. "I'm going to keep you safe for the rest of our lives."

"Forever?"

"Longer, if possible." I press a small kiss against her lips.

"Wentworth was always my favorite Austen hero." She exhales, and the tightness leaves her body. We're joined. Connected. Back together, forever.

CHAPTER THIRTY-FIVE

Lucy

Hunter turning up and declaring his undying love for me wasn't what I was expecting this sunny New York day. But it was exactly what I needed. I thought handsome men making grand declarations of love was the kind of thing that only ever happened to women like my sister or in the novels of Jane Austen. Up until recently I've felt like a supporting character in everyone else's life. Today, Hunter made me feel like a leading lady. The heroine of my own story.

Hunter explaining how his perceptions of the world have shifted rang true for me too. His honesty, his vulnerability, the pain I saw in him when he talked about his father. Hunter is no longer running. And that's what it took for me to believe everything that Hunter was saying about loving me was true. Maybe that's also what it took for me to accept my own feelings about him. All I know is that Hunter collapsed every single one of my defenses today, but I've never felt so safe. So loved.

He believes in me when I don't have enough faith for myself. And I know he's going to be brilliant even when he doubts himself. We understand and accept each other's flaws and are better because of them.

We're far from perfect, but we fit together like each one of us doesn't quite work without the other.

I've met the love of my life. And he loves me back. I'm not sure life gets better than that. It's more than I could have ever hoped for myself.

The thing about New York is that even when you reconcile with the love of your life during your lunch hour, capitalism still calls. Five minutes after Hunter told me he wanted to be with me forever, I headed back to my desk and he to his.

In buildings next door to each other.

I tried to leave on time, but a last-minute motion in a live trial meant I had to work late.

I finally buzz up to Hunter's apartment, exhausted from what feels like the longest day ever.

"I don't want to live in Brooklyn," he says as he opens the door.

A surge of energy moves through me. It's so good to see him. So good to know we're moving forward and not taking steps back. Now is the beginning of our shared life together. The path to get here has been difficult and treacherous. But somehow, looking at Hunter, I know everything's going to be a little easier now. "I want you to move in."

"Move in?" I say, wondering whether I misheard him. "When?" Presumably he means eventually, when we get to that point in our relationship. Or maybe he doesn't. Maybe he feels this sense that I have, that everything finally fits. Everything works. Everything's finally in place now.

"We could go back to your place now and get some stuff if you want to."

"Are you insane?" I laugh at him. He's moving at warp speed. We've only been back together since lunchtime, but Hunter's impatient. "It's nearly nine at night."

"Okay, so maybe not tonight. But there's no point in delaying things. Why would we not live together? We both work incredibly demanding jobs. We should make the most of the time we're not in the office."

I smile up at him. I'm barely across the threshold, and he's got all these ideas for the two of us. I get it. We know what our future holds. Why wait? I close the door behind me, and he pulls me into his arms. "With that logic, you'd have us getting married a week from Tuesday."

"Fine with me," he says like it's no big deal. Maybe it isn't. All the big decisions have been made. We're better together than apart. We'll love each other forever. We'll care for each other until the day we die. What's left but to get married? I watch him as he talks animatedly about which parts of the apartment could be changed or remodeled.

"Maybe we should just move. We could get something a bit closer to work. And the park. Portis is making more money now. We could get something nice. Bigger." He drops a peck on my lips, and I push my hands into his hair.

He closes his eyes in a long blink, and his entire body relaxes. "My mind is working overtime."

I laugh. "I can tell."

"It's good to have you here," he says, pressing a kiss to my neck.

"It's good to be here," I reply. Wherever he is, feels like home. As we hold each other, I realize I've never felt this . . . at peace with someone. Hunter is so solid. So warm. He's always been this rock of a man. And now he feels like mine. "God, I really love you."

He grins at me. "You say that like you're surprised."

"I think I am a little," I say honestly. "I'm not sure I ever thought I'd meet someone I felt so sure about. It feels as if I've been waiting for you and now you're here."

"That's because there have been too many people in your life that you should be sure of but you weren't. But that's changed now." His grin widens. "You can be sure of me."

"I am," I say. "And you can be sure of me."

He nods, slowly, an expression of lust unfurling on his face. His hands snake up my back and find the top of my zipper. He pulls it down and off my shoulders until it pools at my feet. I don't have matching underwear on, and I don't care. I know Hunter isn't focused on my underwear.

I reach for his belt, and he groans before pulling my hands away. He lifts me up and over his shoulder and marches us into the bedroom. My ass is in the air and there's nothing I can do about it. He launches me onto the bed and crawls over me. I can't help it, I'm wet already. Probably since before I rang his buzzer. Probably since lunchtime.

"I've missed you so much," he says, pressing kisses between my breasts. "So much."

I sigh, content to let him explore me. I love how reverent he is with my body. How he treats me like I'm precious. It makes me feel adored. And to be adored by a man like Hunter feels better than anything I could possibly imagine.

I grab at his T-shirt, desperate to feel more of his warm skin against mine.

"So impatient," he says.

"Yes. I want you. I want all of you."

"You have me," he breathes, sitting back on his heels, pulling my ass up onto his lap. "And I have you. Body and soul."

I think he took my soul way before he took my body.

"You have both," he continues, before I can confess that he owns me entirely. "And I've given them willingly. And I want to be with you and marry you and tell the world how I feel, but I can't possibly feel more for you than I do in this moment."

He plunges his fingers into me and I gasp. I'd forgotten how good he feels, how he knows exactly what he needs to do to unlock my bliss.

"Jesus Christ." He sucks in a breath. "You're always so wet."

"I'm always ready for you," I say.

"Even when we're in line for sandwiches?"

I nod. "Anytime I'm anywhere near you."

He grunts and curls his fingers inside me. My back arches and I grip the sheets beside me. My orgasm is just a breath away, but I'm not ready for it. Not yet. I want to feel more of Hunter. I want to feel all of him.

"Please, Hunter," I say. I don't need to explain myself anymore. He tears open a condom packet. He knows what I need. When I manage to focus again, he's over me, naked, gazing into my eyes with pure love.

I open my legs as wide as they will go. Ready for him. Ready for forever. His tip teases at my entrance, and I want to be teased, but not now. Now I just want to feel him. And he knows. We lock eyes and he slams into me with such force, he drives me up the bed.

It's exactly what we both need.

I can barely breathe, I'm so completely full of him. I can't move because I know that the slightest movement will send me over the edge. My clit buzzes with anticipation, crying out to be touched, but I know even a breeze could make me come right now.

"You okay?" he grunts into my ear.

"More than," I say.

"You're so tight, so fucking tight." His voice is strained with the effort of not coming. We're both so tightly wound, so aware that this moment is full of meaning because it's the start of forever.

"I love you," I whisper on an exhale.

His chest heaves between us. "I've always loved you," he says, sliding out, slowly, carefully, like I'm made of glass.

His eyes are molten lava. Full of heat and energy. It's me that's doing that to him. It's my body, my pussy. Me. I reach around to his ass and hit bliss as he pounds into me again. Except this time, he doesn't stop to revel in me. He doesn't stop for anything. It's like he's tripped a switch and can't stop what he's started. But I don't want him to. I want more of him. I want all of him.

My body sheets with goose bumps and sweat at the same time, and my fingers dig into his flesh. The tendons in his neck strain, and I know he's trying not to come, or just trying not to feel some of what's between us.

But it's impossible.

The drag of him between my thighs is the only thing I can think about. My entire body starts to vibrate, and I cry out, a deep guttural noise I've never heard myself make before. Hunter brings out a side in me that I didn't know was there. It's always been the case with him, and I think it always will be. He sees the best in me because he sees the whole of me. And he loves it all.

I lift my hips from the mattress, desperate for him to be as deep into me as possible. He groans as our bodies slam together. I feel him inside me and hear him whisper my name like he can't quite believe this is real.

But it is real and it's forever. I have no doubt about that.

"Fuck, Lucy. I can't hold out much longer."

My hand slides up his chest to cup his jaw. He looks down at me, and our orgasms spiral around us like both are joined as one, lifting us higher and higher, binding us tighter and tighter.

We wrap ourselves around each other as our climax ebbs away, knowing that every time we're physical, it binds us closer.

"You feel so good," he mumbles into my ear.

"I think we needed that," I say as he slides to my side, pulling me to mine.

"I always need you," he says, and I can't help but smile. I can't believe the man I'm lying in bed with right now is the same man I put into an Uber at Ed and Katherine's engagement party all those months ago. He really feels like he's a part of me now.

He gives me no time to catch a breath before his fingers are tracing circles on my skin, bringing my nipples to attention. He bends down to suck, scraping them with his teeth as he moves from one to the other. I want his teeth on me, his mouth. I want his dick inside me. I'm so greedy for him—I want all of him, in all the ways.

He works his way down my body and settles between my legs, lapping at my clit, like he's soothing it, preparing it, getting it ready to explode again. I squirm into the mattress, wanting more but not being able to handle even half of what he's giving me.

He grips the tops of my thighs, holding me in place as he paints me with his tongue, over and over and over. It feels like I'm corkscrewing to another place, one filled with light and heat and Hunter.

All I can feel is Hunter. His hot breath as his tongue works relentlessly through my folds is all I need to have me bucking against his hands. He lays a hand flat on my stomach, pressing, holding me in place until I can't take any more.

I'm not sure if I'm making words as I choke out his name. I grab at him, wanting him closer as I climb toward the peak. With my hands in his hair, his tongue darts into me, and I'm lost. I'm falling down, down, down, bursting over and over and over.

When I finally manage to open my eyes, my legs are still wide and Hunter is still lying between them, his gaze fixed on my pussy. I don't have the energy to be embarrassed.

"You have a beautiful pussy. I feel like the luckiest guy alive to get to see it close up like this."

"You need medical attention," I say, letting an arm flop over my face.

"I mean it," he says. "The way it throbs, it's like a flower opening up, showing me how pretty it is."

Hunter worships me. And not just my pussy, but all of me. I know it.

"You're right," I say. "We should move uptown."

He leans up on his hands so I'm looking right at him. "You trying to get me hard again?"

"Are you telling me it's difficult?"

He grins. "So you'll move in with me?"

"Of course I will," I say. "We'll move in *together*."

"We can walk to work together," he says.

"And have lunch together," I say.

"And kids."

I laugh. "You want our kids to walk to work with us?"

"Sure," he says. "The nanny can walk them to work with us so we don't miss out on anything we don't have to. Although you might still be in law school, so maybe we can alternate days when the kids take you to school one day and me to work the other."

I smooth my hand over his cheek. He doesn't assume having kids is going to slow me down. He just sees our future together in the sunniest way possible.

"You think I'm actually going to make it to law school?"

He looks at me with a frown. "Of course. If that's what you want to do."

"It's going to be a lot. You working all the hours. Me studying and working too."

"But we can handle a lot. A lot is what we're used to."

I smile at him. He's my partner in this. He wants for me what I want for me. And he believes I can have it. I feel the same about him. I have no doubts that he and Ed are going to keep growing Portis into a real power player. There's no end to the possibilities now we're together.

"Can I get you anything?" he asks.

"I'd like a glass of water," I say, looking up at him. "But I can get it."

He climbs out of bed and heads into the kitchen. When he comes back, he's holding my favorite soda that I always order at the sandwich store.

"You bought these for me?" I ask.

"I did. I want you to feel comfortable here."

"And you thought *you* wouldn't be enough? You thought you better buy the soda as well?"

"I wanted to cover all my bases." He grins at me and sits on the bed, pulling my legs over his lap. "Should we go right into apartment hunting?" he asks. "Do you have an area you like best? If you don't, that's fine. It really is. I get it. Maybe you don't fully trust what I'm feeling yet."

I take his hand and link my fingers through his. "It's not that I don't trust it. I . . . just . . . I'm worried about studying." I glance around. His apartment is small. And it's his. "I think it would be good to find something a little bigger. And something that's been ours from the beginning. A fresh start."

A grin tugs at the corner of his mouth. "A fresh start."

I'm not sure if I ever thought about what this would look like, sharing my life with someone. But he wants me to be happy. Maybe as much as I want him to be happy. That equality makes me feel safe. It makes me feel loved.

"It would be nice to be able to walk to work. Or at least not have to take the subway. I don't mind the bus."

He grins at me. "The bus. Really? In the heels you wear?"

I take a sip of my drink and then flop back down onto the pillows, watching him watching me, his eyes full of kindness and consideration. "Have you thought about where you want to live?"

He shrugs. "I'm happy if you're happy."

"When did we get so agreeable?"

He chuckles. "Maybe when we met each other."

"We turned into the best versions of ourselves for each other."

He crawls over me and presses his lips to mine, before pulling back. "That's exactly it. I want to be the man you deserve."

"You are," I say, circling my arms around his neck. "Already."

CHAPTER THIRTY-SIX

Lucy

I've never been nervous meeting up with Katherine before, but I've been experiencing a lot of firsts in my life recently.

"We don't need to tell them everything," I say.

"What's everything? How fucking sweet you taste on my tongue?" Hunter asks. "How you're permanently wet around me, or how you close around my cock like—"

"Hunter," I say, glancing around to see if anyone is listening to our conversation as we head toward Madison and 63rd.

"This is New York," he says dismissively. "No one's interested in our sex life."

There's no arguing with that. Everyone in New York has enough going on with their own lives without gossiping about perfect strangers.

"I just mean about the move and everything," I say.

"You don't want them to know we're moving in together?" Hunter comes to an abrupt halt on the sidewalk. "How come?"

I scan his face. He looks genuinely confused and maybe a little hurt.

"I'm just worried Katherine will think it's too fast."

"So?" he asks.

"So, I don't want to have to field questions. And have her questioning my judgment. Then she'll tell Mom, and everyone will be in my business. Before I know it, I'll be moving into an apartment I don't want to live in because that's what Mom and Katherine think is the right thing to do."

He shakes his head. "Well, it will be my apartment as well, and they're not going to push me into living anywhere I don't want to live. And . . ."

"And what?" I say. I'm not used to Hunter holding anything back from me. I don't want him to start now.

"I think that's the woman you were. But things have changed, Lucy. I'm not sure you'd be so easily pushed around now. I don't think you want to please them over yourself anymore. You don't have the same need to be liked by your mom. Maybe it's because you know how much *I* like you . . ." He presses a soft kiss to my lips, and I feel his smile against my mouth.

He's right. The old me would have been chastened by my mother. I would have ended up taking another place in Brooklyn because it was cheaper and because that's what my mom thinks is best.

But I've already told Hunter I want to live on the Upper West Side. The lower end. I've been pretty specific with him. So why am I so concerned with what Mom and Katherine are going to say?

"It's just memories," Hunter says like he's reading my mind. "You don't need to question it. You've spent a huge chunk of your life trying to please other people. Now you don't have to. It's going to take some getting used to. Don't stress."

"So you think we should just come right out with it?"

Hunter shrugs. "There's no reason to hide."

I pull my shoulders back. He's right: I have no reason to hide anything about my life from anyone. If people love me, they'll be happy for me. If they don't, they won't. It's as simple as Hunter makes it seem.

Katherine and Ed are already seated in the restaurant when we arrive. It's the first time the four of us have been together since the wedding.

We all hug and take a seat. Katherine is beaming as usual. There's something different about the dynamic between Hunter and Ed. They seem closer somehow. Like a barrier that was between them has been broken down or something. Hunter told me about flying to Boston to get things back on track with Ed after the honeymoon, and it's obviously worked.

"How's the new house?" I ask. "I can't wait to visit."

"You have to come stay soon." Katherine pauses. "Well, not too soon, because the entire thing's a mess. We have so much to do."

"Everything needs changing," Ed says. "But it's our forever home, so we don't mind if it takes a while."

"Just not too long," Katherine says.

"How's Mom with everything?" I ask.

Katherine winces. "I mean, not great. I'm getting the Lucy treatment. She's being snippy and making snide comments." She and Ed share a glance, and I can tell my sister gets strength from the man she loves. Strength to cope with the disapproval of our mother.

I nod, knowing exactly what Katherine is going through.

"She'll get used to it . . ." I stop myself. "Well, she might never get used to it, but you'll get used to her disapproval."

"Ed says I need to train myself to tune it out."

Ed and Hunter exchange a look. They've clearly had a conversation about this: our mom and the power she wields over us. Or at least, she did. Her power is waning as we move forward in our own lives.

"We have news," I say, squeezing Hunter's hand under the table. "We're apartment-hunting."

Katherine squeals. "You're moving in together?"

We're not just moving in together. It's more serious than that, but from the outside looking in, we're taking the next step.

"Yeah, we're looking in this area, actually. A few blocks south."

"So we can both walk to work," Hunter adds. "Eventually, the nanny will walk the kids with us, so we can have as much time with them as possible."

Katherine's eyes flare. "You're pregnant?"

Hunter laughs. "Not yet." He turns to me. "Are you?"

It's my turn to laugh, and I shake my head. "Very definitely not pregnant," I confirm.

"Right," Hunter says. "But later on. When we have kids."

"So this is a real thing," Katherine says.

I shrug. "He's it for me."

Hunter grins, leans across, and kisses my cheek. "She's more than enough for me." He laughs, and I elbow him in the ribs. "In the best possible way. She's the woman I want to spend the rest of my life with. I want her to be the mother of my children and . . . yeah, I want us to grow old together."

Katherine sits back in her seat. "Well, this isn't what I was expecting to hear today. I thought you were going to tell us you'd split up and that it was all amicable, but that was that, or that you'd only ever pretended to be together to keep me happy."

Hunter squeezes my thigh, but neither of us say anything.

"I didn't think that," Ed says. "I knew when Hunter came to Boston that things had changed for him. And Lucy was that change."

"You're right," Hunter says. "Lucy showed me the man I want to become."

I glance across at him. How did I get so lucky? I feel like he plucked me out of a hurricane of desperation. Desperate to be the good sister, the loved daughter, the capable paralegal. And now I'm . . . me. Not desperate to be anything or anyone but who I am.

"You were always that man," I say to him.

"Not until I met you," he replies.

"Good grief," Katherine says. "Who are the two of you? What have you done with my feisty sister and my husband's grumpy business partner?"

I shrug. "We fell in love, I guess."

Katherine reaches for my hand. "I'm so happy for you. And I'm also happy for us, because we get to go on double dates, go on vacations together, live life . . . the four of us."

"Wanna move to New York?" I suggest.

"Wanna come to Boston?" Katherine asks.

"It's not so far away," Hunter says. "We should all go in on a beach house for the summers."

"On Martha's Vineyard," Katherine and I chorus.

"That's where we should get married," Hunter says, his face full of possibility and hopefulness. "We should rent out that house again and get married where we first fell in love."

"You're so romantic," I say. I narrow my eyes. "And did you just propose?"

"I thought I had already," he says. "Are you in any doubt that there's anyone else for me but you?"

I shake my head and try to bite back a grin. Hearing how he loves me still hits me right in the chest. I'm not sure that feeling of surprise and bliss will ever go away. At least, I hope it doesn't.

"Me neither," he says. "I'd like to take your last name, if that's okay, and know we're bound together in law as well as love. I want all of that with you. So will you marry me?"

Contentment unfurls through my body like internal sunshine, leaving me warm and satiated, and I smile at the man beside me whom I'm going to marry. So this is how good life can get. I really had no idea. I stare at him, his cheeks rosy, his hair deliciously ruffled. There's not much for me to say. If he wants to marry me, my answer's yes. Of course it is. "I'll marry you on Martha's Vineyard," I say. "Or at the top of the Empire State Building, or out at sea. I'll follow wherever you lead me."

Hunter cups my head and presses his lips to mine. The familiar buzz is back, and I sink into him, wanting no space between us.

We end our kiss and press our foreheads together.

"Can we get some champagne?" Ed asks a passing waiter. "Our best friends just got engaged."

We turn back to the table, linking our hands and fingers.

"I'm matron of honor, right?" Katherine asks.

I wince. "I mean, yeah, of course, there's no one else. But I don't want a big fancy wedding." I turn to Hunter. "Unless you do?"

He shakes his head. "Just the four of us on the beach in Martha's Vineyard works for me."

I can't think of anything better. Me in a white dress next to Hunter, pledging to love him for the rest of my life, with my sister and Hunter's best friend right next to us. It's all I need. I don't need to be the perfect daughter. The perfect sister. The perfect employee. I just want to be the woman who loves Hunter, and the woman Hunter loves back.

EPILOGUE

Hunter

When Ed told me he hadn't bought Katherine a wedding present, I knew exactly how to solve his problem.

"You think they'll like it?" I take the three steps down from the porch and turn to face the property we just viewed. It's September, but the house still feels like summer inside. Maybe it's the big sky above us, or the ocean in front of us, but it feels kind of magical.

"I think we should show it to them first," Ed says. "I don't want to be making purchases like this without talking to my wife about it."

"You're totally right. They have to see it before we buy it. It's going to be in all our names anyway."

"Right," Ed says. "I thought for a second there you were thinking we should buy it as a surprise."

"I value my nuts," I reply. "I'm not making financial decisions like this without speaking to Lucy." My cell starts to ring. "Speaking of."

"Hey," she says. "We got back to the house and the car is gone. Where are you?"

"We're about a mile down the road. Is Katherine there?" I glance at Ed, getting his go-ahead to invite the girls over right now. There's no time like the present, right?

"Yeah, of course. You want me to put her on?" she asks.

"No, it's not that. But could you meet us? We've got something to show you."

"Sounds ominous."

"Not at all. You'll see." I give her directions, which doesn't take long because we're just up the street.

Ed's staring at me as if I'm about to tell him something he didn't just hear on the phone.

"What are we going to say?" he asks.

I shrug. "I can say something about how the love story between Lucy and me started here. About how Martha's Vineyard was an incubator of our love and that we want that warm, soft, safe environment to be with us on our journey—"

I stop short, in part because it looks like Ed is going to give himself a hernia trying not to laugh, and in part because Lucy pulls into the drive. She and Katherine are dipping their heads so they can take in the house through the windshield. They turn to each other and exchange words before getting out of the car at the same time.

"Shall we buy it?" Lucy asks immediately, leaving my romantic speech about our love in pieces over her shoulder. "Is it for sale?"

"Oh, heck, it's right on the beach," Katherine says, looking out over the water. "The location is just perfect."

I glance at Ed. Why was he nervous about what to say? We didn't have to say anything at all.

"I thought maybe it could be a wedding present," Ed says to Katherine.

"But for the four of us," Katherine says without missing a beat. "I mean, the four of us have to buy it together, right?"

Ed laughs. "Right. Actually, there's enough land on this plot to grow into. So further down the line, if we wanted to build a second property or demolish this and start again and build something bigger . . ."

"But this is darling. From the outside, anyway," Lucy says. The outside of the property needs sprucing up a little. Some of the paint is peeling, and the deck needs revarnishing. If she likes it outside, she's going to love it inside.

"Can we go in?" Her face lights up. I never get tired of seeing her happy.

We all head inside, and I can tell by the way Lucy doesn't say anything that she's blown away. She grabs my hand and squeezes. "Look at these counters," she says, eyeing the pale marble in the kitchen. "From the outside, I expected it to be a fixer-upper."

"The family who had the place was just putting the finishing touches on it when they had to relocate for work. Everything's newly refurbished apart from the outside."

"So what's the plan?" Lucy asks. "Who does Ed need to bang to get us this house?"

I chuckle while Ed looks on, his mouth open, expression horrified.

"Ed says he hasn't found the right wedding present for Katherine yet, and I'm going to need to find one for you as well. So . . . we thought the house."

"Let's explore," Lucy says. She leads us through the house, she and Katherine exclaiming over the views and the layout. Upstairs, the four bedrooms are beautiful, with en suite bathrooms in the two primaries and a Jack and Jill between the other two.

Ed and I are on the landing when we hear Lucy's outraged voice from one of the guest rooms. "I don't believe it," she says. "That's it! There's no freaking way I can stay in this house." We stumble into the room to see what the problem is, expecting to see a nest of vipers or a collapsed ceiling or something.

I scan the room. I can't see what they're talking about. Katherine looks concerned and Lucy looks furious.

"What's the problem?" I ask. Ed and I have scoured the real estate listings over the last couple of months to find something on the beach. Properties like this don't come up a lot. This house is perfect, with room to grow too.

"Seriously, Katherine. You can't make me. I can't bear it."

"What?" I ask, trying to make sense of what's going on.

"We'll strip it off before we move in," Katherine says.

"What?" I ask, looking around for the lead piping or asbestos tile. What on earth has Lucy spotted that Ed and I didn't see on our first tour through here?

"Well, we'd better. I'm not stepping a foot into this house again while that wallpaper is here."

"You don't like the wallpaper?" I ask, trying to connect the dots between her reaction and the innocuous, beachy motif on the walls. Three lighthouses are spaced at intervals around the room. I really don't see the problem.

"Of course I don't like the wallpaper," Lucy says, like her reaction is entirely rational. I scan the walls, trying to figure out what's so offensive.

Katherine and Lucy exchange a glance. Lucy turns to me. Katherine turns to Ed. "It's perfect," they say in unison.

I have no idea what the hell is going on, but relief runs through me, and I start to laugh. "You're always so surprising, Lucy Jones. But I'm glad you like it."

"But seriously, we need to change that wallpaper," Lucy says.

"If that's what will make you happy, then that's what we will do." Lucy's happiness is my priority now. And I'm her priority. We're both looking out for each other. We're each other's safe harbor. The rudder in each other's boat. I've never felt so safe and sure about . . . life.

"There's one condition, though," Katherine says. "No one gets to use the house unless we're here. We can't have Mom and Dad in this place without us, or Mom will have re-papered the entire house in this wallpaper or something worse."

"Agreed," we all say together.

I'm not sure whether it's just because I'm spending more time with her or because she seems to have changed a little, but I like Katherine more than I did when she and Ed were just dating or engaged. Maybe I've changed. Now she's not the person keeping Ed from being chained to his desk twenty-four hours a day. She's now the woman who makes my best friend happy and the sister of the love of my life.

"This is our place," Lucy says, wrapping her arms around my waist. "It's where our love story started. It's where I started to believe that I could love someone and they might love me back."

My heart balloons in my chest as I pull her closer. Being with Lucy has made me more *me*. A better version of myself. A version capable and worthy of the woman in my arms. And I get to be with her forever. I think that makes me the luckiest man alive. "And it's where we'll spend the rest of our lives living our love story."

Acknowledgments

This is one of my favorite books I've ever written, and it means the world to me that you read it. Thank you! Also, just the author's opinion here, but Wentworth *is* the hottest Jane Austen hero and severely underrated. Just like Hunter. Please contact me on social media to debate this with me in my DMs!

Kimberly, thank you for being the best of the best. We should lobby for a law to mandate working from bed.

Thank you, Lauren, for pulling me out of my funk and coming up with the idea that doesn't just solve a problem but makes the book better. Thank you so much to Lauren, Charlotte, and the entire Montlake team for making this so easy for me.

Thank you, Autumn, for keeping me sane and handling me all the stuff that's really tricky. I couldn't do it without you. Scarlett: 4k, baby. Let's do this! And thanks to you, we did do it!

Lenora, your namesake got Wentworth in the end—against the odds. Remember, you'll always figure it out.

About the Author

Louise Bay is the *USA Today* and international bestselling author of contemporary romance novels that make you laugh. Louise was inspired by such bonkbuster authors of the eighties as Judith Krantz and Jackie Collins, but wants to be Emily Henry when she grows up. Writing is just a side hustle to her full-time career as a personal butler/driver/chef to her kid. IYKYK. For more information, visit www.louisebay.com.